W9-BCZ-715

HAVE YOU SEEN ME?

Other Books by Alexandrea Weis

Realm
The Secret Brokers (Book 1)
Sisters of the Moon
The Christmas Spirit

By the Multi-Award-Winning Duo
Alexandrea Weis with Lucas Astor

The Magnus Blackwell Series
Blackwell: The Prequel (A Magnus Blackwell Novel, Book 1)
Damned (A Magnus Blackwell Novel, Book 2)
Bound (A Magnus Blackwell Novel, Book 3)
Seize (A Magnus Blackwell Novel, Book 4)

The St. Benedict Series
Death by the River (A St. Benedict Novel, Book 1)

Forthcoming by Alexandrea Weis

A Locket of Time

Forthcoming by Alexandrea Weis with Lucas Astor

The Chimera Effect
The Secret Salt Society
A River of Secrets (A St. Benedict Novel, Book 2)

HAVE YOU SEEN ME?

ALEXANDREA WEIS

Have You Seen Me?

Cover design by Gabriel De Leon
gssdeleon.com

ISBN: 978-1-64548-075-4

VESUVIAN BOOKS

Published by Vesuvian Books
www.VesuvianBooks.com

Printed in the United States
10 9 8 7 6 5 4 3 2 1

Tall stalks whipped against Lindsey's legs as she ran. Her ragged breath broke through the silence of the dark, isolated field. She put everything she had into maneuvering through the deep weeds. Her chest burned, but an icy dread kept her desperate to outrun the beam of light following her.

Exhausted, Lindsey paused and kneeled by a thicket of grass, hoping to remain out of sight. But then a flashlight locked on her position. She startled and stumbled backward, tripping over something.

Falling to the boggy ground, weeds slapped her face, and her leg scraped against a sharp object.

Son of a . . .

Lindsey grabbed her leg but kept silent as a sting flared above her ankle. When she reached down, the spot was wet to the touch.

Blood. Crap. That will leave a trail.

She discovered the cause of her fall—a marker built of stone.

Lindsey had heard stories about the famous battlefield and the single marker left to remember the fallen soldiers.

"Where are you going to run, Lindsey?"

The nondescript, guttural voice seemed to surround her.

Lindsey hurried to get up while scouring the trees. She judged the distance it would take her to get lost in their shadows.

She surveyed the endless acres of grass. There was nowhere else to go.

A tickle raced across her neck, awakening an intense dread. The locket she kept close—the one containing pictures of her and Marjorie—had slipped off.

Not my locket!

She wanted to search the grass for the prized memento, but there was no time. The rays of the flashlight found her.

Lindsey summoned her courage, determined to lose her tormentor.

The hurried whoosh of trampled weeds drew closer.

Lindsey cursed. She took off, dashing for the trees, not looking back. She ran into pockets of thick mud and her legs tired as she struggled.

A ray of moonlight broke through the clouds. Lindsey examined the outline of the land. The grass thinned before the line of trees.

She kept going, and when she broached the trees, relief rolled through her.

Branches scratched her face. The sting they left brought tears to her eyes, but she pushed on.

Almost there.

The pine needles crunched beneath her feet, alerting her pursuer to where she was.

Then another sound rose in the air—churning water. The bend in the fast-moving Bayou Teche was ahead. She lunged for the end of the tree line.

Around her was more tall grass, and then ahead, piers poked out of the swirling waterway.

A structure appeared on her left. Rising against the dark sky, its craggy outline hinted at crumbled walls and a collapsed roof. A smokestack rose like a column into the night.

Lindsey ran, glimpsing trash piles and abandoned machinery around the site of the old sugar mill.

A darting orb of light swept past her.

She charged toward the river's edge.

The piers got closer, and she spotted the remains of the old dock, its rotting planks poking out along the shoreline.

Lindsey closed in on the water, knowing she had no place else to go.

A light behind her danced along the water's surface, heightening her fear.

The riverbank came up quickly. Lindsey paused on the edge, staring into the churning current at the river's bend.

She looked back over her shoulder. "I'll see you in hell."

Lindsey dove into the swirling currents. The cold shocked her just as an undertow pulled her down. She fought to get to the surface. Panic ate up her oxygen as she kicked hard, but she wasn't gaining any ground.

Darkness closed around her, engulfing Lindsey in blinding terror.

CHAPTER

The humid fall breeze drifted in the open window of Aubrey's beat-up Accord, cooling her flushed skin. She gazed out at the grounds of Waverly Preparatory School, where majestic oaks provided shady havens for the students dressed in their blue and gray uniforms. She wiped her brow, anxious about her new job. Her memories of the private school were not the best. She hoped teaching the students turned out to be better than being one.

She got out of the car, making sure to lock her luggage inside. After the long trip from Baton Rouge, she welcomed the chance to stretch her legs. The sun beat down as she walked the path from the main parking lot. The occasional heavy-based thump of a song from somewhere on campus drifted by, along with the sweet succulence of magnolia trees. Students strolled across grassy patches, carrying book bags weighed down for a day of classes. In the distance, a faint whinny from one of the horses in the stable carried across the sprawling grounds. Waverly prided itself on offering physical education programs that included riding, fencing, tennis, swimming, and even lacrosse.

The atmosphere reeked of privilege from BMWs in the parking lot to the pricey array of laptops students toted to class.

Aubrey chuckled. *Nothing has changed.*

She progressed along the walkway, recalling the days on campus when she had been an unsure adolescent, afraid of being rejected because she was too chubby, too smart, or too dark. While self-consciousness about her skin color had faded, returning to her roots had reawakened her insecurities.

Ahead were the granite steps of the imposing two-and-a-half-story antebellum home that remained the centerpiece of the school. With a sweeping second-floor balcony and sprawling porch, the plantation home formed the entrance to a quad where several square brick buildings rose against the sky, dwarfing the original 1832 structure.

Walkways on either side of the house led to the inner quadrangle or heart of the school. Stone benches and a large round fountain adorned with a flashy silver sculpture glistened in the morning sun. *The Quad* was where students went to decompress or meet with friends.

Aubrey patted her stomach, assuring herself that her experiences at the school—both good and bad—had prepared her for her new job. But as the historic home loomed, its french windows and smooth white plaster finish only added to her nervous butterflies. She admired the detailed scrollwork running along the balcony's white iron railing, while smooth columns set off the gray shale roof. A bricked chimney rose on either side and the arched front doors topped with a fan transom of leaded glass seemed to ooze a warm Southern welcome.

Elaine House, as it was known, was home to the principal or headmistress of the school and was the one place on campus that Aubrey dreaded to enter. Not so much for its rumored past of ghosts and strange occurrences, but for the woman who occupied the French Creole structure—Sara Probst.

Aubrey adjusted the wrinkles in the front of her formfitting dress, wishing she had worn something more comfortable. October in Louisiana could be brutal.

The languid breeze, and buzz of life around the campus, infused Aubrey with determination. She wasn't a student anymore, but an educated professional and no longer subject to her former principal's tirades. Aubrey steadied her shaking hands as she walked the last few feet to the granite steps.

A breeze caught several fliers pegged to an announcement board along the walkway, and Aubrey became distracted by a young woman's picture.

A pair of green eyes edged with despair called to Aubrey amid the notices for tutoring help and laptops for sale. *Troubled* was the first thing that popped into her head. The tightly drawn line of the girl's mouth, dark circles, and sunken cheeks stirred a tide of sadness in Aubrey. But the note and name at the bottom quickly piqued her curiosity.

Have you seen me?
Lindsey Gillett is missing.

The name was one Aubrey didn't know, but the eyes she'd seen before. A million unhappy memories returned as she examined the flier. All the angst her time as a student at Waverly had brought returned in a heated rush.

"Ms. LaRoux, I'm glad you're on time."

The cold, gruff voice sent a chill through Aubrey.

She turned toward the steps and put on her best smile.

Sara Probst, wearing gray tweed despite the heat, stood on the airy porch and glared at Aubrey. The former athletic director remained as lean and shapely as when Aubrey had attended the school ten years ago.

Sara had climbed to the esteemed position several years before Aubrey enrolled. The assertive woman with the brassy blonde hair had led Waverly into the twenty-first century, without forgetting the school's esteemed seventy-year reputation of providing top-notch college-preparatory education.

Aubrey stepped closer, noting the subtle wrinkles of middle age across Sara's brow and around her mouth. Sara's killer stare was still there, making Aubrey reconsider returning to her alma mater.

"Ms. Probst," she said, speaking clearly and succinctly, just like the woman had taught her. "It's good to see you again."

Sara came down the steps, her square-heeled pumps tapping the stone.

"I was surprised when I received your application. I didn't think when you left here, you would ever want to come back, considering all that happened."

The comment rekindled the image of the pretty field hockey team captain who had gone missing in Aubrey's senior year. Marjorie Reynolds had a reputation for a sharp-tongue and quick right hook. Aubrey had avoided the svelte brunette, eager to stay out of her line of fire.

She turned to the poster of the girl. Then it struck her why the woman's eyes had stood out—the girl reminded her of Marjorie.

"I'm sorry to see you have another missing girl. Waverly has had more than a few in the past as I recall."

Sara motioned to the board. "Yes, there were the three girls who vanished in the nineties. But their tragedy is nothing like this. Lindsey is a precocious troublemaker. The police believe she ran away, just like Marjorie did when you were here."

The comparisons rattled Aubrey. "Not everyone believed Marjorie ran away."

The headmistress came alongside her, and her wide-eyed stare withered Aubrey's self-confidence.

"What else could have happened?" Sara's expression cooled. "Marjorie ran away several times while she attended school here. Or didn't you know?"

Aubrey straightened her back, attempting to appear resilient. "I'd heard rumors, but Marjorie and I weren't close."

"Yes, I remember how she bullied you. Several of the faculty called her out on it. You were suspected in her disappearance, as I recall, because of the bad blood between you."

Aubrey squirmed. "I was questioned, but I wasn't a suspect."

Sara tilted her head. "Marjorie always was a pigheaded girl. Lindsey was the same way. Same bad seed ran through both."

Shock ruffled Aubrey's system. "Excuse me?"

"They're sisters." Sara turned away from the board. "Well, half sisters—same mother, different fathers. Lindsey was sent here by her father. He hoped getting her out of New Orleans would settle her down. She had some run-ins with the law. Of course, I didn't learn about any of that until after she ran away. I wished I would have known sooner. Might have avoided a difficult situation for everyone involved."

The woman's cold analysis didn't surprise Aubrey. She had been the same way when Marjorie had disappeared.

But keeping up a stoic attitude when faced with tragedy was

something Aubrey understood. Dwelling on something of which no one had control didn't change anything. And when you're responsible for the well-being of hundreds of students, forbearance was the best course of action.

"Do they know where she went?"

Sara motioned to the open front doors of the home. "Not a clue. Officers came to the school, questioned several students—with parental permission, of course—and then went on their way. I get updates, but I don't pry. I have other students who need my attention. I can't let the school fall apart for one flighty girl."

"What about the students?" Aubrey argued. "This can weigh on young minds. They might need counseling or at least access to some professional help. I find getting students involved, and not cutting them off from a crisis, helps them cope."

Sara's lips thinned into an unamused smile. "This is not a crisis. And they already have access to all those things. Discussion groups, counseling, advisors—whatever the board sees fit. I don't want this unfortunate event distracting students from their studies and overtaking the school. We have kept things quiet and will continue to do so."

Aubrey remembered the time after Marjorie disappeared. Keeping quiet had not helped anyone cope.

"Is that a good idea?" Aubrey demanded. "Some students might want to do more."

"It is all they will get, Ms. LaRoux."

Sara marched up the steps, exhibiting the same military precision with her movements as Aubrey remembered.

"Come inside and let's go over my expectations," Sara called over her shoulder. "You've got a lot of catching up to do."

Aubrey followed the school director to the entrance of the historic home.

God, give me strength.

CHAPTER 2

T he frigid air caressed the dew on Aubrey's skin, sharpening her wits. She breathed with restraint as the heavy perfume of lavender coming from blooms inside the front door accosted her nose. The royal blue walls with white wainscoting dulled the appearance of the old oak hardwoods. The floors groaned under her weight, and then the heavy doors creaked closed behind her, sending a shudder through her.

"You may have noticed we are coed now." Sara motioned to the open office to the left of the entrance hall. "We started taking on boys right after you graduated. The state forced my hand."

Aubrey got a peek at the ornate white and blue Chinese vases positioned on walnut stands by the door. "I'd heard something about it. Do they live on campus?"

"Goodness, no." Sara waved her hand in the air, almost snorting with displeasure. "We have a block of apartments in town where a few of our male faculty supervise them. Have to make sure they stay far away from the girls."

Sara entered what would have been a formal parlor but had become the principal's office. The intense shade of dusky gray complemented the thick, almost masculine furniture. A red rug sat below a large walnut desk with carvings of lions' heads caught in mid roar on each corner. Gold-framed portraits of previous schoolmasters adorned the walls—all men.

Sara had become the first female school director, but her family name had given her an edge.

Aubrey took in the portrait of a man with the same long face and hard eyes as the woman behind her desk. Sara had not inherited Warren Probst's dark curly hair or small chin, but they did share the same long, slender frame.

"You look like him."

Sara got comfortable in her chair. "Many people say that when they see his portrait."

Aubrey took one of the brown leather chairs in front of the desk. "You don't find it creepy? Having him watching you work?"

Sara furrowed her brow. "Why would I?"

"But didn't he die in this room?"

"Yes, he shot himself in here, but contrary to what everyone has whispered on campus for years, there are no ghosts in this house." Sara pulled out a folder from her desk drawer. "And I like having his portrait there. His approval is important to me."

For Aubrey, the comment was classic Sara Probst. The woman had never seemed to care about her standing with anyone—student or faculty. She had been an enigma on campus, living in her creepy home, and running the school with an iron fist. Perhaps the disturbing portraits gave her solace in her lonely job. Aubrey accepted it as another quirk.

Sara flipped open a folder on her desk. "You received your master's in history two years ago from Northeastern University. Quite impressive."

Aubrey folded her hands in her lap. "Ah, yes. And I got my undergraduate from Brown."

"Good schools. I know you have little experience as an educator, but I feel you have what it takes to teach at Waverly." Sara sat back. "You were always a quick study and that will serve you well. I knew you would go far."

Aubrey chuckled, overcome by the compliment. "Ah, thank you, but I didn't think you even noticed me."

"I noticed, but you lacked confidence when you went here. I suspect you found some while away at school." She tented her fingers. "Teaching at Waverly is a challenge for all faculty, considering the setup. Having both day students and boarding school students presents many difficulties. And the boys are a problem unto themselves." Sara rolled her eyes. "You will take up Ms. Levi's old quarters. I'm sure you remember the housemother's responsibilities from when you stayed in the dorms."

"Will she be coming back after her leave?"

Sara faced the window that looked out over The Quad.

"She asked for a one-year LOA—that's why I took you on and didn't hire a local substitute. If you work out, you can have her position. Legally, I don't have to hold it for her after her three-month medical leave is up."

"I hate to think I'm pushing a fellow teacher out when she's ill."

Sara turned back to her. "Be grateful you have the chance to work at our esteemed institution because of Ms. Levi's poor mental health. The woman was always slightly off-kilter, so it's good she's gone."

Aubrey clasped her hands in her lap. "Thank you for the opportunity."

"Ms. Levi taught history and coordinated on-campus activities like picnics and weekend trips to New Orleans for the girls who live in the dorms. You will take up those duties."

Aubrey sucked in a fortifying breath. "So, you explained on the phone. I would prefer to plan more stimulating activities such as trips to homeless shelters and volunteering at hospitals or nursing homes. I feel it would give the girls a broader perspective to become involved in the community."

"Just keep track of your girls. I can't afford any more bad press." Sara leaned forward. "The newspapers are already bringing up the old unsolved cases of the girls who disappeared in the nineties during my father's tenure as headmaster."

"I heard rumors about those missing girls," Aubrey said. "But I never learned what happened to them."

Sara set her hands on the desk. "No one knows for sure. The police believe they wandered off campus. Drinking may have been involved— alcohol was found in one of the girls' rooms. Or they got involved with the wrong sort of people from town."

Aubrey swallowed hard, attempting not to laugh. Franklin, the small town five miles down the blacktop road, wasn't somewhere young girls went missing without a trace.

"Franklin is hardly the epicenter of crime. It was a quaint, quiet town when I attended school, but I can't imagine any unseemly characters living there way back in the nineties."

"The decade doesn't define the atrocities of men, Ms. LaRoux. In five thousand years of recorded history, their appetites have not changed. You're a history teacher and should know that better than anyone."

The cutting remark quelled Aubrey's rebuttal. Sara had the propensity to slice a person in half with her words. The Eviscerator, they called the headmistress back in her day. No one on campus—student or faculty—was spared her scathing comments. Even Aubrey had suffered her principal's caustic wit.

She had won an award for distinction in English. Sara had been there to offer congratulations and something else.

"It's a good start, Ms. LaRoux," she had said in her unpleasant way. "But a low bar to set for yourself. Aim higher."

The words still stung but had set something off in Aubrey. Perhaps her resentment was why she had come back to Waverly. To show Sara Probst that she had aimed higher.

"What do you think, Ms. LaRoux?"

Sara's question brought Aubrey back to the present.

Aubrey cleared her throat. "I'm sorry?"

"I said I was teaching at Waverly at the time those girls went missing. It was a difficult time for students and faculty. I suspect it was especially hard on my father."

Aubrey stiffened. "I'm sure it was hard on you when Marjorie went missing and now this new girl. I don't envy your job."

Sara waved a careless hand in the air. "After I was appointed headmistress, following my father's death, I often pondered the fate of those girls. I believe they ended up in Bayou Teche. I have lived in this area for over thirty years and have seen dozens of people pulled from Bayou Teche." Sara's tone hardened. "But for goodness sake, don't discuss anything you learn about Lindsey's case with your students. The last thing I need is them spreading more rumors. Your job is to keep them in line."

Aubrey wanted to butt heads with her viewpoint, but something else bothered her more.

"What do the authorities have to say about all this? Aren't they curious if the past disappearances are related?"

Sara chuckled, sounding more like a man than a woman. "The local sheriff, Mason Dubois, isn't worried about Lindsey. She had run away from campus before. He expects she will turn up soon."

Aubrey thought her attitude a bit cavalier. "And if she doesn't?"

Sara leaned back in her chair. "I never figured you to be one prone to panic, Ms. LaRoux. Don't give in to the hysteria students generate. Faculty is expected to set the example and promote calm."

Aubrey sank into her seat, feeling fifteen again. "Yes, Ms. Probst."

Sara stood and smoothed her tweed skirt. "Now, let me walk you around the campus. A lot has changed since you were a student."

The shady oaks on the path from the headmistress's house offered brief respites from the sun as Aubrey struggled to keep up with the energetic Sara. The woman's brisk stride would exhaust a ten-year-old wired on sugar. Aubrey dabbed the sweat from her forehead, worried about her makeup. She nodded at students who checked her out as they passed.

The confused and discerning looks she received were the same she'd given to new faculty. She knew all students loved having newbies to taunt and manipulate out of assignments.

"Don't let the students bully you," Sara advised as they walked past a group of girls, their heads bent in avid whispering. "I know you were prone to that when you were here as a student."

"That was a long time ago, Ms. Probst. I've worked for East Baton Rouge Parish Public School system for a year. No one bullies me anymore."

Sara cocked her head. "You're still an inexperienced teacher, and this is your first assignment at a private institution. These kids aren't like the ones you encountered before. Sons and daughters of the wealthy sometimes have larger chips on their shoulders to knock off. Be careful how you approach them."

Hot anger stirred in Aubrey's chest. "Is that how you saw me when

I came here?"

Sara glanced ahead to the red brick buildings surrounding The Quad. "You came here thanks to a scholarship. The Creole Catholic Society, if I remember correctly."

Aubrey held her head high. "My parents worked hard to get me here, even with that scholarship."

Sara nodded. "Your parents were good people. I heard of their passing."

The mention of the most horrible day of Aubrey's life tore through her like a blowtorch. The drunk driver who had taken out her father's car on the way back from an anniversary dinner still sat in Angola Jail, serving out his twenty years. The memory of the remorseful father of two dragged from the courtroom in chains always roused a bitter taste in her mouth. No one had won, as her lawyer had promised. Now she not only mourned her parents but the life of the man who had killed them.

"I didn't realize you knew."

Sara sized her up. "I read about the trial in the Baton Rouge newspaper. That must have been difficult for you."

Aubrey knew that formidable gaze. She'd encountered it numerous times during her four years at the school. It was another facet of Sara Probst that remained fresh in her memory. The school director's lack of compassion and her intolerance for emotional outbursts were legendary.

"I survived," she said in a deadpan voice.

"We all survive, Ms. LaRoux. It's the scars that get us in the end." She motioned to one of the red brick buildings. "I will show you to your room in the dorms first. We've added a wing since you were here."

Aubrey struggled to get the lump out of her throat. "Ah, yes. I thought that looked new."

"It is." Sara moved ahead. "Along with the indoor swimming pool, tennis courts, and a renovated gym. The stables are the same, but we won't be going there. I can't stand the smell."

The admission didn't surprise Aubrey. The headmistress she remembered from her high school days had an affinity for cleanliness and disliked horses.

"How did you pay for all the new additions?"

Sara chuckled, and the dark sound brought a frown to Aubrey's lips.

"The main job of being head of this school is making sure you get enough money through donations to keep the board of directors happy, and the parents believing you're involved with educating their children."

"Aren't you involved in educating the students?"

Sara glanced at Aubrey and grinned, showing her sharp, pointed teeth. "Hiring educators is how I stay involved. Your job is making sure the students learn."

A burning trickle of intimidation twisted in Aubrey's gut. "No teacher can make a student learn. They have to want to."

"Then you'd better make sure they want to, or we are both out of a job."

She let Sara pull ahead as they walked briskly toward The Quad. The woman's determined stride matched her harsh tone. It suddenly became apparent that the infamous headmistress probably put as much pressure on her staff as she did her students, making Aubrey question if she would make any difference in her old school.

Even the students she encountered reinforced her uncertainty. Cliques of smart girls, wearing glasses and tight braids, poured over iPads and notebooks, as they sat by the fountain, ignoring everyone around them. Clear-faced girls with perfect smiles huddled on benches, shared lip gloss, and took selfies as they laughed and pointed at those not cool enough to join their ranks. Good-looking boys—all with a swagger only the omnipotence of youth could generate—stood on the grass and gawked at the pretty girls, no doubt challenging each other about which bitch they could bed first. Along the shadowy inlets between the buildings, the outcasts kept their shoulders hunched and their heads lowered while taking fleeting glances of the popular kids.

Aubrey's heart ached for the outcasts. She, too, had suffered through the inequality adolescence brings. Class, race, or the financial status measured in the adult world could not compare to the popularity, beauty, and physical prowess prized among the younger set. She wanted to assure them that everything changes in college, but she knew they would not believe her. Aubrey wouldn't have accepted what any faculty member said during high school. They had been the enemy then.

That's what you've come here to change.

"We have more students than when you attended," Sara boasted as they approached a glass door with a keypad to the side. "Applications go up every year, so we have gotten stricter in our selection criteria."

"Wow." Aubrey hid her surprise. "I thought the selection process was pretty strict when I went here."

"It was." Sara stopped and punched a code. "But we must always set the bar higher. It's the only way to stay the best."

The door buzzed and popped open.

Sara reached for the metal handle and then turned to Aubrey.

"Codes for the dorms are given to each person allowed inside. The logs are checked by our security people daily to make sure no one is gaining access who shouldn't. Last year we caught one of our male students sneaking in. A girl gave him her code. I expelled him to set an example."

"And the girl? What did you do to her?"

Sara tilted her head. "Lindsey Gillett was the girl in question. After her suspension, I'd hoped she would come back a better student, but I was wrong."

Sara stepped inside, and the knot in Aubrey's chest tightened.

"This way, Ms. LaRoux."

Aubrey cringed at the way she said her name. There was a hint of distaste sprinkled with an overbearing formality, just like when she had been a student.

The inner lobby reminded Aubrey of a hotel with its comfy sofas and assortment of old photographs of the grounds. A bulletin board crowded with fliers about parties, workshops, or field trips sat next to an array of locked mailboxes. Instead of fluorescent lights, chandeliers with soft blue bulbs added a tranquil mood while throw rugs, in the school colors of blue and gray, enhanced the casual atmosphere.

"We let the students decorate the lobby. The only stipulation is they must use the school colors. Can't risk letting the girls get too wild."

Aubrey pressed her lips together, fighting her grin. "You don't want them to express their creativity? It might be fun to see what they can do."

"Students need structure, not freedom." Sara approached a single pair of silver elevator doors. "Letting them take the reins in any situation only ends up hurting them."

"I disagree. Projects that encourage creativity always give students confidence."

Sara pushed the elevator button with the ferocity of a field general about to go to war. "You need to reprogram your idealistic mindset, Ms. LaRoux. What you may have learned in college about teaching will not prepare you for the ruthless world of the classroom. Students get into trouble when given too much creativity. And faculty often suffers for it."

The rebuke turned her stomach. Aubrey did not consider herself idealistic but progressive. Though challenging her boss was not the way to promote her ideas, and she had to stay on her good side as much as possible.

The elevator doors opened, and Sara stepped inside.

"It's hard enough to get our students to stick to the dress code, I can't imagine what they would do if we let them run amok with creative pursuits," Sara admitted. "I had to fight the board tooth and nail on the issue of girls wearing ribbons in their hair."

Aubrey hesitated at the doors. "What's wrong with ribbons?"

"Nothing as long as they are not obnoxious, frilly, too long, or detract from the school uniform."

Aubrey stepped inside the elevator. "Most students are just trying to assert their individuality. That's common in adolescence."

Sara stood with her hands gripped behind her back. "This is a prep school, Ms. LaRoux. Individuality is for assignments and sports. Not attire."

The elevator doors closed, and the tightness in Aubrey's chest made her want to run, gasping for air.

Not on the first day. That would make a bad impression.

CHAPTER 3

The morning light coming through the eastern facing windows warmed the room to an almost stifling degree. The harshness of the white floor, walls, and cabinets almost hurt Aubrey's eyes. She wasn't sure how long she could live in such a sterile environment.

The bleak one-bedroom apartment drained Aubrey's enthusiasm. With an efficiency kitchen composed of white appliances, a tiny bathroom, and the sitting room barely wide enough to accommodate the small desk, Aubrey debated if her sanity would survive in such a dismal place.

"I know it isn't as nice as an apartment or cottage you could get in town, but it is rent-free, and the school pays all utilities." Sara went to the kitchen and opened the small refrigerator. "You also get a stipend for groceries every month. We have a local grocer in town who will make deliveries when he brings up the weekly school supplies."

Aubrey went to the windows. "Free food is always an incentive."

Sara shut the fridge door and wiped a finger along the white Formica countertop.

"You will supervise all the girls on this floor and the one above. About fifty in all. Ellen Baptiste oversees the top two floors. She joined us last year, teaching English literature to our juniors and seniors. You will like her. She went to Northwestern as well."

Aubrey wanted to laugh at the slip, but let it go.

"I look forward to meeting her."

Sara went to the sitting area and picked up an iPad. "This is for you. All your classes, after school activities, and the handbook have been loaded in here. There are also forms to fill out for disciplinary problems with students, along with grading criteria and your syllabus for the semester. Make any changes you see fit. As long as our students get outstanding ACT, SAT, and AP scores, that is what matters."

"Amazing how a person's entire education can come down to a bunch of worthless tests."

Aubrey waited for a scathing rebuttal, but Sara simply grinned.

"I wholeheartedly concur, but until the day comes that state governments, colleges, and federal officials ask teachers what students need, we're stuck with their limitless streams of bullshit paperwork."

Aubrey chuckled, a swath of relief streaming through the room. "I don't think I've ever heard you so … frustrated, Ms. Probst."

"Everyone in education is frustrated. They have just learned how to keep silent about it." She set the iPad down. "I suggest you grab a few of the students lollygagging around The Quad and have them help you unload your car. That's a good way to break the ice."

She wiped her hands on her skirt and marched toward the open front door. Before she stepped across the threshold, Sara paused.

"Things are different for you now, Ms. LaRoux. Remember, you're not their friend, can never be a confidant, and must sometimes violate their trust to keep them safe."

The air in the room grew thick with Sara's warning.

"I understand," she said with a heavy sigh.

Sara walked out the door without a second glance.

Aubrey should have felt slighted, but she had spent too many years under the headmistress' watchful eye to know the woman was not sentimental, or the kind to wish anyone well. Blunt, businesslike, and not shedding an ounce of regret over her actions, Sara Probst had been the backbone that had held Waverly together through many storms.

Aubrey dropped her suitcase onto the blacktop of the parking lot and sighed at the boxes she'd packed in her trunk. She had brought too much stuff, but she'd wanted to give her roommate, Ella, additional space to enjoy while she was away. Aubrey's hefty salary and free board offered her the chance to keep up the rent on her old apartment, in case the new job didn't work out. What concerned her was how long she could stand living in a dorm with a bunch of girls before craving the company of adults once again.

"You're Ms. Levi's replacement, right?"

Aubrey turned her head to the side and spotted a tall young man with broad shoulders, a thick chest, and arms that looked like he spent most of his time lifting weights. The ruggedly handsome, blond, blue-eyed stranger stepped closer. He moved like an athlete, swift and confident.

He slipped his hands inside the pocket of his blue slacks and cautiously inspected her car.

"I mean, I heard the crazy old bat had finally lost it, but I never thought Probst would replace her so quickly."

Aubrey slowly rose to her full height, staring him down with the calculating gaze she'd perfected during her short time in the public school system.

"You shouldn't call her an old bat, and whatever issues she had were none of your affair."

The young man's grin reminded her of other cocky young men she'd encountered throughout her short career as a teacher.

"I'm sorry, but Ms. Levi was pretty wacko."

A lean, toned girl, with long brown hair and a dazzling smile on her heart-shaped face, slid in next to the boy.

"Ignore Hartley. Everyone else around here does."

"Bite me, Bella," Hartley grumbled.

"Please," Bella shot back. "Like I would lower my standards to a dumb jock who talks about his four-wheeler more than a girlfriend." Radiating light from her bold brown eyes, Bella came forward with an extended hand. The rebellious purple ribbon in her hair and her regulation-length, purple glitter socks brought a smile to Aubrey's face.

"I'm Bella, Bella Simone. You're going to be my history teacher."

The way her personality exploded from her slender figure, like erupting popcorn, fascinated Aubrey. She had always struggled to maintain her cool reserve, believing it made her appear more mature. Now, she felt old.

"I'm Ms. LaRoux." She shook her hand, eager to know one of her students. "And I look forward to teaching you, Bella."

"I saw your picture in the old yearbooks they keep in the library." Bella edged closer and peeked in the trunk. "You graduated from here."

Aubrey reached for a box. "Yes, I did. Ten years ago."

Bella took the box from her hands. "Hartley, get some of your buddies to help Ms. LaRoux."

Hartley's mouth dropped, but he quickly recovered. He took off across the lot, appearing almost intimidated by Bella.

"Hartley's nice, a big star on the track team, mega-popular, but he's like most of the guys around here." Bella set the box on the ground. "He thinks with his dick."

Aubrey almost laughed out loud but decided she had to take the higher ground. "A pretty young girl like you shouldn't say such things."

"Even if it's true?"

"I won't comment on that since it's my first day." Aubrey reached into her trunk for another box. "Where are you from, Bella?"

"Baton Rouge." Bella leaned against the car's bumper. "My family has a few grocery stores there. My dad has high hopes for me going to a big Ivy League school, getting a business degree, and taking over the stores."

Aubrey wrestled a box out of her trunk and rested it on the bumper. "And what do you want to do?"

Bella twirled a lock of hair around her finger. "Microbiology. I'm fascinated by stuff under microscopes. It's so cool."

Not having any affinity for science—she'd barely passed biology in college—Aubrey decided to stay positive and encouraging.

"I'm sure your father will be happy with whatever you study."

Bella's throaty chuckle filled the air. "Yeah, right. He wanted a son but got stuck with me. He even had me try out for peewee football. But what else could he do? My mom took off when I was two. He's been raising me alone and is totally clueless about a girl."

Her refreshing honesty took Aubrey back a bit, but in her experience, teenagers tended to be a lot more forthright than adults.

"Well, fathers usually have a tough time understanding their daughters. Mine did, too."

"What's your father do?"

The question brought the lump back to her throat. "He was a lawyer in Baton Rouge. He died two years ago."

A glint of concern flickered in Bella's eyes. "That must have sucked."

Aubrey liked her bravado. "Yes, it did."

The heavy thud of shoes rose around them, and then a blur of gray and blue came rushing up to the car.

A young man swallowed up by his large pants and wrinkled shirt stood in front of her, breathless, a little sweaty, and brandishing an awkward smile. He had blue eyes, dark curly hair, a pronounced nose, and the longest lashes Aubrey had ever seen.

"I'm Cal Broussard." He immediately took her hand and pumped it. "I'm going to be in your history class. I'm so excited to meet you, and that you went here, so you understand all the crap we deal with. I hope you plan on lecturing about the history of the school because I—"

"Cal, stop frightening the poor woman to death." Bella removed his hand from Aubrey's. "You come across as a total stalker."

"I'm not a stalker." Cal's voice cracked. "I was being polite."

Bella picked up the box at her feet and shoved it into his chest. "Stalker. You're too scary to be polite."

Aubrey was about to assure Bella that she appreciated Cal's kind gesture when Hartley returned—without any help.

"Hey, the guys want to know if—"

Bella shoved a box in his chest. "Figures. Send a man to get help, and he comes back with excuses."

Aubrey covered her mouth when she snickered. The girl knew more about boys at that age than she did.

With the skill of a field sergeant, Bella took over the operation of unpacking Aubrey's car. Her efficiency, knack for piling boxes in the boys' arms until they couldn't see over the top, and her commanding presence, even had Aubrey a little intimidated.

With every box and suitcase removed from the car, Bella led the boys to the dorm, barking at them not to drop Ms. LaRoux's things along the way.

Aubrey trudged behind the young men, hauling her suitcase and overnight bag behind her.

"Where did you learn to take control of a situation like this?" Aubrey whispered to Bella as they approached the dorm entrance.

"Stock room," Bella replied in her no-nonsense way. "Boss men around in a grocery stock room, and you can conquer the world."

When they arrived at the glass door, Bella told them to leave the boxes since no boys were allowed inside.

Cal and Hartley wiped sweat from their brows, appearing thankful their hard work had come to an end.

"Thank you for helping."

Cal's cheeks pinked, and he dropped his gaze, but Hartley shoved his hands back into his pockets and nodded.

"Sure thing, Ms. LaRoux," he said, sounding confident.

Cal stood there, looking a little lost.

Aubrey watched as Cal slowly scurried away, darting to a patch of shade while Hartley casually sauntered toward a pack of giggling girls.

Bella clucked next to her. "God, do you think he could be more obvious?" She motioned to the girls keenly eyeing Hartley. "What is it with popular people sticking together? They're like elephants."

Hartley zeroed in on one girl—a leggy blonde in a school shirt that was a tad too tight around her full breasts. Her porcelain skin appeared luminescent beneath the morning sun, but her dark red lipstick and heavy black mascara detracted from her innocent round face.

"See, I was right," Bella announced. "Dickthinker."

Aubrey punched her newly assigned code into the keypad by the doors. "You sound jealous."

Bella's roaring laughter almost seemed to echo throughout The Quad.

"Of London Dumont? You must be joking. The girl is known as

the Maneater on campus. Her favorite thing is hunting for fresh meat. She's like a predator—tracks down every good-looking boy she can get—dates them and dumps them."

Aubrey struggled to get the door open while holding onto her suitcase.

Several students by the dorm entrance turned their way.

"Perhaps we should discuss this inside," Aubrey whispered.

Bella rolled her eyes. "Whatever."

Aubrey sighed, already suspecting her tenure at the prep school was off to a rough start.

CHAPTER 4

Hartley kept his eye on the new teacher. He watched the sway of her butt as she disappeared into the girls' dorm. The way she moved reminded him of a gazelle—the ones he'd seen on *Discovery*.

Aubrey LaRoux had not been what he'd expected and nothing like her yearbook photo. The image he had built up in his head—tough, forceful, a no punches kind of bitch—wasn't the woman he met.

That changed things. It would also make what he'd resolved to do harder.

"That her?" London kept smiling as she spoke, putting on a good show.

"Yeah, she was the one questioned after Marjorie's disappearance. She's prettier than her yearbook photo."

London teasingly patted his chest. "Did you come up with that assessment before or after you checked out her ass?"

He didn't like it when she got catty. Her claws were so much uglier than her pretension. Attractive and assertive girls never bothered him. It was the backstabbing ones who got under his skin. It made him miss Lindsey even more. She had been a straight shooter and fun to be around. A born leader, Lindsey had inspired others and helped give him a purpose.

The first day he'd met the pretty brunette in biology, he'd fallen hard. He still couldn't believe she was gone. He hadn't told anyone about the tears he shed in private. He didn't want people to think he was a wimp.

"I have to agree with you. She doesn't look like a murderer." London twirled a lock of blonde hair around her finger. "Still, she arrived at the school right after Lindsey disappeared and was at Waverly when her sister was killed. Seems rather suspicious."

Her breathy voice got on Hartley's nerves. "We don't know if Marjorie was killed. Lindsey never said she was."

"But she suspected." London glanced behind him toward the dorm. "Even if they never found her body, she could still be dead. Remember, we vowed to help Lindsey uncover the truth. The teacher might even lead us to Lindsey. That's why we need to stick close to her."

Hartley studied her perfect profile, debating if he wanted a chance with her. London's looks turned him on, and most of the time that was enough, though part of him longed for Lindsey. But London was no Lindsey and never would be. She could never fill the void left by the girl with the heartwarming smile.

"You get word to the others?"

London flashed her sharp gray eyes at him. "Yep, they're ready. Bella is already doing her part, and Jenna is intimidating everyone to drop Ms. LaRoux's first-period class. So, we should have her all to ourselves."

"Good. It will help us carry out our plan." He kicked at the grass, nervous about the course they were about to take. "Remember to watch your back. We can't afford to go missing like Lindsey. She got too close to the truth and look what happened."

London's lips formed a grim line. "You're convinced the person who got Marjorie got her, aren't you?"

Hartley didn't want to think of Lindsey being hurt or dead. He refused to give up hope she would come back to him.

"Until we find out who it was, we have to treat everyone like a suspect."

London's wicked grin elicited a ribbon of admiration. She had her moments.

"Even Aubrey LaRoux?"

Hartley turned toward the dorm entrance, no longer interested in

London but the attractive woman with the creamy dark skin. "Especially her."

Aubrey grimaced as she lugged her suitcase and overnight bag inside the building, frowning at the bleak gray and blue on the walls. A few girls sat on comfy sofas in the common area to the side, their gazes locked on their phones and tablets. The dreary décor that plagued the lobby carried over into the sitting area. Aubrey yearned for a can of yellow paint and a brush.

The glass doors closed behind her, and Bella appeared at her side, hugging one of the smaller boxes.

"So, tell me what you have against this London …?"

"Dumont," Bella said, filling in the blank. "A lot. She's a stuck-up bitch who thinks men worship her. Which I can't figure out. I mean, what guy wants a girl who will use him to get what she wants and then dump him?"

Aubrey wiped her brow, feeling like she had stepped into quicksand. "Why don't you tell me how you really feel?"

She walked toward the elevator, reviewing a list of techniques to use when encountering a student's hostility. Usually, bullying or a boy was the reason for heated emotions between girls.

Aubrey pressed the call light. "You can't dislike a girl because guys find her attractive."

The doors opened, and Bella stepped inside, balancing the box in her arms. "Yes, you can. There are lots of people you can dislike from the moment you meet them. Dogs can sense bad people, right? Then consider me a pit bull who can't stomach London's BS."

Aubrey struggled to roll her suitcase over the deep groove where the elevator doors came together.

"You will have to work with people you don't like someday. And coming up with a strategy now will help you in life."

"I don't plan on working with liars and cheaters."

Aubrey pressed the button to her floor while rethinking her game plan. The girl almost sounded a little too adamant. She wondered where her animosity came from. Bad experiences? Probably. Aubrey had felt the same loathing toward Marjorie. After her disappearance, she had made a pact with herself never to judge again. It had worked for her so far.

"What happened between you and London? There must be something."

The doors closed, and Aubrey held her breath, waiting for Bella to speak. The floors ticked by, and when the elevator came to a stop, she had given up hope of getting an answer.

"I hated someone once," she said in a soothing tone. "I eventually discovered all it did was tarnish me. I'd wasted so much energy on rage; I'd made myself miserable and not fun to be around. Giving someone that kind of power over you only hurts you, not them. Hate deepens your scars and keeps you from healing."

Aubrey pushed her suitcase out, done with her first lesson as a Waverly faculty member. Her stomach muscles knotted at the lingering scent of floral air freshener in the gray hall. How many times had she been forced to inhale that obnoxious odor while being taunted, kicked, or bumped against the wall hard enough to put a lump on her head? Bitter memories of life in the dorm still haunted her, but she wasn't that scared girl anymore. Aubrey had come to slay the demons of her past, not dwell on them.

"You ever play sports in school?" Bella asked from behind her.

Aubrey played down her surprise and headed along the dimly lit corridor. The small window at the end of the hall added to the prison-like feel she had experienced in her youth.

"I never got into any of that." She walked to her room door, close to the elevator.

"Well, I was on two swim teams in junior high and came here because their program is one of the best in the state."

Aubrey retrieved her keys from the pocket of her purse. "Yes, Waverly has always had a competitive swimming program."

She worked the lock, waiting for Bella to say more, but not wanting to push her. The silence became so frustrating she kicked the door open with her foot. She had worked with students who needed to talk before and knew giving Bella time and encouragement would help her—the girl seemed to have a lot on her mind. Aubrey never expected such a conversation while moving into her apartment.

Aubrey maneuvered into the room, checking out where to leave her suitcase, mindful of when Bella entered the room.

"I got on the team my freshman year," Bella said from the doorway. "Backstroke is my best event."

Aubrey went to a table in her living area and set down her purse and overnight bag, attentively listening and hoping Bella would trust her. Sometimes strangers were safe havens for confession, but bartenders, priests, and teachers were the best at keeping secrets.

"London was on the team, too, but she wasn't as good as me and she knew it. To make sure I didn't get in the way, she pushed me off one of the start boards in the pool. I slipped and hit my head. She claimed it was an accident, but I ended up in the ER with a concussion. My father refused to let me swim after that."

Aubrey slowly faced the girl, her insides shrinking. She had not expected anything so dramatic.

"So, I quit." Bella set the box on the table next to Aubrey's overnight bag. "The funny thing is, if I hadn't been injured, I might not have discovered how much I like microbiology." She put her hands on her hips. "So in some ways, I hate her, and in others, I don't. But no matter what, she's a bitch."

Aubrey had a seat on the heavy wood table, looking up at her. "I'm sorry you went through that."

Bella scanned the small apartment, appearing over her heart-wrenching disclosure. "Nice. I've never been in here before. Ms. Levi never allowed anyone in her rooms."

Aubrey watched as she inspected the kitchen appliances and small sink. She had professed so much in such a short time that it made Aubrey wonder if Bella needed a friend. And Aubrey was desperate for information. Perhaps they could help each other.

Aubrey recalled the missing Lindsey Gillett and Sara Probst's mention of her love for swimming.

"Bella, did you know Lindsey?"

Bella faced her, and her shoulders drooped. "Yeah, everyone knew Lindsey."

Aubrey stood, shaping her questions in her head. "Do you have any idea what happened to her?"

The girl shook her head. "The police think she ran away, but Lindsey wasn't a runner. She told me once she came here because her older sister did. It was after she disappeared that someone dug up the information on how her sister went missing."

Aubrey took a step, hoping to break the ice. "I was here when Marjorie went missing."

"Wow, what are the odds? It seems weird; two sisters disappearing like that." Bella paused and glanced up at Aubrey. "What do you think that means?"

Aubrey sucked in a deep breath, worry cutting through her. "I don't know, but there's been almost ten years between the two disappearances."

"Everyone around here blames the ghosts of the dead soldiers."

Aubrey furrowed her brow. "What dead soldiers?"

"The ones who died here during some battle. There have been rumors floating around for years about how the ghosts are responsible for taking the girls. Ms. Probst rides everyone's butt for talking about it. She doesn't want anyone to think the school is haunted. She hates hearing that crap."

Aubrey remembered the lectures and constant emails Ms. Probst had sent to faculty and students during her years in attendance.

"Yes, she always wanted to downplay the dark history of the school. She felt highlighting its past as a sugar plantation upset black students like me."

Bella rolled her eyes. "More like it would cut into the bottom line. Everything to her is about money or the school's reputation. She doesn't care about the students' feelings."

Aubrey had to agree. Part of her job in Baton Rouge had been recruiting from prominent families. School boards vied for wealthy patrons to offset the cuts the parish and state continued to make in their budgets. Money was the bottom line in education. Students were often a distant concern.

"Well, Ms. Probst wants only the best for Waverly."

"Do you think they will ever find Lindsey, Ms. LaRoux?"

Aubrey wanted to encourage Bella, but the past had taught her false hope could be just as debilitating as the grief it tried to suppress.

"I'm sure the authorities are working very hard," she said, sticking with the truth. "They understand there's nothing worse than not knowing what happened to someone you care about."

"Unless you find them dead," Bella countered. "That would suck."

A chill enveloped Aubrey, and she hurried to end the discussion. "Let's get the rest of those boxes up, shall we?"

She ushered Bella to the open apartment door, unnerved by what she had discovered.

Coming to Waverly was her new start, but it seemed like Aubrey had stepped back in time. Another girl was missing.

There had always been something off about the school. Aubrey wasn't sure if the land's horrific past or the school's remote location were to blame, but five missing girls was more than coincidence. She wished she could solve the mystery and put to rest her years of doubt. Unfortunately, Aubrey didn't consider herself brave enough to risk her job and career to get any answers. She'd keep her head down and teach her students. It was a simple plan, and one she prayed would keep her out of trouble.

CHAPTER 6

The crisp morning air disintegrated Aubrey's fatigue. The aches from her late night of unpacking receded as she took her time walking from the dorm to the liberal arts building. The tickle of nerves was different from her schooldays. She was a teacher, and her future no longer hinged on a specific grade or achievement tests.

Students already crowded The Quad, skimming notebooks or typing into computers. Part of her wished she had started the school year with them instead of coming in two months later, but she was there, and could finally make the changes she'd sworn to accomplish.

The ear-splitting clang of the first bell came from the speakers above the liberal arts building door.

Aubrey grimaced. *Damn thing is still too loud.*

Inside the main hall, banging lockers, the murmur of hurried conversations, peals of laughter, and the intermittent honk of a trumpet or clarinet filled the air.

The energy was electric and carried through the halls as Aubrey went to the staircase and set her hand on the oak banister. The smooth wood brought back so many warm memories. She could close her eyes and go back in time—feel her uniform skirt brush against her thighs, smell the perfume of the other girls rushing past, and register the tremble of the steps with the weight of students scurrying to make it to class.

She climbed, moving slower than the students, taking her time, and at each landing, sneaking a peek out the large windows that overlooked the school quarter-mile track, Olympic-size swimming pool, and stables.

Another jarring clang from the final bell shook the window.

Frantic steps echoed along the stairwell. Aubrey felt swept up in the furor, but now, she was a teacher, and the lessons began when she was ready.

She reached the landing on the third floor, a little winded. The climb had seemed like nothing when she was eighteen.

Last minute banging of doors carried along the hall as she made her way to class. The tingle in her belly grew more insistent. She clutched her briefcase, nervous about her first day.

Ahead was room 304, her classroom for the coming semester.

Aubrey held her breath as she walked up to the door and peered at her reflection in the frosted glass.

Bella's fists clenched, and she bit her lower lip, holding in her anger. She leaned away from the window and checked the other students in the room—the ones in on the plan. She had done her job feeling Aubrey LaRoux out. Her story about the swim team confrontation had been a bit too contrived, but it had gotten the sympathy and false pretense of trust she wanted to establish.

London sat next to Hartley's desk, leaning on him like a security blanket—something she'd done since Lindsey had gone missing. She was sure Hartley loved the attention, but Bella suspected his flirting wasn't legit. He'd cared too much for Lindsey to go with a flake like London.

Cal was at his desk in the front of the room, his open laptop, along with a notebook and selection of pens. And the fiery redhead, Jenna—the real oddball in their group—sat as lookout close to the classroom door.

She returned her attention to the chubby guy in the back of the classroom—the unexpected addition. He wasn't part of their group and could jeopardize their plans.

"What's Pussbucket doing in here?" she complained to Hartley. "You said you got rid of everyone."

Hartley slapped his hand on his chest. "Me? Like I would ever talk to that disgusting loaf." He jabbed his thumb toward the dark-haired, chunky boy blowing his nose. "Cal was supposed to get him to drop."

Cal stood from his desk.

London rolled her eyes. "The geek heard you."

Cal came rushing over, his face scrunched together and looking as ferocious as a rabid hamster. He stopped in front of London's desk. "No one wants to get within six feet of Pussbucket. He's the walking plague." He pointed at Hartley, frowning. "Anyway, his job was emptying the classroom, and my job was research. None of you would have known about those girls from the nineties if I hadn't found it online."

London sneered. "Oh, like looking shit up on your laptop is a real feat. Are you going to do anything to help this operation, Geek, or will we have to carry you just like Lindsey did?"

Bella stepped between Cal and London. "Shut up, both of you. We have a plan to shake down this Aubrey LaRoux, and we must stick to it. We're doing this for Lindsey, remember? So cut the crap and do your jobs. Find a way to get Pussbucket out of here before—"

"She's at the door," Jenna frantically whispered from her desk. "Sit down, quick."

Bella scurried back to her desk just as the door slipped open. Her heart thudded.

That was close.

Aubrey's love for teaching vibrated through her fingers while she turned the doorknob. It was a good sign. Every year that started with such a feeling became momentous. She took in a deep breath.

Here we go.

The moment she crossed the threshold, she exhaled her disappointment.

Only six students occupied the twenty desks allotted to the room, well short of the fifteen in her class list. Their dreary faces, slack with boredom and the dullness emanating from their eyes, added to the weight of Aubrey's dismay.

Bella grinned at her from the front row with rebellious hints of purple glitter catching the light on her uniform.

Hartley had a desk closer to the windows covering the far wall, but his gaze remained glued to London. The leggy blonde giggled as he bobbed his eyebrows, entertaining her.

A round male student filled out the last desk in the back row. Dark circles rimmed his dull brown eyes, and his jet-black hair dipped low over his forehead, partially covering his puffy face and red cheeks.

A slender young woman, with more stud earrings than Aubrey could count, flipped back her shocking mane of bright red hair. She took up a spot by the door, keeping her cautious green eyes on Aubrey. Sara Probst railed against students coloring their hair in fanciful hues. The handbook Aubrey had gleaned the night before had four whole pages devoted to the subject. But on the girl, the brilliant color struck Aubrey as a bold attempt to reveal the fiery personality behind her exquisitely carved features and lightly tanned skin.

Her head held high, Aubrey walked toward the front of the room, feeling like an inmate about to face a death squad.

She dumped her briefcase on the dingy brown teacher's desk. "Good morning, I'm Ms. LaRoux, and I will be replacing Ms. Levi for the rest of the school year."

Hartley broke out in a round of applause.

"Woo hoo," London called out. "Ms. Levi was so boring."

Aubrey opened her brown leather briefcase and rustled out her iPad. "Somehow, I thought there would be more of you."

Bella slapped her tablet on her desktop. "Everyone heard there was a new history teacher, and they changed their classes. People are pigs."

"You should know," London snapped.

Bella faced the young woman, rage brimming in her gaze. "And when I say pigs, I'm referring to you."

Aubrey walked around to the front of her desk. "That's enough."

Bella faced front, but her dislike remained etched into her features.

Aubrey sat against her desk, gauging the tension in the room. "I take it you are London Dumont. So, Ms. Dumont, tell me why you didn't drop this class."

London shot a quick smile at Hartley. "Well, Hartley said he met you, and you were cool, so I decided to stick it out."

"What a crock," Bella barked.

Aubrey ignored her. "And what do you like about studying history?"

Cal's hand went up. "Can I answer that?"

Aubrey ignored him and motioned to London. "Do you have any interest in studying history after you graduate?"

London's shoulders caved. "Me? Ah, no." She nervously glanced around the room. "I want to study oceanography and save the whales. I think history is a waste of time, but I need it to graduate."

"History is not a waste of time. It teaches us not to repeat the mistakes of others," the redhead by the door said in a distinctive, gritty tone.

Aubrey tilted her head, studying the young woman with interest. "What makes you say that, Miss ...?"

"Jenna Marchand." She folded her arms, revealing the edge of a tattoo under the cuff of her shirtsleeve. "And I like history, but I don't plan on studying it in college. I want to study equine veterinary medicine. I'm into horses."

"We already know you love horses more than people," Hartley grumbled.

Jenna sat back in her chair and stared him down. "It's better than spending all my time on four-wheelers and driving drunk through the woods."

The heavyset boy in the back raised his hand. "Can I go to the nurse? I don't feel well."

Bella spun around from her desk to face him. "You never do, Pussbucket."

The chubby, young man's cheeks turned a deeper shade of crimson. "It's pronounced Puce-bouquet, bitch."

A rattled Aubrey checked her class list, anxious to find the student's name. She almost gasped when she saw it—John Pucebuquet.

"Yes, John." Aubrey motioned to the door. "You may go to the nurse."

The grating of his desk against the white tile floor as he struggled to get out of it carried across the room. John tugged his book bag out from under his desk and grunted while hobbling toward the door. His ill-fitting shirt rode up his back, exposing the top of his white jockey shorts.

He made it out the door, leaving the room drenched in awkward silence.

"He's always sick," Cal said. "John misses more school days than anyone I know."

Aubrey took a step toward the desks. "Skewering his name was uncalled for, Bella."

She gave a smug grin. "I can't help it if he has a crappy name."

The others in the room chuckled, but Aubrey felt cut to the core.

"There's nothing funny about bullying." She went back to her desk and set the iPad down. "Waverly has a strict anti-bullying policy, and I will send you to Ms. Probst if you do it again."

"She's the biggest bully of all," Cal stated. "She's the first to cut you down to size if you're not taking part in the proper after-school activities."

"Or wearing the appropriate school attire," Bella added.

"Or have the wrong colored hair," Jenna continued.

"Or are the wrong sex." Hartley folded his arms. "She never lets any guy on campus forget being in her school is a privilege."

Aubrey sank onto her desk, astounded but also alarmed. Nothing had changed. The complaints from her students mirrored the ones she'd heard when attending the prep school. She'd returned to Waverly to make a difference and be the kind of teacher she'd never had—encouraging. What could she do to turn the situation around?

"Ms. Probst wants the best for the school, and though her methods may be a little hard to take, she means well."

"Then why hasn't she found Lindsey?" London's voice trembled, as she twisted her hands tightly together. "She has done nothing to help organize a search for her and has continually refused our requests for vigils. She won't even let us set up a grieving group."

Hartley's deep laugh reverberated through the room. "Like Probst would give a damn about us."

London wiped a tear from her eye. "I was Lindsey's friend. We shared a lot, but I never got to say goodbye."

"The investigation is still ongoing, and there's still more to discover, so why don't we leave it there," Aubrey insisted, wanting to get her students back to history. "Ms. Probst would not do anything to stand in the way of the law."

Bella leaned away from her desk, commanding Aubrey's attention. "Did Probst keep everything quiet when Marjorie Reynolds disappeared?"

Aubrey's stomach shrank to the size of a pea. She'd not expected her past to become a topic of conversation. Perhaps she had underestimated Bella.

London sat up, and her tears vanished. "You know about Marjorie?"

Bella put on a condescending sneer. "Ms. LaRoux was a senior here when Marjorie Reynolds disappeared."

"Whoa." Hartley gaped at her. "You knew Lindsey's stepsister?"

The lesson plan in Aubrey's head vanished, and her apprehension rose.

"I didn't exactly know her," Aubrey grumbled, feeling as if control had edged away from her.

Cal stood, smiling. "Do you know what happened to the dead girl?"

"Nobody knows if she's dead, pea brain." Jenna glared at Cal. "Her body was never found."

Cal sat. "It's been ten years. Safe to say she's dead, Jenna."

A rumbling of conversation overtook the room. Aubrey returned to her desk, debating what to do. She'd never encountered this situation before. Then again, few teachers had. Perhaps the best way to get her students back on track was to satiate their curiosity.

She raised her hands, demanding quiet.

"All right, settle down. Yes, I went here when Marjorie Reynolds disappeared, and though it is a coincidence, her sister disappearing right when I return, I'm sure it's not related."

Jenna blew out a loud hiss. "Please tell me you're not that dumb. It's always related."

"Shame they're not out to get you, Marchand," London said across the room.

Jenna shot London the bird.

Aubrey went to London's desk. She needed to assert her authority over the classroom. Otherwise, she would never get her students focused on their lessons.

"Stop this bickering." She waited as the students sank deeper into their desks. "I would think you'd want to work together to help Lindsey, not waste your time arguing about petty things."

"What did you and your friends do when Marjorie disappeared? How did you try and find her?"

London's grilling brought a rush of guilt to Aubrey. She had known Marjorie would come up, eventually, but Lindsey's disappearance had pushed the topic to the forefront of everyone's mind. Maybe allowing the discussion had been a bad idea. Students would want to know more about her relationship with Marjorie and her experiences with the case. Should she address the questions, or ignore them?

She turned away from the class, unsure of what to do.

Back behind her desk, she sat and reached for her iPad, settling on her decision. She would rather put her students' questions to rest now instead of letting them turn to gossip for the facts.

"We didn't do anything."

"Did you guys ever search the grounds?" Cal asked her. "Check out any of the old sites from when the land was a sugar plantation? The family burial ground? Or the battlegrounds? Elaine House is where the Battle of Irish Bend was fought in 1863. Union soldiers took over the house, and the dead are buried all around here."

Jenna groaned and rolled her head back. "Only you would know that."

London sat up. "But all the old gravesites are off-limits. Lindsey got suspended because she got caught around the mill ruins at the bayou."

Aubrey paused her hand over her tablet as a twinge of doubt rose from her gut. "I thought Lindsey was suspended for attempting to sneak a boy into her dorm room."

The entire class laughed. Aubrey sat back in her chair, a heavy weight settling on her chest.

"Lindsey wasn't that stupid," London said, still smirking. "She knew Probst watched her like a hawk."

"Why did …?" Aubrey's voice floundered.

Sara Probst had knowingly lied to her, and the reason behind such deception began to eat at Aubrey.

She turned off her tablet and put it aside, mulling over how to get her class back on track. It was apparent her students were never going to get their head around history at this point. She had learned that sometimes it was better to address a situation of distress for students, rather than ignore their feelings. Perhaps it was time to put that lesson to the test.

"What else can you tell me about Lindsey?" She eyed her class, searching for any hint of emotion. "Perhaps we should talk about her and her disappearance. It might help many of you cope with the stress of losing her."

"I'm not stressed." Jenna flipped a curl of red hair out of her round face. "She was a bully. Everyone on campus talked about it. Her sister was too. Do you know anything about that, Ms. LaRoux?"

Acid rose in the back of Aubrey's throat. She clenched her hands. "I heard Marjorie was unfair with several students. She had individuals she liked to seek out and was particularly harsh with them."

"Did she do that to you?"

Hartley's probing rattled Aubrey.

"I know Lindsey was pretty mean to me," Cal said. "She called me a lot of hurtful names."

"She could be a real bitch sometimes," Jenna agreed. "Try living in the same dorm with her."

"Stop attacking her," London shouted. "She was my friend."

"You think everyone is your friend," Bella edged in. "And then you stab them in the back."

The agitation in Aubrey snapped.

"Enough!" She reined in her anger. "I know some of you may have differing opinions on Lindsey, but let's focus on what we know about her case."

"What we know?" Hartley laughed, sounding angry. "Not a whole hell of a lot. Nobody tells us anything."

Aubrey stood, taking in the unflinching faces staring back at her. If she didn't know better, she would swear her students were the ones in control, not her.

"And what if the police had come to all of you, what would you have told them about Lindsey's last day?"

Then she saw it. The one thing that had not been there when she'd walked into the room—the spark of enthusiasm.

Aubrey settled down, glad her education had given her the right course of action. Discussing the case would help her class. What her students needed was comfort, and Aubrey wanted to provide that.

London coolly set her hands on her desk. "I would want them to know what she was struggling with. She had problems and being at this school didn't help the situation."

The hooks of curiosity sank into Aubrey's flesh. The teacher in her screamed to return to her lesson plan, but the student in her, the one who had lived for years with Marjorie's strange disappearance, wanted answers. She remembered that helpless feeling of not knowing what was going on and being considered too young to handle the truth. She didn't want her students to spend years wondering as she had.

"What kind of problems did Lindsey have?"

London took a deep breath, and her shoulders relaxed. "She often told me being at the same school where her sister disappeared scared her to death. She felt like she was next."

A pall settled over the classroom.

"Did anyone ever threaten her?" Aubrey demanded.

London shook her head. "It was just something she felt."

Jenna settled her elbows on her desk while cupping her cheeks. "What happened the night before they found her missing? I heard there was a fight up on the third floor."

Bella turned around in her chair to face Jenna. "Lindsey lived next door to my room. There was no fight. But I do remember hearing her leave her room after we were locked in for the night."

A tickle of anticipation crept up Aubrey's spine. "What did you hear?"

Bella nodded. "Something woke me up about three in the morning. Then I heard the thud of her door."

Aubrey ran her hand over her brow; nervous about the path the conversation had taken. "And you never spoke to the investigators about this?"

Hartley snickered. "None of us did. And we're the people she talked to most on campus."

Aubrey folded her arms, debating what to do. The discussion had taken an unexpected turn, and she was out of her depth. Getting herself and her students involved in a missing person's case was not a good idea, but her students had expressed their concerns. Aubrey hated to miss an opportunity to help them. Indulging her class this one time wouldn't hurt, would it?

"Perhaps we should be writing this information down."

Cal's arm shot up. "Way ahead of you, Ms. LaRoux. I figured if the police aren't going to do anything, maybe we should."

Hartley hurled a wadded piece of paper at Cal. "Asshole."

Cal pointed to the laptop on his desk. "There's a lot of evidence the parish guys don't have, but we do. Why not use it to launch our investigation?"

Jenna nodded. "That's not a bad idea. We have better access to the campus and can talk to anyone we want without raising suspicion."

Aubrey held up her hands. "No, you can't do this. None of you, or me, for that matter, are trained for that. You could hurt the chances of finding Lindsey if you tamper with the investigation. I'm here to teach history, not how to investigate a missing person case."

Hartley gave a curt nod to Aubrey. "You ever see that series *Don't*," he cleared his throat, "mess *with Cats*. It was on Netflix."

London snapped her fingers. "Yeah, I saw that. Some people found a killer with only their computers and a lot of detective work. The boys in blue didn't do crap."

"Exactly." Hartley pointed at London, a gleam of exhilaration in his eyes. "They went around law enforcement and cracked the case. Why can't we?"

"Because it's illegal and unethical." Aubrey raised her voice. "Not to mention that all of you are under eighteen."

Bella frowned at her. "What difference does our age make?"

Aubrey massaged the knot forming in her left temple. "It will make a great deal of difference when I lose my job, or worse, end up in prison for influencing minors."

"That's if they find out." Cal stood and approached her desk. "If we find anything, it can all be sent to a tip line. No one would have to know any of us were involved."

Aubrey wanted to throttle him for the suggestion, but there was something cunning about what he'd proposed—a way to uncover a mystery without getting caught.

"I like the sound of that." Jenna stood from her desk, her cheeks almost the same color as her hair. "We could finally do something."

"And find out what happened to Lindsey." London's voice ratcheted higher. "She deserves our help."

Cal took a step closer to her desk. "If we discover that mystery, maybe we can figure out what happened to the other girls."

Aubrey tensed, not sure how to interpret Cal's steely gaze. The burn of worry in her stomach heightened. She had become so caught up in the discussion about Lindsey Gillett, she hadn't seen the mention of the other girls coming.

"What do you know about that?"

Cal waved to the classroom. "We all know what went down in the nineties. Perhaps you might tell us more than what we read about in the archives."

Aubrey sagged against her desk, feeling cornered. "Over eight years, three girls went missing. It happened when Ms. Probst's father, Warren, was headmaster at the school. The press and pressure to find the girls took a toll on him and he shot himself not long after the last girl went missing."

"Damn." Bella slapped her hands on her desk. "I heard he did it in the headmaster's house. Is it true?"

Aubrey sighed. "When I went here, rumor was he haunted Elaine House, but no one ever saw him."

"Who were the missing girls?" Jenna asked.

"Marion Caldwell, Tracey Lowe, and Jeanne Caron." Cal glanced up from his computer. "They were all seventeen, blonde, blue-eyed, and about the same height."

"Serial killer?" Hartley offered. "They all look alike, so there had to be a serial killer on campus."

Bella went to Cal's open laptop. "That doesn't explain why Lindsey and her sister are missing."

London nodded in agreement. "Lindsey was a brunette, and so was her sister."

"Maybe the guy changed hair color preferences," Hartley joked.

Bella gleaned the pages Cal had pulled up on the missing girls. "Serial killers have a specific type they like. They rarely change their MO."

Aubrey stared at her students. "How would you know?"

Bella never glanced up from the computer. "Serial killers are a hobby of mine."

Jenna walked back to Cal's desk. "That would explain a lot."

Fed up, Aubrey tossed up her hands. "We can't do this."

Cal looked up from the laptop. "Yes, we can. What would you rather do? Teach us about history we can Google or solve a mystery that people have been talking about in this area for a long time?"

The practical teacher side of Aubrey wanted to protest and insist the class get back on track. Still, the disappearance of Marjorie Reynolds haunted her, and she wanted to get to the bottom of whatever mystery plagued Waverly. It was a big risk. She could be putting her career on the line if Sara Probst found out, but solving the puzzle might end the questions that resurrected her guilt in the middle of the night.

She shook her head. "I have assignments we have to cover. The history we study will—"

"Be the history of Waverly instead." Cal beamed at Aubrey. "History can be nothing but boring dates to many, but when you study the portion that relates to you, all the circumstances and characters come alive, and suddenly, you're on the inside. And that's when you stop listening to history and start learning it."

Aubrey walked up to Cal's desk. "Why are you selling this so hard, Mr. Broussard? Is this to get out of doing something constructive in class?"

"I wasn't selling," he said. "I was merely suggesting."

Aubrey weighed the determination in his face. "And how will the history of Waverly help you with your SAT, ACT, and AP tests? Preparing you for those tests is part of my job. Ms. Probst has high hopes for your class, and I don't want to disappoint her."

Cal leaned toward her, his grin never faltering. "We're not asking you to forgo your teaching plans, just put them off for a short while.

We'll make up for any lost time. We're asking for a chance to find out what happened. Aren't you curious? Wouldn't you like to know what happened to Marjorie and her sister?"

His conviction almost swayed Aubrey, but still, she doubted if she could pull off such a scheme under the watchful eye of Sara Probst.

Bella looked up at her, lines of worry popping up on her brow. "Lindsey was beautiful, smart, and a troublemaker, but when she wasn't found in her dorm room that morning, even I was scared. I don't want to feel that way again, ever."

The hard-line Aubrey had maintained faltered as Bella's assertions settled over her. The morning she'd found out about Marjorie, Aubrey had lived in fear until graduation day. The sleepless nights, the sick feeling in her gut, had always been there, and she was tired of experiencing that continual gnawing stitch of uncertainty. This could be an opportunity to heal herself and her students.

I can't believe I am doing this.

"Fine." She held up her hands, capitulating. "We will do some digging into the disappearances, but only as an assignment. If anyone asks, we are investigating the past of Waverly, and nothing more. Furthermore, this will only be for a few days, and then it's back to my lesson plan. Agreed?"

She walked back to the whiteboard, encouraged by the smiling faces and nodding heads she saw in the room. She picked up one of the dry-erase markers, formulating her plan.

Aubrey drew six columns on the board and put each one of the student's names at the top.

"Why are you putting Pussbucket's name up there?" Hartley demanded. "He won't participate."

"I agree." Cal walked closer to her desk. "He's a snitch. If we're going to keep this between us, he can't know about it."

Aubrey rested her shoulder against the board. "What do you suggest? He's part of the class. We have to involve him."

Cal picked up the eraser and removed John's name from the board. "When he's here, you teach your history, and when he's not here, we study ours. The guy's notorious for skipping class."

"And what if he finds out?" she demanded, already regretting her decision.

He handed Aubrey the eraser. "We can keep John quiet. We have enough on him to guarantee he won't be a problem."

A cold stab went through Aubrey's chest. The depths of her students' handling of the situation scared her.

With an icy, indifferent gaze, Cal walked back to his desk.

"How do you propose we do this?" Jenna asked.

Aubrey regained her composure and faced her class.

"We break everything down into parts. There are six elements of any investigation—who, where, what, when, why, and how. We will each take a question and search for clues that will hopefully find us some answers."

Under each student's name, she wrote one of the six elements. In place of John's name on the board, she put hers.

Bella pointed the pen in her hand at the board. "And how do I answer the *what* in my case?"

"What means what happened. In other words, did Lindsey disappear or was she taken? To ascertain that, you would need to search her room, collect evidence from people who knew her. Each of these elements will need evidence to prove or disprove them, interviews to add to timetables, and help uncover possible motives. Plus, a lot of this will involve good old intuition—following your nose."

London waved to the board. "How do you know this?"

"Her father was a detective with the Baton Rouge Police before he became a lawyer," Cal asserted. "I read about it on his obituary."

Aubrey coolly eyed the young man, impressed by his research but alarmed by his interest. Students had never checked up on her before, and the revelation sent a tingling sensation along her spine.

Jenna slapped the side of Cal's head. "Stalker much?"

A burst of playful laughter filled the room, but it didn't ease Aubrey's concern. She felt set up. She attempted to push the feeling aside, but the paranoia stayed with her.

"I was just doing my homework on our new teacher."

Aubrey's inner bullshit alarm went off. *Yeah, keep your eye on that one.*

"Save it for our investigation, Broussard," Hartley scolded. "We have to work together on this, and I don't want to deal with your usual creepy shit."

An icy chill enveloped Aubrey. *What creepy shit?*

London twirled a lock of her golden hair around her finger while eying the board. "When do you want us to start?"

Aubrey clasped her hands. "You can take out your computers and start now."

"Cool," Bella said, heading back to her desk. "And what do we do if we find something? I mean, like something important."

Aubrey gulped. She hadn't thought that far ahead.

"This is just an assignment, remember? Let's see if we find something first. If the parish investigators aren't coming up with much, we might arrive at the same dead end."

CHAPTER 8

London sat back on her bench, eating up the last bits of sunshine. She raised her face to the sky, glad her long day of classes had come to an end. The homework waiting for her brought a dull throb to her chest. Lindsey had made homework fun—she'd made school fun. When would this empty feeling go away?

"Hey, there."

The deep voice encouraged her to open her eyes.

Hartley sat next to her—a little too close—on the bench. She wanted to shimmy away, but they had an image to keep up.

At that moment, Aubrey appeared, walking from the liberal arts building.

London admired her beauty and the way she walked along, lost in thought with her pretty mouth downturned and amber eyes lowered to the sidewalk. Her long ponytail of jet-black hair flowed behind her.

She'd thought she would hate the new teacher, especially after everything Hartley had learned about her past with Marjorie Reynolds. Still, the woman was far from the cold, calculating student presented in the investigation interviews when Marjorie went missing.

Perhaps the officer who had questioned her about Marjorie had not given her a chance. The thought surprised her. It sounded like something Lindsey would say. Lindsey would have liked the new teacher—Lindsey liked everyone.

Like the Pied Piper, everyone had flocked to Lindsey. The girl with the glittering personality and big heart had won over everyone she met. London had loved her like a sister, which only made the pain even more debilitating. Everything she did, she wanted to share with her best friend, but Lindsey wasn't there.

I miss you.

"Did you do it?"

Hartley's request brought her back to the present.

"I put it where she won't miss it."

He edged closer, the coffee on his breath curling her nose. "Where?"

London sighed, knowing how much he liked details. "I put it someplace sure to get her attention." She turned to him, grinning. "If she doesn't notice, let's just say things could get hot in her apartment."

He chuckled and shook his head. "I knew you would pull it off. Now we have to see what she does."

"If she does nothing at all? I'm not convinced she wants to solve the mystery. Bella may think she can win her over, but Ms. LaRoux is a teacher. Her career and job are on the line. She has a lot more to lose than we do."

Hartley's upbeat smile never wavered. "But she won't be able to resist. She was a suspect in Marjorie's disappearance, and then she just happens to show up here right after Lindsey goes missing. If our tactic doesn't reveal the truth about what she knows, nothing will."

London's breath caught in her throat as she thought of all the chances they were taking—the shitstorm they were fighting to uncover. "What if she doesn't have a clue like the rest of us?"

Hartley's gaze stayed with the graceful woman as she approached the doors to the dorm. "Then we might have found a new ally to help us. Either way, we'll soon know where she stands. She doesn't have a chance against all five of us. Lindsey made us a force to be reckoned with."

The achiness smarting Aubrey's back made her smile. It was the result of chasing students in the halls, teaching her six history classes, and heading the weekly dorm room meeting to get acquainted with the young women in her care. After an exhausting day, she might have pulled out a book to relax before bedtime, but the excitement generated by her morning class kept her mind from settling.

She opened her laptop on the coffee table while her frozen lasagna dinner warmed in the microwave. Aubrey glanced at the pile of empty moving boxes by her door, waiting to go to the dorm's dumpster. Fatigue kept her glued to the gray sofa, as the hum of the microwave blocked out the giggles of girls in the hall beyond her door. She inspected the modest room with its stark white walls and dreary gray furniture. Even her knickknacks and pictures did little to help the apartment's gloomy atmosphere.

"I can see why Ms. Levi went bonkers."

Aubrey focused on the flashing Google cursor on her page and typed in *Waverly School*, eager to see what she could find.

When her search returned over fifty thousand hits, she wilted into her seat.

She eventually stumbled on the news of Lindsey's disappearance.

The first article was from *The Franklin Herald*. The reporter had written a piece about the missing girl. The article quickly turned biased when Lindsey's sordid past, along with her previous arrest in New Orleans, was highlighted more than her sudden disappearance.

The beeping of her microwave made her glance up. Wafts of white smoke swirled above her Formica countertop.

Aubrey leaped from the sofa and sprinted into her kitchen area.

She opened the microwave door, expecting to find her dinner burned to a crisp. However, the smoke wasn't coming from inside the oven, but from behind it.

Aubrey searched the counter for a towel and then quickly removed her hot dinner. She then turned the microwave around to inspect the back panel. That was when she saw where the smoke was coming from— the electrical socket.

She quickly unplugged the oven and moved it out of the way so she could get a better look. The smoke dissipated, and the outlet cover had no signs of singeing. The white plastic appeared utterly intact.

Aubrey stood back from the counter, trying to figure out what had caused the smoke.

She went in search of her tool kit. The small black bag of tools had been with her for years, ever since she'd discovered nothing worked in college dorm rooms.

After testing the socket cover's heat, she unscrewed the plastic top to check the wiring inside.

With the last screw removed, Aubrey removed the cover and gasped.

A wave of smoke whooshed out of the outlet. There, crammed next to the wiring, was a folded piece of paper. The edges were brown, but the rest remained intact.

"What the hell?"

Aubrey carefully reached in and pulled the paper out, then checked to see if anything else was in the outlet. She was about to set the scrap aside when she noticed the handwriting.

Aubrey put her screwdriver down and carefully unfolded the scrap.

Her curiosity quickly turned to disbelief, shrinking her stomach. She held her breath and read the scribbled writing.

> *I am afraid. Someone is after me because I know too much and am close to uncovering the truth. Let everyone know I did not disappear. They wanted me gone. Find out what happened to Marjorie and the others, then you will find me.*
> *Lindsey Gillett*

Aubrey read the note three times. She reached for the counter, a wave of lightheadedness coming over her.

"Holy shit."

She covered her mouth and took the note back to the sofa, debating what to do.

She peeked at her purse on the table by the door, her phone inside. She should call the sheriff and hand the note over, but something inside Aubrey hesitated.

What if it isn't Lindsey's handwriting but a prank?

If her students knew about her questioning for Marjorie's disappearance, then someone else on campus could have put the note there to scare her or set her up.

If she went to the police, it could bring her unwanted attention, especially if the note wasn't real. The last thing Aubrey wanted was to dredge up her past with Marjorie.

"But why would someone put it in here?"

The outlet could have easily caught fire and burned down the apartment, but perhaps Lindsey knew that. Someone else would replace Ms. Levi, someone new to the school, and hopefully free of Sara Probst's influence.

Aubrey tapped the note, going through a long list of ideas of what to do, but only one felt right—she had to share the letter with students investigating the disappearances. They could tell her if the note was genuine, and then Aubrey would decide how to proceed.

"Always check for smoke before yelling fire," her father had once said.

Aubrey had uncovered more than a fire with Lindsey's note—she'd unearthed a problem. Who could she trust? Sara Probst would brush the letter under the rug and destroy it if she could, all in the name of protecting Waverly. But her first period students would have a keen interest. Lindsey was their friend, and they seemed adamant about finding out what happened to her.

Then there was the additional problem of involving the parish authorities. Would they treat this like Sara Probst dictated, or could they be trusted? Her head spun with possibilities, but Aubrey felt assured of one thing—if this blew up in her face—it would cost her more than her job. It would destroy her career.

The round eyes staring back in the classroom created an uncomfortable burn in Aubrey's throat. She stood in front of her desk, holding Lindsey's note in her trembling hand, debating if she had done the right thing. Aubrey had not planned on scaring her students with the sudden disclosure, but she also didn't want to lie and not tell them what she had found. If they were going to do this as a team, all the evidence needed to be shared.

London's sniffles broke the unnerving silence.

"She was right," she softly said. "Someone was after her."

"But she found something. We were hoping for that." Cal's enthusiasm upended the heaviness in the room. "Now we have to find out what that was."

Bella turned to him, sneering at his exuberance. "Isn't it obvious? She figured out what happened to her sister."

"Perhaps more than that." Aubrey leaned on her desk, worried about what her students would do next. "She might have discovered what happened to the other girls who went missing in the nineties."

Cal got out of his desk and marched up to her. He snapped the paper from Aubrey's hand. "Are we sure it's her handwriting?"

London scrambled behind him. She took the note and scanned it. She sniffled once more and then thrust the paper into Cal's chest.

"It's her handwriting." London walked back to her desk.

Jenna rocked back her head, appearing bored, and let go of a long sigh. "So what do we do with it? Go to the police?"

Cal held up the note to the class. "No, we use the information she gave us. We find out what happened to Marjorie and the other missing girls. That will lead us to Lindsey."

London flopped in her desk seat. "So we do nothing?"

Hartley opened his laptop. "Not nothing." He typed on the keyboard. "I was assigned the *where* in our case. So I did some digging into the school and its past."

"I've already done that," Cal complained, his voice cracking.

Hartley flipped his laptop around to show the class. "Yes, but did you make a map of where they found clues when those girls disappeared in the nineties?"

Everyone in the class, including an intrigued Aubrey, gravitated toward Hartley's desk.

"How did you do that?" she asked, eyeing the screen.

"I checked in the local newspaper on those three girls we talked about yesterday in class. They didn't have much, but then I remembered a connection in town."

Hartley's beaming grin made Aubrey glad she had shared the note.

"I hacked into the St. Mary Parish Sheriff's Department database and got their records. Took a while to find them because the cases are so old, but they're still open."

A shockwave of astonishment took Aubrey's breath away. When she recovered, she glared at Hartley.

"That's highly illegal. What if you get caught?"

His grin didn't lessen as he eagerly observed her surprise. "A daughter of an officer in town would do anything for me. She swiped her father's passcode for me."

London punched Hartley's arm. "You cheating dog."

Hartley nursed his arm while shooting her a dirty look. "I only took her for a ride on my four-wheeler. Why would I mess with her? She goes to Franklin High."

Aubrey shifted the laptop around to get a better look at his map.

She felt a tingle in her gut as she examined the red X's marked through the detailed layout of the entire school campus.

Elaine House was at the bottom, with the bayou's blue waters at the top of the page. The campus buildings, crowded around the plantation home, covered the lower portion of the document, with only a few buildings positioned close to the bayou, including the stables and the track field.

Most of the top of the map had no other indications of modern structures. Only the ruins of the old sugar mill and the cemetery of the family who had built Elaine House remained earmarked. The concentration of red X's in that area bothered Aubrey. The girls had ended up far away from the dorms, in a place no one on campus usually dared to venture.

"So what did you find? What evidence is in this locale?"

Hartley touched the mouse to the first X near the water, and a picture of a scrap of cloth popped up on the screen.

"That's a piece of Marion Caldwell's uniform." He moved the mouse to another X and clicked. "That's a barrette Tracey Lowe wore in her hair." Then he tapped another X, and another picture appeared. "And that is a shoe identified as belonging to Jeanne Caron." He waved at the screen. "That's what's all over here. Pieces of clothing belonging to those three girls. But there's nothing reported to have belonged to Marjorie. They never found a trace of her."

Jenna moved closer to the computer. "Why the other girls and not her?"

Bella leaned in, her head next to Jenna's, examining the pictures on the screen. "Maybe our killer got better at it. Learned how to cover his tracks."

Cal touched the upper corner of the computer. "Most of your X's are close to the Bayou Teche River."

Hartley nodded. "Just past the battlefield."

"Gross." London grimaced. "Tell me we're not going there."

"Might have to," Jenna argued.

"Yeah," Bella agreed. "We have to check it out."

Aubrey held up a dissenting hand. "Our project does not involve field trips. This is a classroom assignment only."

Cal faced her with his lips set in a thin angry line. "You said we had to find out the answers to the questions we were assigned. So how do we do that without a field trip to the sites where clues were found?"

The students surrounding Aubrey looked at her for an answer. They had talked her into allowing them to participate in the investigation assignment, but she wasn't about to take their work outside of the classroom.

"No way. Those places are off-limits to students."

"But not to faculty," Bella sweetly countered. "You could take us there on a field trip to discover more about whatever battle took place there."

Cal glowered at Bella. "It's called the Battle of Irish Bend or Nerson's Woods. But it was more of a skirmish between the Confederate and Union army who wanted to secure the Bayou Teche River."

Aubrey paused, questioning his information. "What exactly took place if it wasn't a battle?"

"A mistake," Cal admitted with a grimace. "Union divisions ran into the Confederate forces moving through the area. It wasn't planned, and no one was prepared for the encounter."

"Only a geek would know that." She pointed at Cal, frowning. "We need to go there and check it out. Whoever took the girls must have known it was once a battlefield and hoped no one would search there. And if they did, they would chalk up any bones to the dead soldiers buried there after the battle."

London flinched. "We aren't digging up dead people, are we?"

"No, we're not because we're not going." Aubrey paused, considering Cal's story. "I'm sure no one is buried at the battlefield. It's just a story."

"The Confederate soldiers who died on the field were rumored to be buried by the Union army in a mass grave, but no one knows for sure." Cal coolly drummed his fingers on Hartley's desk. "Maybe that is why Waverly is cursed. The dead aren't happy."

Aubrey had heard enough. "All right." She clapped her hands. "Everyone back to their desks. You have assignments to get to."

The dejected faces staring back, she expected. The heaviness her students' disappointment gave her was a surprise.

"We need to go to the battlefield." Hartley stared, imploring her with a wicked grin. "We'll look around and come right back. All we need is an hour, tops. We could go during class."

"Are you insane?" Aubrey pinched the bridge of her nose. "It's bad enough I agreed to this."

"But think of what we could learn." Cal stood next to Hartley's desk, narrowing his gaze on her. "We could find the marker, document it, maybe discover if troops are buried there. Think of what we will add to the knowledge about the site. That's educational, isn't it?"

Aubrey put her hand on her hip. "But we aren't going for the sake of the battle. This has to do with your investigation assignment."

"So does that mean we are going?" Bella asked, sounding hopeful.

"No," Aubrey bellowed, determined not to give in.

Hartley closed his laptop and folded his arms, a dangerous glint in his eyes. "If we don't go, what will be the point of our investigation? Our hands will be tied by what we learn in the classroom. Then we might get bored, tell other students about our assignment. And then other faculty might hear."

London leaned against his shoulder, a devious grin spreading across her lips. "Take us to the battlefield, and then we will know you're committed to helping us succeed with this project. It will show that we can trust you. In return, you can trust us to keep everything we find quiet."

Aubrey's stomach burned, and the bitter taste of bile rose in her mouth. "That's blackmail."

Cal chuckled and joined London's side. "That's education. You can't teach anyone without trust."

Aubrey leaned on Hartley's desk, sick over her predicament but knowing she would have to go along. It wasn't out of fear of discovery, or her students' strong-arm tactics that motivated her—it was curiosity.

She reexamined his map, no longer hiding her interest. What if they did find something? She would have to inform the police, and then everything would get revealed.

Then again, you might get the answers you've been craving for years.

"I'll submit the permission slip to Ms. Probst. I'll tell her we're researching the battle, and I want to show you the site."

Bella folded her arms, and a pensive line crossed her brow. "What if she says no? We won't be able to go."

Cal gestured to Bella, nodding. "She's right. We can't let anyone know we're going to the battleground."

Aubrey's frustration gnawed at her. "I have to request permission to take you guys on any field trips."

Hartley grinned, making his eyes two specks of blue light. "It's only a field trip if we leave campus, right? So, we're not leaving campus."

"He has a point," Cal agreed. "The handbook says we are allowed to go where we want on the grounds with faculty supervision."

Aubrey tossed her head back, unable to argue with his logic, but uncertain Ms. Probst would see it the same way.

"All right. Tomorrow. Get here half an hour before classes start so we can sneak away without being seen."

Hartley high-fived with Cal. "Now we are getting somewhere."

Aubrey headed back to her desk, the tension in her shoulders becoming as taut as a drawn bow.

"Yeah, you guys are going to get me fired."

CHAPTER 7

Two cups of coffee churned in Aubrey's stomach as she made the trek across the dark quad. Lights shone through dorm room windows, lighting her way along the sidewalk. She tugged the pack she had brought closer to her shoulder. Loaded with flashlights, water, and a first aid kit, Aubrey wanted to make sure nothing happened to her students during their illegal jaunt to the battlefield.

When she arrived at the glass entrance to the liberal arts building, all that greeted her was the school's mascot—a blue and gray wolf— depicted on the doors.

"Shit." She searched The Quad, cursing her students' tardiness.

"I heard that." Jenna stepped out of the shadows.

Aubrey calmed her racing heart. "You scared the crap out of me."

Jenna checked the time on her phone. "You said six thirty."

Aubrey's hope for a stealthy getaway slowly faded. "If the rest don't show up on time, this will—"

The bouncing beam of a flashlight approached. Her heart rose in her throat. She prayed it was her students and not someone coming early to the building.

"I thought we would beat you guys."

Hartley turned off his flashlight, allowing Aubrey to get a glimpse of London and Cal at his side.

"Cal and I drove in together from town." Hartley nodded to London. "We just ran into her."

Aubrey was relieved to see Cal had a pack on his back.

"What did you bring?"

Cal shrugged his pack around his shoulder. "First aid kit, water, bug spray, and my Cannon. In case we find something, we'll need a better camera than what's in our phones."

London lifted her five-gallon purse. "I have water, Coke, Sprite, Diet Coke, chocolate bars, power bars, and snack packs in case we get hungry."

Jenna chuckled. "It's a fact-finding mission, not a picnic."

A chuckle came from the dark to the right of the doors.

Aubrey spun around, searching for the culprit.

Bella walked up, smiling. "You all look guilty as hell, and we haven't even done anything yet."

Aubrey glimpsed the first rays of sunlight streaking across the sky. They needed to get moving.

"Everyone stick together. No wandering off. If anyone does spot us and asks where we've been, you tell them we were at the stables, or the track, getting some exercise. That will sound believable."

Bella pointed at Cal. "No, it won't."

Cal glared at her. "I exercise."

Aubrey raised her hand, demanding quiet. "Let's go. No talking until we are away from these buildings and don't use flashlights. People will spot us."

London meekly raised her hand. "What about snakes?"

Hartley chuckled. "It's October. They're hibernating."

"They're not hibernating yet," Cal insisted. "It's too warm."

"Oh, for God's sake." Aubrey shooed them along the sidewalk. "Let's get moving."

She led the way along the sidewalk, heading toward a break in the buildings decorated with a garden of posies and fresh red mulch. It was the fastest way she could think of gaining access to the long patch of grass that led to the rear portions of the school.

When she stepped over the stones marking the garden's edge, her students stopped and watched.

"What are you doing?"

Aubrey looked back at Cal. "We go this way, between the buildings and avoid getting close to Elaine House."

Cal followed her into the garden, mindful of not tromping on the posies.

The others followed his lead, and within minutes they were behind the liberal arts building and hiking across the grassy field that led to the stables.

"Why can't we walk on the path?" London complained.

Aubrey waved at a passing fly. "Because the paths have lamps to light the way. And we don't want to be seen."

"You thought this out," Bella said with a snicker. "I'm glad. It shows you have a devious mind."

"No, it proves I would like to keep my job, and you guys from getting in trouble with Ms. Probst."

"Little late for that." London moved her big purse on her other arm. "There's not a person on campus that hasn't landed in hot water with her at some point."

Light from the morning sun trickled across the sky as they crossed the manicured grass.

"That woman loves to create drama," Jenna said. "Last year, she planned to suspend me for my hair. It took a note from my parents threatening a lawsuit to get her to back off."

Cal scooted closer to her. "I was wondering about that. All the guys figured you wouldn't last the semester when you came back with your fiery hair."

"She tried to get me to admit I put detergent in the swimming pool last year." Hartley took London's bag from her arm. "Remember when they found a ton of suds in it?"

"That wasn't you?" Bella asked.

Hartley shook his head. "Not my idea. I know who did it, but I wasn't going to rat them out to make Probst happy. So I took the week of detention she gave me and kept my mouth shut."

"She did the same thing to me," London admitted. "She wanted me to roll over on the girl who pulled the fire alarm in the dorm last semester."

"You did that," Bella roared. "Everyone on campus said you did."

"No, I didn't." London bit her lower lip. "It was Lindsey. She claimed it was an accident, but I know she did it on purpose."

Aubrey went up to London and put an encouraging hand on her shoulder.

"Why didn't you tell any of the faculty about that? They could have handled the situation."

"I was afraid for Lindsey," London mumbled. "She was all freaked out about someone following her, so I didn't want to make matters worse."

Aubrey kept a wary gaze on the land surrounding them. "But why did Lindsey pull the alarm?"

London's loud sigh carried in the humid air. "She was pissed with Probst about something. She never told me what."

Aubrey came to a dead stop, floored by the admission. "Is that why she ran away?"

London shook her head. "Lindsey didn't run away. We all know that."

Hartley hurried and came alongside Aubrey, blocking her view of London.

"What about you, Ms. LaRoux? Did Ms. Probst ever do anything to you when you attended the school?"

The odd question put off Aubrey's interrogation. She suspected London knew more than she wanted to admit, but perhaps it wasn't the time or place to push her. Aubrey needed to establish trust with her students. Even if their tactics had rubbed her the wrong way, she still wanted to learn more about Lindsey.

"It wasn't like what you guys suffered. With me, it was more about never being good enough. She never spoke to me or addressed me when I went here. I was a scholarship student. One set up by the Catholic Creole Society. I could never figure out if it was because of that, or my skin color, or she just never cared for me. Then when she offered me this position, I thought perhaps I had exaggerated it all. I think Ms. Probst's manner more than her position makes her difficult to understand. She has a stressful job."

"You're making excuses for her," Jenna said in an irritable tone.

"After my parents made a stink, she ignored me as well. To this day, she won't speak or acknowledge me. Not like I care, but I think that's how she copes with those who get the best of her. She pretends they don't exist until she needs them. And my guess is she needed you."

"She's a bitch," Hartley mumbled. "Everyone at school knows it."

"You have to be respectful of where she comes from." Aubrey peered ahead; glad she could make out the landscape in the early morning light. "Ms. Probst spent her whole life at this school. Her father came here when she was eight, and short of the years she spent away at college, Waverly is all she has ever known. I think that's why she took over after he died. She's protective of this place."

"You're too nice, Ms. LaRoux." Jenna slipped the pack from Aubrey's back. "I bet you try to see the good in everyone."

Aubrey let her have the pack, grateful for the break. "Not everyone."

"I'm sorry I snooped on you," Cal said while walking next to her. "I was curious. I wasn't stalking."

She patted his shoulder, feeling she was making headway with her students. "I was flattered, even if it was a bit stalkerish. Don't make a habit of it."

"Where are we going first?" London asked as she checked the lightening sky.

Cal removed a tablet from his pack. "We'll head to the battlefield first. That's where the investigators found the most evidence. Then we can head to the mill next to the bayou. If we have time, the cemetery."

London held up her hands. "No cemetery. I refuse to go there. The battlefield is bad enough."

Cal shrugged, not appearing too concerned. "I guess we can skip it. Nothing was found there, anyway."

Bella snuck closer to Aubrey and whispered, "Do you think we'll find anything?"

Aubrey sucked in a deep breath, attempting to hide her nervousness. "I sure hope not."

The grass got thicker and higher after the group passed the edge of the pristine grounds. The sun had risen, turning the red streaks into gold and illuminating the sky. Clouds occasionally blocked out the sun, allowing a cool breeze from the nearby river to wash over Aubrey's warm skin. The long hike made her regret her decision to indulge her students' curiosity. She preferred a comfortable classroom to the remote area where every breed of Louisiana insect seemed to flourish.

"According to the map, we should be on top of the battleground," Cal told her. "I'm going to fan out and get a better look."

"You go right, and I'll go left," Hartley suggested. "We can cover more ground that way."

Aubrey stayed with the girls, maneuvering through the eerily quiet grounds.

"Have you ever been here?" London asked. "Before, when you went to Waverly."

Aubrey shook her head. "I never ventured past the stables. This is all new to me."

Jenna surveyed the grounds. "They say this is where Marjorie Reynolds disappeared."

"Is it?" Aubrey hooded her eyes against the sun. "I never knew that. They never told us she disappeared around the school buildings. Not out here."

"I'm glad to hear that," Bella muttered.

Aubrey stared at her. "What's that—"

"I found something."

Cal's cry sent a shockwave through Aubrey. She hurried to where he stood in a patch of thick weeds. He had his hands pushing back the tall stalks as a mass of flies swarmed around him.

She got closer, wary about what awaited. Then a chunk of dark black cut stone caught her eye. It rose about two feet off the ground and had a square cement base.

"It's a monument," Cal excitedly announced. "I never knew this was here."

Hartley came charging forward, sending up a cloud of gnats.

"Sure seems like nobody was meant to see this," he said. "I thought these sites were protected."

"Unless they're on private land." Aubrey ran her hands along her arms, overtaken by a chill. "There are quite a few battle sites still owned by families and not open to the public."

Cal cleared away the weeds blocking the bronze plaque secured to the stone.

"*On this spot on the morning of April 14, Major General Richard Taylor and his men met Brigadier General Cuvier Grover's Union brigade. An unknown number of Confederate soldiers died on this site and were buried in an unmarked grave. This marker is dedicated to their memory and sacrifice.*"

London lifted her feet. "Are you kidding me? We could be standing on dead men?"

Jenna raised her head to the clear blue sky. "That's sad. Those men died here, and all they get is that plaque. No gravestones?"

Aubrey surveyed the grounds, an uneasy feeling settling over her. "A lot of men were buried where they died during the Civil War. They never made it home."

Hartley approached the memorial. "What happened after the battle?"

Cal patted the marker. "Taylor withdrew. Grover's men took the site and ended up living in Elaine House for a few weeks. This victory, along with the one at Fort Bisland, two days earlier, assured the success of the Union expedition into West Louisiana."

Aubrey turned back to Cal. "So why would someone bring those girls here? Are they making a statement against the Civil War? This site was chosen for a reason."

"So they wouldn't be seen or heard." Jenna looked at her as if analyzing her reaction. "You could do what you want and never have to worry about interruptions."

Her intense gaze set Aubrey on edge.

London hugged herself. "That's creepier than the dead guys."

Hartley slapped at the flies around the monument. "We'll never find anything under all these weeds." Then he paused. "What's that?"

Cal eased in closer, appearing fixated.

Aubrey pushed between them and spotted what had sparked their interest.

On a corner of the monument, flecks of dark red stained the off-white base.

"That looks like blood."

Cal touched it, but the stains did not smear.

"It's dried but could be from a kill. There are foxes, coyotes, and bobcats on these grounds. We've all heard the coyotes before."

"You would have to analyze that to know for sure," Bella said, as she leaned over Aubrey's shoulder.

"Doubt that would help us." Hartley dug out his phone and held it up to the monument. He took a quick photo of the blood. "Whatever was here is long gone. Let's head to the old mill. Perhaps there's more blood there."

London faked a dramatic shudder. "Please, let's hope not."

Cal dug out his tablet and held it up. He pointed toward the right to a thicket of trees.

"That way. We should run into the bayou soon."

Cal set off first while Aubrey stayed behind, covering the rear and making sure the rest of the group followed him.

Hartley quickly eased back to join her, his lips pressed into a concerned line. "You seem rattled. Is this too much for you?"

The question struck her as intrusive. "No, I'm fine. I can't help but think about those young women."

He turned to her with a hard, penetrating stare. "The killer knew about this place and had been here before. He or she knew no one would hear them cry out."

"She?" A knot had manifested in her stomach. "You think a woman could have done this?"

"Possibly. Someone who knew the girls or had a problem with them. Could have drugged them, knocked them out, and brought them here."

His cold, flat delivery chilled her despite the warm breeze.

"If you believe that, why don't the police? They never mentioned anything about the missing girls when Marjorie was abducted."

Hartley winced. "If you found three girls missing and probably dead in an all-girls' school, wouldn't you try and keep it quiet?"

"Do you think Warren Probst had something to do with that?"

Hartley reluctantly nodded. "If he wanted to keep this school open, he didn't have a choice. I would have done the same."

She studied his profile, a wary twinge rising in her chest.

"What an odd thing to say."

His grim expression never wavered. "If you want to find a killer, you have to think like one."

"But you're a seventeen-year-old boy, Hartley, and hardly a killer."

He raised his gaze to the others ahead of them. "Age has nothing to do with the thirst to kill. That's something you're born with."

The cold detachment in his voice unnerved her.

"And you think our guy has this thirst to kill?"

"I hate to break it to you, Ms. LaRoux, but that's something all men possess. Some just keep it in check better than others. But when we get mad or are pushed too hard, it comes out. Controlling it is key."

Uncertainty clouded her judgment. Hartley was a student, a young man on the brink of adulthood. What could he possibly know about such things?

"And how do you control it?"

"Like every other kid my age—I worry about school, partying, date pretty girls, and sometimes drink."

She held up her hand. "I didn't hear that."

Hartley chuckled. "Yeah, you did, but unlike the other teachers at our school, you understand. Just be careful, Ms. LaRoux. Not everyone at school wants to be your friend."

Hartley walked ahead, leaving a bewildered Aubrey questioning her instincts.

She might have considered the visit to the battleground a way to appease her students, but it did give her some new insights into their behavior. There was still something off with the picture presented to her. These students seemed too collected compared to other seventeen-year-olds. It made her wonder what they were scheming.

CHAPTER

Water roared around her while the humidity pressed against Aubrey's skin. Her feet sank into the mud, making it harder to walk. Her white tennis shoes were red with clay, but she didn't complain. Her students seemed so intent on reaching the mill. She had to tough it out.

"We must be close," Hartley said, as he checked his phone. "We should be able to see it by now."

"We don't know if the structure is still standing," Cal admitted. "The last documented picture was back in the 1990s."

"How do you know that?" Aubrey asked.

He pulled up the photo on his iPad. "Insurance assessment. Or so the internet says."

Aubrey peeked at his tablet. "You sure do seem interested in this place."

He swept the picture aside on the page and returned to his map of the grounds. "When I look at a rundown mill or an overgrown battlefield, I see what it can tell us about the past."

"I don't like to think about this plantation's past." Aubrey noticed a tall structure, like a smokestack, meeting the sky ahead. "A lot of misery was inflicted on this property. Slaves worked this land, and they died here, too."

London's pink lips disappeared as she smashed them together. "Sorry, I didn't think about how hard this might be for you ... Maybe we shouldn't have come."

"No, it's fine," she assured her. "And Cal has a point. To see a place, really see it, you must understand the people who lived and died there. When you grasp their triumphs and tragedies, you learn to respect the past. History is more than dates and battles—it's people. Remembering and respecting what they went through is what matters."

Hartley picked up his step and pointed to the roofline breaking over a patch of pine trees.

"That's the mill."

"Hartley, don't wander off," Aubrey suggested, adding a hint of irritation for emphasis. "Stick with the group."

Cal shook his head and muttered, "I'll get him."

Aubrey watched as the two young men ventured ahead, getting lost under a few trees.

"Great," Jenna complained, knocking some of the red mud from her shoes. "The guys take off and leave us to fight off the snakes and bugs."

"Snakes!" London spun around, looking at the ground. "Where?"

Aubrey patted her arm. "Come on."

She urged the girls to break into a brisk walk. The high grass whipped against their legs, making Aubrey thankful for her long slacks.

They came to a line of shade that stood before a thick outcropping of trees. The roar of rushing water accompanied the birds singing in the trees.

Aubrey kept up the rear as the girls forged ahead. They worked through thick piles of leaves, and then the soggy ground turned firmer. The shade offered a break from the intense sun, and the essence of evergreen revived her. The burn in Aubrey's thighs told her they were climbing a ridge. When the light once again broke through the thinning branches, she pushed forward to stay close to the girls.

She popped out along the shoreline at a bend in a churning, muddy river. Shiny quartz rocks cluttered the bank as eddies swirled and then drifted out to the middle of the waterway.

The current was swift, and the few massive logs floating by let

Aubrey know that the undertow would be deadly.

"Over here."

She followed the sound of Cal's voice and gasped.

He stood in front of a vast mill made of brick with a single black smokestack coming out of one end. Part of the wall was missing on one side of the square structure, and the windows and doors had vanished long ago. The top of the stack had crumbled in, leaving a rough, uneven opening at the top. Ivy and plants grew up the side of the remaining building. Still, through the jumble of brick and greenery, you could see an assortment of sugar processing equipment, including the gear mechanisms of the rolling sugar cane press.

Cal waved to her and the others as he stood on top of a mound made of rust. "Look at this place."

Aubrey searched for Hartley amid the ruins. He stood atop another mound close to Cal.

"They're the old iron boiling pots," Hartley called. "I can't believe they're still here."

The girls ran ahead, looking to explore.

Aubrey did not share their enthusiasm. What they saw as an adventure, she saw as a place of hard work and misery. She felt heartsick as she moved closer. She imagined the building with the furnace boiling and sending steam to the piston engine used for operating the cane press. The heat must have been unbearable, and the conditions inhumane.

"Be careful," she called to the boys. "Don't cut yourself on anything."

The closer she got, the more menacing the building became. Hundreds of slaves must have worked day and night to keep the sugar production going.

The remains of several piers dotted the side of the river. The old dock had fallen away, but the thick beams used to build its foundation still rose out of the water, meeting the menacing current head-on.

The excitement in her students' faces eased her discomfort. Their wide eyes and exuberant smiles momentarily washed away the horrible images of the past.

"I read the Confederates used these old sugar boiling pots to make salt during the Civil War." Cal jumped down from the top of the inverted pot. "Perhaps they used these for that same reason. Maybe that's why they're still here."

Aubrey scoured the area around the mill, amazed at so much still left behind. "I never knew this was here. I read about the sugar mill here in a book once, and how the slaves operated the machinery, but I never imagined ..."

Hartley arrived at her side. "I wonder why the school never demolished it."

"Because it's still considered a historical site." Cal held up his tablet. "The house and all its property are registered with the National Registry of Historical Landmarks. To tear it down would create a whole lot of legal headaches."

"So they just left it here," Bella commented. "But what does this have to do with our missing girls?"

Hartley waved his hand over the dilapidated building. "Seems to me this would be a perfect place to hide anyone away for as long as you want."

London squinted at the mill. "Hide them where?"

"I bet inside we can find some rooms, maybe partially intact and—"

"No, we're not going inside," Aubrey asserted, cutting off Hartley. "That structure isn't stable. And the last thing I need is someone injured on this expedition."

Jenna scratched at a bug bite on her arm. "You act like there is something you don't want us to see."

"What? No." Aubrey took her pack from Bella's back and set it on the ground. "We came here to see where those girls were last seen. And now we have a possible place where they could have been kept." She removed the first aid kit from her pack and unzipped it. "There was nothing else we were going to find, considering everything happened almost thirty years ago." Aubrey handed some calamine lotion to Jenna. "Put that on your arm."

Bella stood over her. "So how does this help us find Lindsey?"

"Well, we know she's not here. If she were, we would have heard her."

Hartley faced the river, analyzing the fast current. "In the case reports, there was a belief the girls might have drowned in the river. What do you think of that theory, Ms. LaRoux?"

Aubrey found his tone unsettling. "Did they ever drag the water for bodies?"

Hartley shook his head. "Nope. It was spring when they disappeared. The water was too high, and the undertow too strong."

Bella took the first aid kit from Aubrey. "No one drowns in that river unless they're pushed in."

"There have been suicides on Bayou Teche before," Cal argued. "The Franklin Library has dozens of newspaper articles."

Jenna stared at him. "Is that what you do for fun?"

London shook her head, appearing as if she didn't buy any of it. "Lindsey didn't kill herself."

"Neither did Marjorie," Aubrey said softly.

The students all faced her, their brows pinched in a questioning look.

"Is there something you know that we don't?" Hartley demanded.

Aubrey shook her head. "I doubt it. Marjorie was popular, a tad pretentious, and known as a prankster, but she wasn't depressed, or ever spoke about hurting herself. If anything, I think she got off on hurting others more."

Bella picked up Aubrey's pack from the ground and wiped some of the red mud from the bottom. "Did she hurt you?"

"Hey, what you kids doing out here?"

Aubrey flinched and turned toward the trees, where the man's gravelly voice emanated from.

Her heart thudded at the horror of getting caught with her students at a strictly forbidden location.

A man with light brown skin, dressed in blue overalls and a red cap, walked toward the group. His baggy clothes and sinewy figure accentuated his lanky gait. His sculpted cheekbones, long nose, and penetrating dark-brown eyes brought a smile to Aubrey's face. Her heart warmed with recognition.

"Mr. Samuel?"

His stern features lifted, and a pearly white smile broke through. "Is that you, Aubrey LaRoux?"

He was almost on her when Aubrey saw his wrinkled brow and the slight jowl that jiggled as he moved, but when he held out his arms, she ran to greet him.

The hug he gave her was the sweetest welcome she'd received since returning to Waverly.

"I heard you had come to teach. I couldn't believe it when Probst told me, but it's good to see you."

"You know Mr. Samuel?"

Cal's question reminded Aubrey of her students. When she turned to see their bewildered faces, she became serious once more.

Always be the teacher.

"We are old friends. He worked here when I was a student."

Cal gave the older man a welcoming wave. "Hey! Remember me?"

"I remember you, Cal Broussard." Samuel gave each one a thorough scolding with his eyes. "I followed you all when I saw you from my office window at the stables. You know Ms. Probst doesn't want you out here." He pointed at Jenna. "And I know you, Jenna Marchand, don't want to lose your riding privileges. You're already on thin ice."

"It's my fault." Aubrey stepped in front of her students. "We have been studying the history of the plantation, and I suggested we see the original battlefield site and the mill. Sort of a field trip on campus."

Samuel nodded, but the lines of suspicion around his mouth remained. "You expect me to believe that? This is about that missing girl. Only reason anyone would be out here."

Aubrey hesitated, questioning if she should lie. "If I said yes, would you tell Ms. Probst?"

Samuel's chuckle reminded her of a smoky, dark whiskey with hints of mystery hiding beneath the surface. "I may work for the woman, but I'll be damned if I'm gonna be her spy."

The students let out a collective sigh of relief.

Aubrey kept her grin hidden.

"But you guys shouldn't be out here," he scolded, attempting to sound menacing.

"We were heading back," Aubrey said. "They have to get to their next class."

Cal puffed out his chest. "Yeah, I have a trig exam in another hour."

"Liar," Bella muttered. "The test is tomorrow."

Aubrey motioned to the trees, anxious to head back. "It's time to go."

Samuel waited by her side as the students started toward the pines.

"What are you really doing out here?" he whispered to her.

Aubrey shot him a dirty look. "I told you."

"No, you told me you brought them kids out here for class, but I know you, Aubrey. I saw the same look in your eye when that Marjorie Reynolds disappeared. You wanted to find out what happened to her."

Aubrey kept her attention on her students, and not Samuel's probing gaze. "You know why I wanted to find her. And did you know Marjorie and this Lindsey girl were sisters?"

"I heard." Samuel walked a few steps and waited for her. "Not much you can keep hidden in this school." He motioned to the students disappearing into the shade of the trees. "Do they know about you and Marjorie?"

A wave of tension coursed through her shoulders. "No, of course not."

"Are you going to tell them about how she bullied you, and after she disappeared, how everyone suspected you got rid of her?"

A thin film of sweat broke out on her upper lip. "That was just talk."

"But it would explain why you came back ten years later, right when Marjorie's sister has up and disappeared."

"I didn't know about the missing student until I arrived on campus and saw her picture plastered everywhere."

They approached the line of shade, and her self-doubt erupted. Nervous needles plagued her feet and fingers.

Samuel waved her into the dense covering of trees. "But the moment you found out, I bet you wanted to solve the mystery just like when Marjorie vanished."

"It was my students, not me, who wanted to go. I thought, by letting them do a little digging, they might feel more in control. God knows I remember how helpless I felt." She pushed a low hanging branch out of her way. "Samuel, do you remember when those three girls went missing in the nineties?"

"Sure do. I was a groundskeeper then. My father was head caretaker. Caused a lot of problems for all the guys on campus. The sheriff's men questioned all of us dozens of times. I remember how worried Mr. Probst was. I don't think the man ever slept during his tenure here."

A trickle of anticipation zinged through her. "Do you remember anything about their cases? Anything at all that could tie those missing girls to Lindsey?"

He removed his red cap and scratched the mane of straight black hair pulled into a long ponytail.

"That seems like a stretch to me, but I can see where you're going. Three missing girls then, one ten years ago and now, but I find it hard to believe it could be the same person."

"There have been serial killers that went on sprees that lasted decades. Gary Ridgeway killed from 1982 until 2000, so it's feasible."

Samuel chuckled. "Where did you learn that?"

"I've been doing some research on the subject."

"Sounds like you've been doing a lot of research." He kept his voice low as they walked through a path lined with leaves. "What you're suggesting ain't likely. Franklin is a small town and people notice strangers."

"What if the person who took those girls isn't a stranger?"

He went quiet and stared toward a break in the trees. "Then I'd say we have a big problem."

When she was a student, Samuel had been a rock of support, but now he didn't sound so resilient.

By the time they reached the edge of the trees, her students had started across the vast field, heading back toward the battle memorial.

Samuel walked next to her, swiping at the tall grass. "I always sensed there was something off about this land. The Chitimacha Indians inhabited this region way before the plantation was built. They believed the area was cursed. They might have been right."

Aubrey directed her attention to her students a few feet ahead. "A curse didn't take all those girls."

"Whatever happened, it's related somehow."

The admission sent a wash of iciness through her. Her gaze lingered on her students.

"Do you think Lindsey ran away, or did she disappear because of what happened to Marjorie?"

Samuel raised his head to the sky as they stepped from the trees. "I suspect that's what you and your students plan on finding out." He glanced at her. "Be careful. If the person who had anything to do with those girls vanishing is still around, they won't like you digging into their business."

A rush of ice-cold dread momentarily incapacitated her. She had never considered herself in danger, but he was right. If they pursued their investigation, the wrong someone might eventually notice.

Samuel adjusted his cap and set his gaze ahead. "I'd better head back to my office and get some work done. I'll see you again, Aubrey."

He set off, heading to the west toward a thicket of brush.

"See you later, Mr. Samuel," Cal called to him.

Samuel gave a casual wave and then turned away.

Bella slowed and came alongside Aubrey. "Are you okay, Ms. LaRoux?"

Aubrey plastered on a fake smile. "Sure. Why?"

Bella tugged at Aubrey's pack on her back. "You just looked upset."

She took the pack from the young woman and slipped it over her shoulder. "Just in desperate need of coffee. That's all."

The sunlight glistening off the glass of the liberal arts building was a welcomed sight after Aubrey's sojourn into the wild. Her muscles ached for more caffeine, and she longed for some water on her face before dealing with the rest of her classes. The time away might have been brief, but she felt as if she had traveled to another world.

However, her students didn't appear as uplifted as she felt on returning to the circle of buildings. Their gaits had slowed since leaving the battlefield, and their constant chatter had faded.

"Can we do that again?" Cal asked next to her. "Get out of class."

"Yeah," Jenna said. "It was nice to be away from this place for a while."

"Can we go someplace without mud next time." London lifted her foot. "I'll never get this red crap off my school shoes."

Aubrey could commiserate. Her shoes were caked with the red stuff as well.

"Perhaps our next trip could be somewhere more informative, and a place Ms. Probst might approve of."

"Like the police station?" Bella asked, sounding determined. "I'd like to check out those records Hartley got access to."

"And blow that I hacked into the sheriff's database?" Hartley howled. "Are you insane, Bella Simone? Then I'd get arrested."

"Not necessarily." Cal got between the two, deescalating the mounting tension. "If you covered your tracks with an IP converter, they could not trace your server."

"Of course, I did that," Hartley shouted. "I'm not new to hacking."

Aubrey raised a hand demanding quiet. "I don't want to hear any more about hacking. I think we've done enough illegal things for one day. I was thinking more about going to the library in Franklin where Cal found those old articles. Might help to read the first-hand accounts of what people reported back then."

Cal's hunched shoulders perked up. "I could set something up with Mrs. Caveletti. She runs the library's historical records."

To see the bounce in his step was too much for Aubrey to say no. "Why don't you do that, then. I will get permission from Ms. Probst to take a field trip."

A round of cheering rose with the news of another reprieve.

Hartley picked London up and twirled her around. "See? I can be useful and romantic."

She slapped his shoulder. "Put me down. I'm not impressed."

"Let it go, Hartley," Bella said, snickering. "She isn't into you or your sexy computer skills."

Cal pointed his thumb at his chest. "My computer skills are far sexier than his, and I don't chase every skirt on campus."

"Watch it, Broussard." Hartley's voice dropped to a growl. "I could say a few choice things about you, too."

Aubrey grabbed Cal's shoulder and squeezed. "If you don't play nice with each other, how do you expect me to want to take you off campus?"

London's unexpected, "Oh God," carried across the well-mowed grass. "Please don't say that. I'm dying to get away from these depressing buildings."

The groans of assent got louder as they approached the shadows cast by the tall liberal arts building.

Aubrey glanced up and immediately felt like her students. She found it odd how she had never viewed any place where she worked as a prison, but there was something about the square brick building. She pictured herself a nun returning to cloistered life.

The lively conversations of students hurrying to classes created a distressing picture in her mind—all that exuberance shadowing so much death. Aubrey felt the lies of Waverly could not be kept secret for much longer.

"We'd better head back around to the front," Aubrey suggested. "Break up into smaller groups, so we don't look suspicious."

The looming gray roof of the plantation home escalated Aubrey's apprehension.

They stepped onto the walkway that led into The Quad. Aubrey scoured the grounds for anyone appearing overly interested in their party.

They broke into two groups and strolled toward the liberal arts building, but no one paid attention.

She reached the glass entrance, with the snarling blue and gray wolf staring back at her, and sighed.

We got away with it, thank goodness.

She opened the doors. Cal gave her a crafty smile, Hartley a secretive wink, and Bella nodded before getting lost in a sea of students.

London and Jenna stayed with Aubrey on the staircase. They did not speak but seemed to share Aubrey's exhilaration.

The girls parted ways on the second floor, leaving Aubrey to trek to her classroom to prepare for her third period class.

CHAPTER 9

Bella waited at the base of the stairs, scouring the eager expressions of students as they dashed for their classes. She didn't share their enthusiasm. For Bella, high school was an endless parade of stupid subjects she vowed never to use again.

But the journey to the battlefield, the way Aubrey had fielded her questions, and her wavering belief in the woman's guilt improved her mood. Charged with new ideas, Aubrey had been a breath of fresh air, and an ally Bella hadn't known she needed.

Jenna approached her from the side of the hall, displaying her usual vague smirk. Bella's dislike for the competitive girl still bubbled, but she had learned to put it aside. It was something she chalked up to Lindsey and the way she had brought them all together. Lindsey had introduced the misfits and eventually made them fast friends. How she had pulled off that little miracle kept Bella up some nights.

"What do you think?" Jenna asked.

"I'm not sure she did it." Bella eyed a small clique of freshmen as they walked past. "She's just as curious as we are."

Jenna glared at the young girls. "So, what do we do?"

"Why do you delight in scaring freshmen?"

Jenna shrugged, looking even scarier. "Every single one of those girls arrived at the stable thinking they were expert horsewomen. Five minutes

—78—

in the ring showed they were nothing but wannabees."

"We can't all be Sybil Ludington."

Jenna cast her disparaging gaze at Bella. "Who is Sybil Ludington?"

"The female Paul Revere." Bella quietly sighed, amazed at how little students absorbed. "Do you read your history assignments or just cheat on the tests?"

Cal appeared out of nowhere, scrambling toward them from behind a few basketball players.

"She didn't crack. Maybe she didn't have anything to do with it."

Jenna faced Cal, folding her arms. "Do you know who Sybil Ludington is?"

Cal volleyed his gaze between the two young women. "What does the female version of Paul Revere have to do with whether we can trust Ms. LaRoux?"

Jenna rocked her head back, grimacing. "History geeks."

London slid in next to them. She slinked closer to the oak railing as she eyed the last dregs of students hurrying to class. "That didn't go as expected. She seemed pretty composed."

Hartley arrived and crowded in next to London. "I think we need to stop considering Ms. LaRoux as a suspect."

"No way." Jenna sneered at Hartley. "When questioned about her relationship with Marjorie, she admitted to being bullied. That's a motive for murder. We can't let our guard down."

"You bully me," Cal said to Jenna. "And I haven't killed you yet."

Bella snickered. He had a point. Jenna and her caustic attitude had rubbed everyone the wrong way in school. It had amazed her when Lindsey had taken the rebellious girl under her wing.

Lindsey had done the same with her. A loner who preferred a book to the company of others, Bella had found Lindsey's friendship a welcomed change from the hours she spent alone in her room. When she'd met the group Lindsey had created, she wondered what the five could have in common. Still, Lindsey had been kind to her. Bella missed her smile, her laugh, and the way she had listened to her ideas. It was why she'd agreed to go along with Hartley's crazy plan. Lindsey had wanted to find her sister's killer, and Bella wanted to discover who had taken Lindsey. She owed her friend that and a whole lot more.

The final bell traveled down the hall, but no one moved. Classes and studying seemed irrelevant next to murder and cover-ups.

Hartley leaned in and whispered, "Let's just keep pushing with our investigation. If she didn't do it, we should know soon enough."

London frowned. "And if she did? We promised Lindsey we would find out the truth about her sister."

Bella didn't share London's negativity. She wanted to believe in the teacher who had been kind and encouraging. "If we have Ms. LaRoux on our side, I bet we will find out what happened faster than working without her. She's smart and has resources we can't get our hands on."

Hartley rested against the railing. "She's got a point."

Cal nodded. "I agree. Let's work harder on seeing what Ms. LaRoux knows, and if she is innocent, let's see what she can do for us."

"Just be careful what you tell her," Jenna said. "Until we know for sure she had nothing to do with Marjorie and Lindsey's disappearance, we can't trust her."

"Maybe you should ease up on Ms. LaRoux. She's not all bad. Lindsey would have given Aubrey LaRoux the benefit of the doubt."

"But Lindsey isn't here," Jenna snapped. "And until we track her down, watch your back with the teacher. She could turn on us."

Bella bit her tongue, deciding it was pointless arguing with the bitter young woman. No matter what Jenna preached, Bella had already made up her mind about their teacher. She couldn't believe someone who had put so much at risk for her students could be out to destroy them.

The last few steps along the hall were the longest of her journey. The fatigue of her restless night and the exertion of the short trip to the mill had depleted Aubrey's energy.

She put her hand on the doorknob to her classroom. She had fifty minutes to collect herself before her lecture on the Declaration of Independence.

She opened the door and caught her reflection in the frosted glass.

I look like I've been rode hard and put up wet.

Aubrey froze the moment she stepped into her homeroom.

Behind her desk, and sifting through a lesson plan, was Sara Probst.

The woman glared at her through beady brown eyes. "Ah, here you are. I was wondering when you would return from your excursion to the river."

Aubrey's hope of a successful caper siphoned out of her, taking away her strength.

"I watched you, and Hartley Gregory, Cal Broussard, Bella Simone, London Dumont, and that insufferable, Jenna Marchand climb through the gardens this morning from my rear kitchen window."

She went to the desk and set down her pack while her mind went into action, thinking of an excuse. "They are the students from my first period, learning about the Civil War. Ms. Levi neglected to tell them of the Battle of Irish Bend. When I brought up that the battlegrounds were not far from here, my students wanted to see it."

"Your students are well aware of the battlegrounds." She tossed the lesson plan to the desk. "It's in the handbook and also marked as a place they're not allowed to go."

"Alone," Aubrey quickly added. "I'm faculty, and our trip was about research and learning."

Sara folded her hands and squared her sizable shoulders, appearing ready to pounce. "Off-limits applies to faculty and students alike. Our insurance company won't cover us if anyone gets hurt there. The historical value of the land required a separate policy, a very hefty one, our board wasn't willing to buy."

Aubrey fondled the strap on her pack while her stomach nervously fluttered. "I wasn't aware the reason no one can go there is about money. I thought it had to do more with the past."

"If I could open that damned field to tourists and charge admission, I would, but the men who sit on the school board would oppose it."

The indifference Sara Probst emanated became downright icy. Aubrey braved herself for a thorough scolding for disobeying the rules.

"You are not to leave the safety of the school grounds again. If you want to take another field trip, try visiting Franklin instead."

"How can it be a field trip if we never left the school grounds?"

The raised eyebrows on Sara's face told her she had overstepped her bounds.

"I'm sorry." Aubrey remembered she needed her job and softened her tone. "I didn't see the harm in taking my students to visit the memorial and discuss a significant battle in Louisiana history."

Sara stepped closer, her gaze burning into Aubrey. "Consider this your warning. Other teachers are dying to take your place. Smarter ones, who follow the rules. I will not hesitate to replace you if you disobey the rules again."

The slight didn't hurt her. It fueled her anger. "The students are asking questions about Lindsey's case. They're nervous and scared. I've heard you've never addressed her disappearance in an assembly."

Indignation deepened the lines on Sara's face. "And why should I address the entire school about something we know nothing about. Was it a prank? Did she run away? Who knows? And planting such notions in the minds of our student body isn't what I'm paid to do. Until I have something concrete to share, the subject will not be addressed."

She marched toward the door and stopped at the threshold.

"I'm the one who has to field angry calls from parents when their children report what was discussed in assembly. Be careful what you say to these kids, Ms. LaRoux. Despite their raging hormones and egos, they're still impressionable."

She walked through the door before Aubrey could think of something clever.

Aubrey flopped against her desk. While a student at the school, she'd always felt coddled and not allowed to think for herself, now she understood why. Her anger cooled when she put herself in Sara's shoes. Liability made people paranoid and often turned schools that strived for growth into places that suppressed it.

The night chill clung to the sweat on London's face. She darted through the trees at the battlefield's edge, running as fast as she could. Her chest was on fire, her leg muscles screamed for a break, but the raw and eviscerating terror in her system fueled her flight.

She clutched the golden locket—the one she had taken from Lindsey's room. It was her token, but someone had found out she'd hidden it.

Afraid she would collapse if she continued, London ducked behind a cluster of trees and hugged the trunk of a large hickory. She sucked in air, acutely aware that the sound of someone crashing through the brush was getting closer.

The mill lay just ahead. Thank goodness she had come to this place with the others. She could hide there.

"I won't let you have Lindsey's locket. It's mine, so is her secret."

The voice was unnatural, dark, and grisly.

London gripped the necklace tighter, determined not to give up her last remembrance of her friend.

A crash came from the brush close to her. The sound made her flinch. She needed to get moving.

London turned, about to take off into the woods, but came to a sudden halt when confronted by a gaping hole.

The light from the moon sifted through the canopy and disappeared into the deep pit.

She teetered on edge, her shoes sinking into the mud surrounding the rim. London flailed her arms, fighting like hell not to fall in. Her heart pounded in her ears as bile filled her mouth.

A twig snapped behind her.

London wheeled around. Fear pumped adrenaline into her muscles, begging her to run, but where would she go? The dark well lay behind her, and the monster who had chased her through the woods was right ahead.

A shadow came around the side of a tree, lumbering from side to side, reminding her of a troll. But London knew the person on her tail was not some fairy tale creature.

London gulped, jutted out her chin, and dug deep for the resolve to fight her opponent. She had to survive, to warn the others.

"I'm not afraid of you."

The shadow inched closer. She couldn't make out any features, but London could guess who it was.

"I knew you had something to do with it. Lindsey knew, too. That's why you got rid of her."

The shadow dipped behind a tree.

London searched the area, anxious to discover where her tormentor had gone.

Silence.

It permeated every ounce of her being, terrifying London more than the sound of crushing leaves.

London trembled, and the locket in her hand tapped against her palm.

She waited, attuned to any movement, any sound.

A hard smack to the center of her chest knocked the air from her lungs.

London toppled backward.

She was unable to stop her momentum, and just when she should have hit the ground, London kept falling.

Darkness engulfed her, and the light from the opening grew farther away. Time slowed, and she prepared herself for the impact when she hit bottom.

The crack of her bones breaking, the hiss of the last dregs of air leaving her chest, the flop of her body against the hard surface all resonated in her head, but there was no pain. She was thankful for that.

A strange peace overtook her. The fear that had driven her diminished and London reveled in a swell of tranquility.

Dark spots gathered in her eyes, but she could still make out the opening of the well.

A figure shrouded in shadows stood above her, looking down as numbness spread through her arms and legs.

"And now you join Lindsey, keeping my secret safe," a rough voice called into the pit.

London wanted to speak but couldn't find the breath. That was okay. She wasn't afraid anymore.

The light dimmed, but the figure at the top of the well looking down on her remained.

The others will find you.

The certainty of the words circling her head gave her satisfaction. She had done all she could.

Blackness blotted out the world, and London gave in to the overwhelming serenity.

She was ready. She could rest.

A dull thud resonated in Aubrey's head as she tried to squeeze out the last few minutes of sleep before her alarm rang. She repositioned her pillow, but the pounding continued. Her eyes popped open, and then she heard the bang coming from her front door.

She removed her earplugs—a necessity when living in a girls' dorm—and scurried from her bed.

Aubrey grabbed her robe and had barely shrugged it on when she got the chain off the door. Her hammering heart frightened her wide awake.

She was a housemother for fifty girls. Something must have happened. She opened the door to find a waif with bloodshot brown eyes wearing a pink T-shirt. Then Aubrey saw the fresh tears on her face.

Oh shit.

"Ms. LaRoux," the girl got out in between sobs. "It's London. We can't find her."

Aubrey burst through the door and grabbed the girl by the arms. "What do you mean you can't find her?"

The girl whimpered. "I woke up and was supposed to get her up early to study for a chemistry test. But I went to her room, and she didn't answer. Her door was unlocked. I went inside, and she wasn't there."

Aubrey calmed. Alarming the girl with her hysterics wasn't going to help the situation.

She let go of the student. "What's your name?"

"Chrissy, Chrissy Michaels."

Aubrey took a breath, phrasing her words in the shortest syllables possible.

"Chrissy, did you check the common area, the showers, or perhaps she's doing laundry in the basement?"

Chrissy wiped her nose on her sleeve. "We checked everywhere. Me and a few girls searched the entire building. And the alarm is still on, so she couldn't have gone out."

Aubrey's concern intensified, sending a queasy roll through her stomach. "When was the last time you or anyone saw her?"

Chrissy blinked, and another tear snuck down her cheek. "Yesterday evening. She was going to meet Hartley and said she would be back before the doors were locked for the night."

Aubrey stood, gazing at the other girls who had gathered in the hall behind Chrissy. All in their nightclothes, some with sleep in their eyes, their stunned faces reflected Aubrey's mounting trepidation.

"Let me get dressed and I'll unlock the doors. Perhaps London didn't make it back in time."

"I called her cell phone," a buxom brunette admitted coming forward. "She hasn't picked up. It goes straight to voicemail."

Any teenager missing a call wasn't cause for distress, but with one girl missing on campus, Aubrey feared there could be more to London's disappearance.

"Has anyone tried Hartley's phone?"

Bella came forward, holding up her phone. "I called him after word got around about London. She was supposed to study with him at the library last night, but he says she was a no-show."

Aubrey spun into her room and immediately went to her phone. She searched the new numbers she had recently added to her contacts.

She spotted Sara Probst's name and burning ignited in Aubrey's stomach.

She tapped the number and waited.

I can't believe this is happening.

The headmistress picked up after two rings.

"Ms. LaRoux, it's rather early. Is something wrong?"

Aubrey gulped. "London Dumont is missing."

CHAPTER 11

The rising sun warmed the sidewalk as Aubrey paced in front of Elaine House. The wrinkled T-shirt and jeans she'd thrown on before running out of her apartment made her feel frumpy next to Sara, who sat in a rocking chair on the front porch. How the woman had put on her pressed suit, makeup, and done her long brown hair in an upswept bun in five minutes, left Aubrey dumbfounded.

Aubrey walked back and forth, sneaking glances at Lindsey's poster on the campus bulletin board and wondering how she had arrived in such a precarious position.

"You need to calm down, Ms. LaRoux." Sara's stern voice drifted down the steps. "Pacing like a caged tiger will not get the authorities here any faster."

"I just wish I knew where she was."

"I wouldn't worry. I'm sure London will turn up. It's not the first time a girl has spent a night away from the dorm. She might have bunked with another girl."

Aubrey stopped and faced the porch. "Then why did you call the sheriff?"

"Protocol. We do things by the book in this school." Sara stood, nodding her head. "Perhaps her little escapade has something to do with your trip yesterday. Did anyone say anything to set her off?"

"What?" Aubrey rubbed her head, trying to recall everything she had seen or heard. "No. She was fine."

"Then we might have to chalk this up to her upset over Lindsey's disappearance. She has been quite distraught. Many of her teachers have commented on it."

The accusation elicited an odd sense of dismay. "I haven't seen that. She's been resilient despite what happened. She wants to find her friend."

Sara slowly descended the steps. "Two days does not make you an expert with your students, Ms. LaRoux. For instance, did you know the group you went off with yesterday, all put in requests to change their schedules so they could be with you during first period?"

The information took Aubrey by surprise. "How did they find out about me?"

The headmistress reached the sidewalk and continued her measured approach. "That little group of misfits always seems to know the goings-on around here." She turned her attention to the poster of Lindsey Gillett. "Take Lindsey's disappearance. Your ragtag crew of students all had relationships with Lindsey."

An uncomfortable edginess tingled her fingers. "A few of them mentioned that they were friendly with her."

"Friendly?" Sara's chuckle was as cold as her eyes. "They were the five people on campus who hated her most."

The news hit Aubrey like a blow to the chest. "Hated her? That's not the impression I got. You don't know these students, Ms. Probst."

"And you do?" she challenged. "Hartley Gregory dated Lindsey last semester, but the breakup was ugly. London suffered a blow when Lindsey beat her out as captain of the swim team. London eventually got the position after Lindsey disappeared. Cal suffered immense bullying from Lindsey, so did Jenna. We had faculty break up more than one fight between the two girls. And Bella—"

"Bella told me about her accident."

The discomfort in Aubrey's chest deepened. Her doubts about her students' motives ripped her apart. Had she been wrong about them?

Sara folded her hands, appearing formal and reserved. "Every one of those students wanted in your class. Why?"

Aubrey glared at the woman. "I have no idea. I never interacted with any of them until I arrived on campus. You're the one who hired me and—"

Red flashing lights and a screeching siren cut off Aubrey's words.

Three patrol cars came barreling into the parking lot and sped toward Elaine House.

Sara raised her head as the car doors opened. "We'll discuss this later."

"You bet we will," Aubrey muttered.

Four state troopers, three men and one woman, walked toward the porch. The woman carried an iPad as she inspected the plantation home with wide eyes.

The last car door to open came from a cruiser with *Sheriff* in blue emblazoned across the side.

In jeans and a tan button-down, he wore a black gun belt, but his hat was a light brown Stetson, and his boots were black, alligator, and tapped the sidewalk as he approached.

Tall, lean, and with forearms that bulged with ropelike muscles, the sheriff lowered his sunglasses and clipped them on the chest pocket of his dress shirt.

The iridescent color of his eyes captured Aubrey's attention. Then his chiseled cheekbones, square jaw, and the dimple in his curved chin. He removed his hat when he saw her and Sara standing at the base of the porch stairs, but when he flashed a wicked grin, Aubrey took a step back and reached for the railing, unsure if her knees would hold her.

Good-looking men had never evoked such emotion, and that worried her—a lot.

"Ladies," he said, sounding as Louisiana as a dressed shrimp po-boy with a side of hot sauce. "Seems to me, we were just out here a few days ago."

Sara put on a beaming smile—one Aubrey had never seen before.

"Sheriff Dubois, thank you so much for coming." She extended her hand to Aubrey. "This is Ms. LaRoux, our newest faculty member. The girl in question was under her charge in the dorm."

The contempt in her voice grated on Aubrey's nerves.

The sheriff stepped forward and held out his hand to Aubrey. "Ms. LaRoux, I'm Mason Dubois."

She liked the strength of his grip. "Are you the officer overseeing the Lindsey Gillett case?"

"As Sheriff of St. Mary Parish, I oversee everything. Even the Franklin PD comes under my jurisdiction. There's nothing I don't know about, Ms. LaRoux."

"Please call me Aubrey, Sheriff."

Aubrey saw the slightest twinkle in his eyes and immediately began second-guessing herself. Did she look a mess? What about her breath? Then she remembered the missing girl.

Mason ran his finger along the rim of his hat. "Can you tell me why the girl might have skipped sleeping in her dorm room?"

"She was supposed to meet up with another student, Hartley Gregory, to study in the library, but Hartley said she never showed."

"Same Hartley Gregory we interviewed when you reported Ms. Gillett's disappearance?"

Sara came forward. "Yes, same one. He and Ms. Dumont had been spending a great deal of time together."

"But I don't think it was romantic," Aubrey injected, "I got the impression London wasn't interested in Hartley."

The sheriff's blond brows went up. "Why do you believe that?"

Aubrey rubbed her forehead. "I saw her push him away a few times."

Mason dropped his tone, sounding suspicious. "Was she pushing him away forcefully or playfully? Was she afraid of him at the time you witnessed this? I need specifics."

"It wasn't forceful, no. Yesterday when we went to the battlefield, she seemed indifferent to him, not afraid."

He ran his hand through his wavy dirty-blond hair. "You went to the battlefield? You do know that's off-limits to the student and faculty."

Aubrey's irritation bubbled. "Yeah, I heard."

He grinned at her reaction. "I don't seem to remember London Dumont calling Lindsey a friend." He pointed to the female deputy hovering close by. "Laura? Can you read back her statement?"

Laura stepped next to the sheriff and tapped her tablet.

"She called her a, quote, 'backstabbing bitch who wanted me out of the way so she could be the most popular girl at school and the captain of the team.'"

Mason grimaced, accentuating the dimple in his chin. "Doesn't sound like a friend to me."

The disclosure added to Aubrey's nagging uncertainty. She remembered how all the students had presented when she'd gotten to know them that first day. Why lie, and why want to find Lindsey if they never cared for her in the first place?

"This makes no sense. London appeared upset by Lindsey's absence."

Mason pointed to two uniformed men behind him. "Go around, talk to the kids, and see if they know anything." He turned to Sara. "Where is Hartley?"

"He should be arriving soon, along with the rest of the boys living in town." Sara leveled her gaze on Aubrey. "The group Ms. LaRoux took to the battlefield consisted of London, Hartley, Cal Broussard, Jenna Marchand, and Bella Simone."

Mason chuckled. "All the usual suspects."

"What does that mean?" Aubrey demanded.

Mason tapped his hat against his pant leg. "It means, Ms. LaRoux, that those students were the same we questioned when Lindsey Gillett disappeared. According to Ms. Probst, they all had a motive and a profound dislike for the young woman. The headmistress feels the group came together with one goal—to get revenge on the missing girl."

"That's not true." Aubrey's indignation spurred to life. "They want to help find Lindsey and are concerned about her whereabouts."

"And you believed them?" Mason snickered.

Aubrey tossed up her hands. "Yes, why would they lie?"

Sara's *tsk* circled the air. "All students lie, Ms. LaRoux. Perhaps you don't have enough experience to realize that."

"If you believe that, then how can you be an effective educator, Ms. Probst?"

Aubrey's outrage brought a sneer to Sara's lips.

"Students aren't the enemy," Aubrey said, pushing home her point, ready to have it out with the head of the school.

The sheriff stepped in between them. "Let's concentrate on finding London and save this discussion for later."

Aubrey took an abrupt step back, knowing she had to cool off before she got fired. "If you need anything, I'll be in the dorm."

Mason snapped his fingers at Laura, his deputy. "Go with her. Go through the dorm, and then take statements from every girl who knew London."

Sara's mouth slipped open. "That will significantly interfere with our classes, Sheriff."

Aubrey wanted to scream. A girl had gone missing, and all Sara Probst cared about were classes. She didn't care about her students, so why lie to Aubrey? What would it accomplish?

"We'll try to be as quick as we can, but there's another issue we have to discuss, Ms. Probst."

The principal frowned. "Which is?"

"You have two missing girls inside of a week. I'm required to notify the federal authorities."

Sara's eyes widened. "They would shut down the school and send the parents into a panic."

Aubrey stared open-mouthed at her boss. "And a second missing student won't have parents descending on the school once word gets out?"

"They ran away," Sara insisted. "No one has found any evidence to prove otherwise."

The sheriff set his hat on his head, sporting a determined frown. "That's right. They're both missing persons until I find the evidence to say they're not."

Aubrey stuck out her chin. "Then let's find the evidence. I suggest we search the grounds behind the school."

Mason grinned as he adjusted his hat. "Why, Ms. LaRoux, you were reading my mind."

The veins on Sara's neck popped as she stepped forward. "You forget this school has over fifty acres, Sheriff. You don't have the manpower for a search."

"You're right, but you have faculty and staff who can assist us." He glanced up at the sky. "We got a lot of daylight ahead of us. With any luck, your girl will appear before we have to go looking for her."

Aubrey ignored the pounding pulse in Sara's neck, not caring if she annoyed the woman further.

"And what about the students? How do we keep them out of our hair as we search?"

Sara sucked in a deep breath and seemed to calm. "I'll call a general assembly. We can keep them in the big hall while the sheriff and school volunteers comb the grounds."

"Thank you, Ms. Probst." Mason pulled his phone out of his back pocket. "That would be a tremendous help."

He stepped away to make a call, and Sara took the opportunity to ease in beside Aubrey.

"Find this girl, Ms. LaRoux. I need my school back running smoothly."

The woman's obstinance appalled Aubrey. How could she be so cold?

"Have you considered what will happen if we can't find her?"

Sara turned back toward her house. "One problem at a time. I'm sure she will show up soon. London was never one for wandering. She always was a nervous child."

The headmistress climbed the stone steps to her home, appearing as regal as any European queen.

For a few moments in her senior year, Aubrey had admired the woman's strength, but now she suspected Sara's stoicism had all been a sham. Sara Probst was afraid of something, and Aubrey became determined to uncover what it was.

CHAPTER 12

The essence of pine was everywhere. Aubrey navigated the narrow path through the trees, just beyond the battlefield site, anxiously scouring the muddy ground for any sign of London's prints. The racket of the other officers and faculty as they traipsed through the wooded area surrounded her. The flashlight in her hand seemed unnecessary, considering the sun was high in the sky, but the shady areas in the woods heading toward Bayou Teche became so dense in sections that she could barely make out the path.

She walked, fighting against the thick red mud, and keeping her eyes open as Sheriff Dubois had advised. The man's alluring smile and broad shoulders had shaken her. Relationships were something she'd avoided, never wanting to lose sight of her future. All the men who had drifted in and out of her life had been too needy, too immature, or too interested in controlling her. Any romance Aubrey considered appeared doomed from the start.

Reason enough to steer clear of the hunky sheriff.

"You all right out here?"

The deep voice, oozing with sex appeal damn near scared her half to death.

When Mason stepped out from behind a tree, she refrained from throwing the heavy flashlight at him.

"You shouldn't sneak up on people like that."

"Like what?" He came toward her, adjusting his hat. "There are almost two dozen people around you."

She dropped her gaze to the ground. "You know what I mean."

Mason eased in closer. "I came over here because I wanted to ask you a few questions without Ms. Probst hovering over us."

She snickered. "She does tend to be a bit overprotective."

Mason pushed his hat on his head. "The only thing Ms. Probst cares about is Waverly's reputation. I don't think she could give a rat's ass about her faculty or her students."

The accuracy of his statement bothered her. It was what she'd observed as well.

"What did you want to ask me?"

"Why did you bring your students out here?" He glanced around. "Doesn't seem like much of an educational outing to me. It almost looks like you were hunting for something."

"Wow," she drawled. "And what exactly would I be hunting for on an abandoned battleground? Bullets or bones?"

"Clues. Like everyone else in Franklin. Since those girls went missing in the nineties, everyone and their mother have offered theories on what happened. And several of them have come out to this battlefield."

"Well, I wasn't looking for clues. I was trying to teach my students that history doesn't have to happen a thousand miles away. It's right under your feet, alive, and tangible."

"And did your students want to talk about the battle or the missing girls?"

She smiled, knowing he'd backed her into a cunning corner. "They did seem interested in the battle monument, if only for a moment. And yes, after that, their questions were about the missing girls."

He moved a branch out of her way. "It's what everyone wants to know. Death wins out over any subject. It's our macabre nature."

She walked next to him, itching to pick his brain. "So what do you know about the girls that have gone missing? The three in the nineties, Marjorie Reynolds, and Lindsey Gillett?"

He wiped the blond stubble on his chin. "That's a tall order. I think you know what I know, which ain't much."

She liked the way his Southern drawl crept in as he spoke. She bet he was one of those guys whose accent got thicker after a few beers.

"That's not very encouraging coming from the Sheriff of St. Mary Parish."

He rested his hand on his gun belt. "The first day I took office, I read every file I could get my hands on about those missing girls. What shocked me was how shoddy the investigation was in the nineties. Witnesses who weren't interviewed, evidence that wasn't gathered, and federal agencies that weren't notified until way after the girls had gone missing. It may have happened almost thirty years ago, but it wasn't the dark ages as far as police procedure goes."

His honesty was unexpected.

"Any idea why all that happened?"

He stopped and faced her, shifting his hips slightly as he gathered his thoughts.

"The previous sheriff, Hale Perkins, ran this parish for about thirty years before he retired. He was close to everyone here, including Sara Probst's father. It seems the former headmaster of the school helped Hale out of a few legal problems."

"What problems?"

"Hale liked his whiskey. He got arrested more than once outside of St. Mary Parish driving drunk. Warren Probst used his political clout, which some say was quite considerable, to get Hale off." He paused and pressed his lips together. "The reason I'm telling you this is because I'm not Hale Perkins. I have no ties to Sara Probst, but the woman wields the same political clout as her old man, and that makes her a formidable opponent for you and me."

Aubrey almost bent over, waylaid by shock. "Do you think she's behind what happened to Marjorie and Lindsey?"

He shook his head. "No, but I suspect she's going to be a real pain in my ass when I start digging deeper into what's going on around here."

"She'll be a pain in the ass even if you don't do anything."

He took her elbow and encouraged her back along the path. "I'm not the kind to do nothing, Ms. LaRoux. I just wanted you to know that, so if you ever have anything you want to share with me, I can assure you, it will never get back to Ms. Probst."

She weighed his words. "I appreciate that, and if I do stumble on anything, I'll be sure to let you—"

The earth gave way beneath Aubrey's feet, and she fought to keep her balance.

She dropped the flashlight to grasp any branch or shrub she could to keep her upright.

Suddenly, Mason grabbed her, holding on tight as he pulled her to his side.

Aubrey clung to his thick arms, holding on for dear life, panting into his chest, and then she inhaled the faintest scent of his spicy cologne.

"What the hell is that?" Mason murmured.

She peered into his face and saw him looking over her shoulder at something on the ground.

Aubrey held to him as she tilted her head around.

A black pit had opened in the earth next to where she stood. If the sheriff had not been there, she would have tumbled into the large hole.

Mason set her aside, checking her over with his eyes.

"You okay?"

She nodded, still a little breathless. "Yeah." She eased closer to the edge of the pit. "What is it?"

Mason picked up her flashlight and turned it on. He shined the beam into the hole.

The depth amazed Aubrey. She made out the vines and tree roots along the smooth walls inlaid with rough stones. A stench, like rotting meat, wafted up, and she pinched her nose.

"Looks like an old trapping pit. They used them on sugarcane plantations to keep predators away from the fields. Wolves and bobcats would feed on the vermin that lived in the cane. Sometimes they attacked people, too." Mason examined the ground that had given way.

"Someone must have covered it up a long time ago." He leaned over the edge, squinting as he tried to see the bottom.

The look on his face distressed Aubrey. He appeared shaken.

He handed her the flashlight. "Do you recognize her?"

Her? Aubrey didn't understand the question. A slow burn awakened in her chest.

She hesitated before pointing the flashlight into the well, but she could not see a thing once she did. The spotlight danced around as Aubrey attempted to hit on anything. When something shiny reflected from below, she held the flashlight steady.

She squinted into the hole, straining to make out the bottom of the well. Then her beam lighted on a pale hand, clasping a gold locket.

The oddity at the bottom brought the burning in her chest up the back of her throat.

Aubrey didn't want to see any more. The hand was enough, but before she could turn away, she saw her—a young woman's white face, lips slightly parted, and her cloudy, lifeless eyes staring up.

She gasped and dropped the flashlight into the pit. It landed next to the young woman, wearing a blue and gray Waverly uniform.

Bile scorched her mouth, dropping Aubrey to her knees.

"Is that London Dumont?" the sheriff calmly asked.

She kept her mouth covered as she barely nodded. Tears blissfully blurred the gruesome scene.

Hands wrapped around her arms, lifting her from the ground.

Aubrey turned away and buried herself in Mason's shoulder, his spicy cologne filling her nose.

"I'm sorry," Mason whispered, holding her as she trembled.

His embrace roused Aubrey from her emotional outburst. Crying wasn't something she did in front of strangers.

She summoned her courage, untangled herself from his arms and backed away. But Mason kept a steadying hand on her shoulder as if afraid to let her go.

"Over here," he hollered, bringing her out of her stupor.

Shouts of the search party carried across the woods.

Aubrey shut her eyes, but London's white face remained burned into her memory.

Mason ran his hands up and down her arms, bringing life back to her numb fingers.

"I'm sorry," he muttered. "I should have warned you, but I had to know for sure."

Her lips shook as she tried to form words. "Know what?"

He lifted her chin, and his gaze melted into hers. "That you didn't kill her."

CHAPTER 13

Jenna dropped to the bench, the news of London's death echoing in her ears. Bitter waves of guilt, regret, anger, and sorrow rose and fell like tides against a shore. She'd wanted London dead before Lindsey had brought their band of unlikely friends together, and that her wish had come true only added to her devastation.

A hand touched her shoulder. Cal stood over her, his lips moving but the words not registering.

Focus.

She examined Cal's big brown eyes and the patches of stubble on his smooth jaw. The poor guy looked stuck in puberty. Maybe that was why she found him endearing and annoying.

Cal dipped his face closer to hers. "Hey, you look as white as a ghost."

The din of others, the nip in the breeze, and the crush of worried students roused her. The intrusion took a moment to adjust to, but Jenna's disbelief faded as her security blanket of anger popped back into place. She preferred hiding behind her rage than getting waylaid by a betrayed trust. It was a safer way to live, even if it did make her lonely at times.

Lindsey had understood that about her. After long deliberation, Jenna had let Lindsey in but feared the young girl with the bubbly personality would abandon her in the end. In a way, Lindsey had, the moment she disappeared.

"Can I get you something?" Cal sounded sweet as he hovered over her.

She shook her head, chasing away the remnants of her shock. "I'm fine."

Hartley sat next to her on the bench, his eyes red, and his jaw slack. "I can't believe she's dead."

Jenna wanted to give him a reassuring hug, but that wasn't her. She wasn't a hugger.

"Did anyone know about the necklace?" Bella asked. "Did London tell any of you she had it?"

Bella—the voice of clarity and reason—if Jenna ever needed a reasonable opinion about anything, she sought out Bella. Then again, she never asked anyone their opinion because it was usually wrong.

Cal scratched his head. "I never even knew about the necklace until I saw her poster."

Bella paced in front of the bench.

Shit.

Jenna hated pacers. Couldn't she sit and think like a normal person?

"She must've told someone about it or showed them." Bella pursed her lips as she paced. "And whoever she told went after her."

Cal approached Bella, interrupting her pacing.

Saved by the twerp.

"We don't know if anyone went after her. She could've slipped and fallen into that pit."

"London would have never gone there unless someone made her," Hartley muttered. "She didn't like it when we were out there, remember?"

Bella tilted her head. "So she was murdered, and whoever did it might know about us."

A jolt of terror zipped through Jenna's system. She stood, suddenly anxious to move. This wasn't about London or Lindsey anymore. It was about all of them—everyone Lindsey had trusted.

"This is getting dangerous. Any one of us could be next."

Cal faced Jenna. "But we still don't know who went after Lindsey and killed London."

Bella put her hands behind her back and shook her head. "We need help. We need to trust Ms. LaRoux and tell her everything we know."

Cal nodded. "I agree. It's time."

Jenna glanced down at Hartley, who remained on the bench, lost in his grief. He didn't raise his head or acknowledge the others.

Jenna was about to express her opposition when she spotted the slumped figure of Ms. LaRoux on a bench not far away.

She had the same devastating dullness in her eyes as Hartley. If the woman had such regard for someone she had barely known, then there must be something good about her. After all, she had been kind to Jenna and hadn't attacked her ideas or her hair color. Tolerance was a sign of decency in her book. Only those who were accepting of the differences in others were worth the effort to get to know. She had grown up with enough small-minded assholes to recognize those with open hearts.

"I think you guys are right about Ms. LaRoux, but now she looks like she needs to be alone."

Bella stood next to her. "I heard she found London. She and the sheriff. A few others say he practically carried her back."

Hartley put his head in his hands. "Can you imagine how horrible that must have been? To see London so ..." He sniffled.

Jenna suppressed an urge to ruffle his thick mane of blond hair to bring him out of his grief.

"Maybe we should be thankful they didn't find Lindsey."

"Yet," Bella quickly added. "If the killer meant to hide London in that pit, maybe the sick asshole did the same thing to Lindsey."

The thought sent an icy chill through Jenna.

God, I hope not.

The coffee in her paper cup sloshed with her shaking hands. The blanket resting on Aubrey's shoulders did little to take away the cold gripping her body. Around her, officers questioned students and faculty as the light from the afternoon sun dipped over the building rooftops.

She lifted the cup to her lips, but her shaking hand made it impossible to drink. She recalled how Mason had practically carried her back to The Quad, covering her with the blanket, and insisting one of his team stay with her as they saw to London's body.

Aubrey was glad she hadn't witnessed the efforts performed to recover the girl's body from the pit. She had not followed the students as they gawked at the body bag carried to the black van with *Coroner* along the side. Aubrey had experienced enough horror for one lifetime.

She was about to set her coffee aside when a sedate pair of women's black one-inch heeled shoes appeared on the walkway.

Aubrey raised her head to see Sara Probst looking down her nose at her.

"I heard you found her."

There was no warmth in her words, no sense of caring. Perhaps the sheriff had been right about the woman—all that mattered to her was Waverly.

"Yes." Aubrey set her cup aside, suddenly very tired. "I almost fell into the pit with her, if it had not been for Mason."

"You mean Sheriff Dubois." The condescension in her voice didn't waver. "You're a professional educator at this school. We do have standards." Sara removed the cup and set it on the ground, then took a seat next to Aubrey. "I know you must have suffered quite a shock."

"Shock?" Aubrey glowered at her boss. "The girl is dead."

"I'm sure it was an unfortunate accident."

Aubrey held back a frustrated scream. "Are you for real? She was killed. Someone put her there."

"That hasn't been proven yet. The one thing they do know is she was found with Lindsey Gillett's necklace in her hand."

Aubrey remembered the golden glimmer in the dead girl's hand. "It was a necklace—a locket."

Sara motioned to one of the posters of Lindsey not far away on a light pole. "Same one she is wearing in the picture."

"What does that mean?"

Sara placed her hands in her lap. "London and Lindsey had a falling out. Perhaps she was coming from where she left Lindsey, bringing the necklace back to put somewhere or perhaps place with someone."

"Not a bad hypothesis," Mason admitted, coming up to their

bench. "But it doesn't explain who she might have been working with."

"Working with?" Sara frowned. "I don't understand."

"The trapping pit was covered with debris and hidden after London fell in. How London came to rest in there doesn't explain who tried to cover up her accident or their crime."

Handcuffs glinted in the fading sun as they went around Hartley's wrists.

Aubrey tossed the blanket from her shoulders when she stood. "What are they doing?"

Mason glanced back at his men with Hartley. "We're taking the Gregory boy in for questioning."

"But he didn't do anything."

"Not according to my IT guy." Mason wiped his eye, his steady calm not faltering. "He hacked into our database. I want to find out why."

Aubrey squared off in front of him. "You know why."

"Not so loud, Ms. LaRoux." Sara stood next to her. "We don't need to alarm the students."

She faced the woman. "Oh, like a dead body and seeing Hartley hauled away in handcuffs wouldn't alarm them."

Mason took her elbow. "I'd like a word with Ms. LaRoux alone, Ms. Probst."

He ushered her from the bench, but Aubrey didn't take her eyes off the overbearing headmistress. Aubrey never considered herself prone to violence, but she had an increasing desire to punch Sara Probst right in the jaw.

"I'm also getting Hartley out of here," Mason whispered. "Several students have told my officers they know for a fact Hartley killed London."

She eyed his hand on her arm. "You don't believe that?"

He let her go while checking the whereabouts of Ms. Probst over Aubrey's shoulder. "Everyone's a suspect until they aren't."

She took a step back. "What does that make me?"

He leaned closer, grinning. "An ally, I hope." He glanced around at his deputies still interviewing random groups of students in The Quad. "I'm going to need someone on the inside, talking to these kids, getting their take on things. Young people usually say one thing to people in authority and something else to those they trust, like you." He pointed at her. "You can get the information my men can't."

She folded her arms, flourishing an indignant smirk. "And what are you going to do?"

"Study the evidence, keep a close eye on this place, and hope the killer doesn't return."

Her smirk evaporated. "Do you believe the person who took Lindsey killed London?"

He put his hands behind his back, rocking slightly on his cowboy boots. "All I know is London Dumont was chased and then pushed into that pit. Her tracks are all over the forest, along with someone else's."

She eased closer. "Can you tell me anything?"

"No. I'm not going to catch anyone if I give up my evidence." He tapped the side of his hat. "Learned that in detective school."

"You were a detective?"

He dipped his head. "New Orleans Homicide Detective for eight years. I was good at my job, unfortunately."

"And how did you end up here?"

"I answered the ad in the newspaper. I wanted away from the killings. Thought life in a small town would be a welcomed change."

Aubrey began to see the hard-edged man behind the good looks and smooth drawl.

"What else can I do?"

His lingering gaze roused a warm flush on her cheeks.

"I know you and your students went to the battlefield looking for something that could give you a fresh perspective on those missing girls. Hartley hacked into our system and searched the data we had on evidence collected at the site. I can guess you were motivated because of what happened when you attended school here. I read your interview after Marjorie vanished, so Lindsey's disappearance must have hit close to home."

"What are you saying?"

He inched closer and whispered, "Keep investigating. Ruffle feathers, make everyone believe you and your first period students are out to crack the case."

She considered the proposal, and then her mouth slipped open. "You want to use my students and me as bait? If the killer thinks we're closing in, then they will strike again."

"Me and my deputies will be there to stop it."

"How can you be so sure?"

He raised his head, avoiding her gaze. "Because whoever is doing this is eventually going to make a mistake, and then I'll catch them."

"So you believe London's death and Lindsey's disappearance are linked."

He nodded. "And I also believe there's a connection to the past. A killer wanting to mimic the crimes or the same person, I'm not sure."

She came right under his nose, demanding his full attention. "And what if I'm the killer?"

He laughed, and the deep husky sound drew the attention of several people nearby, including Sara Probst. "You're a thinker, Aubrey, like me. Thinkers don't kill; they get answers." He held up a white business card. "My cell is on the back."

She took the card and turned it over, reading the black lettering with his name and title.

"Call anytime," he said before walking away.

She was still holding his card when Bella came up, dark circles rimming her eyes.

"You okay?" Aubrey asked, putting a hand on her shoulder.

"Poor London. I was angry with her, but she didn't deserve that end."

Jenna appeared and gave Aubrey a weak smile. "This is bullshit."

Aubrey wanted to laugh at the assertive redhead's accurate assessment. "It makes me feel so useless."

When Cal arrived, his dour countenance mirrored everyone else's.

"What's going to happen to Hartley?" he asked.

Aubrey rubbed his arm. "He'll be fine. They just want to ask him some questions."

"This shit makes me angry," Bella muttered. "What can we do?"

Aubrey raised her head, considering Mason's advice. "There is something we can do." She waited as her students returned their attention to her.

"We can continue looking into the disappearances, but this time we won't be secretive about it. We'll let anyone join us. Perhaps if we work together, we can find out what's going on."

The fire returned to Jenna's eyes. "Probst will shit a brick when she hears."

A trickle of encouragement steadied Aubrey. Her strength returned as her students' glum expressions brightened. Perhaps by helping them, she could help herself.

"I'll take care of Ms. Probst. You guys spread the word. Our first period class is going to be open to whoever wants to help. Anyone who has heard something, seen something, or just wants to be a part of what we are doing is welcome. It's time we take Waverly back."

CHAPTER 14

T he bumpy asphalt road sent jolts up Aubrey's spine, and she grimaced. While Mr. Jones maneuvered the school bus into Franklin, Aubrey kept her eye on the quaint businesses and stores popping up on the side of the two-lane road. Built out of brick and covered with plaster to survive the torrid summers, the closely arrayed two-story buildings were like structures in the French Quarter but without the fancy wrought-iron balconies, or sensational themes.

Wooden signs with *Mel's Barbershop, Courtney's Bakery, Dale Diamond Hardware,* and *Gloria's Dress for Success* hung outside of doors or in display windows, adding to the small-town feel of the historic downtown shopping area. A few shops still had black iron hitching posts decorated with horse's heads.

People walking in front of stores waved at each other or stopped to chat. No one was in a hurry, no one argued, but when the yellow bus passed, several individuals stopped and stared as if trying to peek inside. Their pensive gazes and stretched mouths told her that news of London's murder had already spread all over town.

She shouldn't have been surprised. Small communities were notorious for their inability to keep a secret. It would just make what she had come to do a whole lot harder.

"I'm not sure how Hartley feels about returning to the station,"

Bella said from the seat behind her.

Aubrey turned to her, eyeing Hartley as he chatted with Cal in the back of the bus. Jenna was with them, frowning at everything they said.

"They only detained him for a few hours," Aubrey told her. "And it had nothing to do with London, but rather that stunt he pulled with hacking into their system. He's lucky the sheriff let him go."

Bella curled her upper lip as she picked a piece of lint off her gray sweater. "The way he talks, you would think he was held in the Bastille during the French Revolution."

Aubrey chuckled, taking a brief respite from her constant worry. Of all her students, Bella had become her favorite. She wasn't supposed to have them, but the young woman's caustic wit, and the way she kept to herself, reminded Aubrey of how she had been as a student at Waverly.

"Hartley does like his drama, but we need him with us. He can point us in the direction of where to locate any evidence the police might have."

Aubrey glanced out the windows as the charming old buildings gave way to more significant structures made of cinder block and steel. Fancy chain stores popped up, fast food restaurants with flashy signs cluttered the roadside, and an array of strip malls stood behind blacktop parking lots.

"You think they're going to share anything with us? A bunch of students from Murder High?"

"Probably not, but our visit will give me the chance to speak to the sheriff off school grounds. He might tell me what they have discovered."

Bella's smirk rattled Aubrey.

"He could tell you where Jimmy Hoffa was buried."

Aubrey didn't press for her meaning but instead looked at the girl anew. "How would you know about Jimmy Hoffa?"

"I'm not only into serial killers but also famous unsolved crimes."

"I'm honestly afraid to ask about your other hobbies."

Bella moved in closer to Aubrey's seat. "What will Ms. Probst do when she finds out we went to the sheriff's station in addition to the library?"

Aubrey didn't want to worry them about the meltdown she was sure

Sara would have. She needed to keep them focused.

"I'll handle Ms. Probst. You have any luck with the other students? Did any of them want to help with our investigation?"

Bella shook her head and rested her arm on the back of Aubrey's seat. "Not yet. London's death has scared everyone. It's only been two days. Give it time, they will come to us."

"I sure hope so. We need to find out if anyone has seen or heard anything. We can't be the only ones London spoke with."

Bella gave her arm an encouraging pat. "Give them time. Once the fear wears off, they will want to join us."

The bus slowed to a stop, making Aubrey slide forward in her seat. She peered out the window to see where they were.

A raised white house, composed of two stories, and decorated with federal windows and gingerbread details stood next to the bus. A blue and white sign out front read, *St. Mary Parish Library System, Franklin Branch.*

"We're here," Mr. Jones announced from his driver's seat.

Aubrey glimpsed the man with the black goatee and turned to the opposite side of the street.

A flagpole displaying a brilliant Old Glory caught in a determined breeze sat in the middle of a parking lot filled with ten cruisers and several unmarked cars. Behind it stood a modern six-story glass building with the Seal of Louisiana—a nested pelican against a blue background— decorating the doors. *The St. Mary Parish Sheriff's Department* sign out front didn't have half the charm or curb appeal as the others in the older section of town.

"Do you want me to stay with you, Ms. LaRoux?" Mr. Jones asked.

Aubrey stood. "Oh, no, Mr. Jones. We'll be fine. We will spend the morning here and then grab lunch before heading back to school."

Mr. Jones removed the latch securing the double doors at the front. A *whoosh* resonated as fresh air rolled through the bus.

"I'll swing back at one o'clock then." Mr. Jones gazed through his overhead mirror to the students sitting in the back of the bus. "Call my cell if you need me sooner. Keep your eye on this bunch."

His warning infuriated Aubrey. She figured Ms. Probst had probably said something to the man and would pump him for information later. She faced her students, hiding her disappointment. "All right, everyone. Let's head inside the library."

Shuffling feet and a few muffled voices accompanied the group as they stepped off the bus and into the morning sunshine. She ushered the handful of students up the sidewalk that led to the library entrance while keeping an eye on the bus.

Once she gathered the students outside the library, Aubrey hesitated, waiting for the big yellow bus to drive down the block.

"Aren't we going in?" Hartley asked.

She held up her hand, counting off the seconds as the bus got farther down the street.

When she could barely see the yellow monstrosity, Aubrey waved to her students. "This way."

She led them back down the walkway toward the street.

"Where are we going?" Cal demanded. "Mrs. Caveletti is waiting for us."

Aubrey stepped into the street. "We have another stop to make."

She headed toward the station, looking back to make sure the students stayed close to her.

"You've got to be kidding me," Hartley muttered.

Aubrey slowed a little and took his arm. "The only way to get the information we need is to go to the source."

He tugged against her grip. "You didn't spend two hours getting interrogated about why you hacked into their system."

Cal arrived alongside them, eviscerating Hartley with his gaze. "You didn't hide your IP address, did you?"

Aubrey pushed Cal aside, not wanting a fight to break out in front of the station. "None of that matters now. We're going to get what we need the right way."

They arrived on the other side of the street and started down the walkway.

"And what's the right way?" Jenna demanded. "Do we use guns, or sleep with whoever can get us the information we need?"

An open-mouthed Aubrey glared at her student. "No, that's not what we're going to do. We're going to ask nicely for help."

Cal and Hartley slapped each other's backs and snickered while

Bella hugged her side and chuckled. Jenna rolled her eyes and smirked without making a sound.

Aubrey marched to the front door and yanked it open. "Get inside and let me do the talking."

A rush of cold air hit her face as she followed her group inside the building. An atrium made of blocks of bluish-gray stone and filled with wooden benches greeted her. Skylights created squares of sunshine, which turned the floor into a chessboard. Potted plants with shiny green leaves hugged the walls, and posters of wanted criminals lined a long pegboard that stretched from the side of a glassed-in reception area.

A female deputy in her dress blues sat behind a desk, scanning an iPad in her hand.

When Aubrey approached the window, the woman glanced up at her. "Can I help you?"

Aubrey put her face closer to the window. "I'm here to see Sheriff Dubois. My name is Aubrey LaRoux from Waverly Private School."

The deputy gripped the revolver strapped to her side as she reached under the desk. "Come inside and sign in." She looked at the students behind Aubrey. "Are they coming in, too?"

Aubrey made sure to put on a friendly smile, hoping to assuage the deputy. "Yes, this is my class. We have a field trip arranged with the sheriff."

Aubrey's heart fluttered as Mason clasped her elbow. He hurried her along a brightly lit corridor with doors on either side. Her students' hurried footsteps came from behind as they passed several open office doors. Curious deputies in their blue uniforms, and some in street clothes wearing badges, watched with amused smirks as Aubrey and her students rushed past.

"You want to tell me why you just show up here and tell my officer we had a field trip planned?"

Mason didn't sound as pleasing as the first day they met at the school. The grip on her arm was firm, and his long strides had her jogging to keep up.

"If I'd showed up and said I needed to speak with you about the case, then everyone in Franklin, including Ms. Probst, would have known about it before the day was over."

He stopped and let her go. "Are you saying my officers are not loyal?"

She rubbed her elbow. "This is a small town, Sheriff. People talk and word gets around fast."

He reached for a door next to him and turned the knob. "Perhaps you're right, but you could have called first."

"Not for what I have to show you."

A sly smile crept across his lips. "Why, Ms. LaRoux, I do believe you have my attention."

She almost stumbled into the room, disarmed by his charm.

The round conference table surrounded by red leather chairs, and walls plastered with safety posters, reeked of old coffee. The somber brown carpet and paneled walls deflated her mood. Aubrey had hoped to get a peek inside his office, or at least the room where they kept their case files.

"We can talk in here." Mason shut the door after making sure the last of her students came inside. He motioned to the table. "Everyone have a seat."

Aubrey pulled out a chair, and to her amazement, Cal, Hartley, Jenna, and Bella sat right next to her.

Mason sat down across the table and eased back in his chair, studying the group. His blue shirt intensified the green in his wary eyes and highlighted his broad shoulders. He was better looking than Aubrey remembered, but she questioned if the interest she felt had more to do with London's case.

Mason folded his hands on the table. The smile he'd shown at the door vanished.

"To what do I owe this visit?"

Aubrey reached for her purse and removed a slip of paper. She slid it across the table to him.

"The other day, I found that hidden in my apartment at the school. It's from Lindsey Gillett."

Mason wiped the grimace from his face and hastily retrieved the note. "Hidden where?"

"Behind my microwave in the wall."

"You can't show that to him," Hartley grumbled. "He's the enemy."

"I'm not the enemy," Mason grumbled while he unfolded the note. "I told you before, I'm here to help."

"Help put us all in prison," Hartley countered.

Aubrey angrily motioned to Hartley. "Stop it. We have to work together to find out what happened."

"Technically, you're working with me." Mason lowered his gaze to the note. "Finding out what happened is my job."

Hartley glared at her as if to say *I told you so.*

She waited patiently for some reaction, but as the seconds ticked by, the sheriff's countenance remained as cold as stone.

"Well, what do you think?" Jenna demanded, voicing Aubrey's thoughts.

Mason took in a deep breath, expanding his thick chest and set the note on the table. "Why didn't you bring this to me when you found it?"

His third-degree hit Aubrey like a punch to the gut.

"I didn't know if I could trust you."

"You still can't," Hartley added.

Mason pointed at him. "Drop it, Mr. Gregory. I let you off easy, but if you push me, I will put you away for hacking into restricted files and interfering with an investigation." He picked up the note and pointed it at Aubrey. "This indicates Lindsey knew her attacker, and possibly London's."

Aubrey nodded, not wanting to show how disappointed she was in his reaction. She'd hoped he'd be grateful. "I know."

He stood and walked over to her. "I'm not sure if I should be livid with you right now or relieved." He eyed the students. "Did any of you speak to anyone about the note?"

The kids sat in silence, looking like terrified deer in headlights.

"Is there any possibility London spoke to someone?"

A thunderbolt of guilt seared Aubrey's insides. She covered her mouth, feeling nauseous.

"You think she mentioned the note to the killer," Jenna said, sounding a little too exuberant. "That's why she ended up in that pit."

Mason stepped up to Aubrey and took her elbow, abruptly lifting her out of her chair. "We are going to have a word outside."

Aubrey barely had a moment to glance back at her students before Mason swiftly escorted her out of the conference room.

He shut the door and guided her down the hall, not saying a word.

The warm rush of relief dancing through Cal's system made him want to dance around the conference room. He held Lindsey's note in his hand, assured he'd been right about the teacher. The first moment he laid eyes on Aubrey LaRoux, he'd wondered if he could trust her, but now he knew she was one of them—a good guy.

Aubrey had brought Lindsey's letter to the authorities, which proved she wasn't the killer. The rest of the gang had to trust her now. They were running out of time and options.

WWLD?

What would Lindsey do? The question ran through his head day and night as he worked through the missing girls' cases. Lindsey had been the first one to teach him about Waverly's past. What started as a difficult relationship soon found common ground with their interest in the missing girls. Then, when Lindsey had confided about her sister being one of them, they became close. He had forgiven her for the taunts and horrible jokes played at his expense long ago. She had shown him enemies could be friends if there was a willingness.

He held out the note to the others.

"See? She's with us."

Bella pointed at the letter. "London planted that note as a test, and Ms. LaRoux passed."

Hartley set his tightly gripped hands on the conference table. "But the police aren't going to help. She should never have shown that dick sheriff the note."

Cal could not help rubbing his nose in his mistake. "I told you not to hack into their database."

"Shut up, Broussard." Hartley thumped his fist on the table. "I don't see you sticking your neck out a whole hell of a lot lately."

Bella pointed at a scowling Hartley. "Don't do that. We agreed on our plan, and you agreed to take the risk, so don't blame Cal about what happened."

Good ole Bella. He could always count on her to have his back.

"I don't know," Jenna whined. "I'm all for believing her, but why couldn't she trust us?"

"She's old school," Hartley explained. "Her generation was taught to turn to the law for help."

Cal covered his mouth, hiding his chuckle. Sometimes he could be as dumb as he looked.

"A generation is considered about thirty years. She's only ten years older than us."

"So?" Hartley's square jaw tensed. "She's still not the same as us."

"Yeah, she's smarter for one." Cal ached to put Hartley in his place. "And a whole lot more patient with stupid people like you."

"Guys, stop it," Bella pleaded. "We have enough going on without you two bickering all the time."

Jenna leaned into the table, creasing her forehead. "Yeah, we have to start working together."

Cal raised his eyebrows, taken aback. "You never want to work with anyone."

Jenna's hands twisted together on the table. "That was before I found out a killer was watching our every move. Someone knows that Lindsey confided to all of us. My guess is they don't want our secret getting out."

Bella sat back in her chair, appearing confident. "So then we have to tell Ms. LaRoux. She has to know what Lindsey found."

Cal hesitated. He wanted to agree, but what if their secret put the pretty teacher at risk? He couldn't live with himself if she got hurt or worse.

"Then we need to find the killer before they come after anyone else."

"How?" Hartley pushed his chair back from the table, angry. "We've found all the clues we can. Lindsey didn't give us a lot to go on. All she knew was it's someone tied to the school. She never gave us any specifics."

"Until we find the killer, we need to protect ourselves." Cal set the note on the table. "We should share what we know with someone the killer might think twice about hurting."

Bella shook her head, frowning. "Psychopaths don't think that way. That's what makes them perfect killers."

A charge of authority surged through Cal. It wasn't something he was used to, but he found the sensation highly addictive.

"But they won't make mistakes. They won't kill someone they think will be missed. So far, they have taken out students, but I doubt they will mess with a teacher."

Cal scoured the faces of his cohorts. Their wide eyes and tight lips told him he was right about their next move.

"What happens if she turns on us?" Jenna asked.

Cal shook his head, trusting the certainty raging in his gut. "She won't."

Jenna's frown cut across the table. "I hope you're right because I hate to think of what we will have to do."

Yeah, I didn't need to hear that.

When Aubrey reached a partially opened door, Mason let her go and motioned for her to step inside. She didn't know what to expect, but pressed her lips into a thin line, ready to defend her actions.

The office she walked into had certificates of merit, framed posters from The New Orleans Jazz and Heritage Festival, and scattered pictures of men on fishing boats. The dark white floor and plain oak furniture contrasted sharply with the touches Mason had added, piquing her interest in the man.

He shut the door as she went to inspect a few of the photos.

She studied the men with cheery smiles holding up trout, redfish, and hefty-sized catfish aboard different boats. In a few photos, she found a shirtless Mason, beaming as he showed off his six-pack abs.

So that's what he keeps hidden under his shirt.

She browsed more pictures scattered around the room, searching for any evidence of a girlfriend or past romantic relationships. She was thankful there wasn't a woman's face to be found anywhere in the office.

The rustling of papers made Aubrey turn to the simple oak desk. Mason sat behind it, watching her.

She pointed at one of the framed photos. "You like to fish?"

"I did when I lived in New Orleans."

She explored the posters and certificates of merit from the New Orleans Police Department.

"Do you miss it?"

He sat back in his chair. "I used to, but I like living here." He pointed to one of the brown upholstered chairs in front of his desk. "Sit."

The command rattled her. She scurried to the chair.

"You should have called me right away with that note. It changes everything. You're no longer safe at that school."

"You expect me to walk away and leave those students alone?" She cut her hand across the desk. "No way."

Mason stood and came around the desk. "What have you found out from the other students?"

She sagged into her chair. "Nothing yet. I told my first period class to spread the word about our investigation, but everyone is staying away."

"They're afraid. I'm sure the students believe whoever took Lindsey and London is watching the school."

"Do you think it could be the same person who took Marjorie?"

He had a seat on the front of his desk. "I'm not sure. The evidence from that case is almost nonexistent."

Aubrey sat up and put on a pleasing smile. "What evidence? I mean, what do you have that you can share? It would help me and my students to know where to start looking on campus."

He observed her for several seconds, making Aubrey squirm in her chair.

"All right, but I'm warning you, this is the unpleasant side of being a detective."

Mason turned to an open file cabinet behind his desk.

Aubrey flinched as he slapped a slender manila folder in front of her.

"That's the autopsy report on London Dumont," Mason said in a flat tone.

She went to open it, but he stopped her. "The pictures are graphic."

She pushed his hand off hers. "I can handle it. I can't help her unless I know everything."

The moment Aubrey opened the folder, she regretted it. The photo on top was of London on the autopsy table, her mouth open, and her eyes staring upward. She had black bruises on her hip, legs, chest, and around her neck.

She closed her eyes, gulping in air, and praying not to be sick all over Mason's desk.

He closed the file and moved it to the side.

"Her neck was broken in the fall, but there were bruises on her body consistent with a struggle. The coroner estimates she was pushed into the well about twelve to fourteen hours before we found her." Mason leaned against the desk and folded his arms. "The necklace in her hand belonged to Lindsey. Lindsey's parents confirmed it was among the things in her dorm but somehow had been misplaced when her belongings were shipped back."

"So someone took the necklace while it was in Lindsey's room."

Mason nodded. "London could have taken it, but we won't know for sure until we catch her killer."

"And London?" Aubrey looked up at the sheriff. "Where is she now?"

"Her remains were returned to New Orleans yesterday."

A queasy roll went through her stomach as she thought of her dead student in the pit.

"And what do you have on Lindsey's disappearance?"

Mason reached across his desk and put a thin folder in front of her.

She opened it and found only a few forms, photos of Lindsey's dorm room and interviews with her friends.

"This is it?"

He nodded. "There's nothing. It's like she disappeared into thin air. One thing I learned, as a detective, is everyone has a tracing. Something they leave behind to let us know where they've been. With Lindsey, there's nothing."

"Perhaps the killer was more thorough," she suggested.

"Then makes mistakes with London?" He shook his head as he took the folder away. "That doesn't add up."

She clenched her fists, hoping she wasn't pushing too hard. "And the girls who disappeared in the nineties? What do you have on them?"

"You've seen enough."

Mason lifted her chair by the arms and turned it around to face him. The show of strength startled her.

He knelt in front of her and took her hand.

Heat flushed her cheeks, and Aubrey's heart rate became like the climbing speedometer of a race car.

"I'm going to stick close to you and your students on campus. The investigation allows me to come and go as I please, and I plan on spending a lot of time at Waverly, but I am asking you to do something for me."

She searched for words, but her mouth only babbled a few unintelligible sounds.

He let go of her hand. "Be careful, and don't trust anyone."

She straightened up and collected herself. "Even you?"

"I'm the only person you can trust. You should know that by now."

She struggled to stand, flustered by his words. Men had hit on her before, but she was never remotely interested. Mason Dubois was another story.

"I should get back to my students."

He took a step back. "Remember what I said. You're in danger. Someone is eventually going to want to find out what you know."

"That's when I'll call you to come rescue me, right?"

He opened the door for her. "Just don't wait too long. I don't want you to end up in a file on my desk."

"I don't want that either." She glanced back at the numerous folders. "That's not the way I want to be remembered."

CHAPTER 16

Aubrey prayed she didn't fall as she stood on her tiptoes, balancing precariously on a desk while clutching a large map. She stretched, attempting to press a taped corner to the classroom wall. Aubrey held her breath, leaned forward to slap the other taped edge in place when a hand reached up to assist her.

"You should have one of your students doing this."

She turned and smiled at Samuel as he wrestled the oversized document into position.

"Thank you, and I would ask, but they're all at lunch."

Samuel held out his hand and helped her from the desk. "And why aren't you at lunch?"

She safely landed on the floor. "Because I just got that in from the printer in town, and I wanted to put it up."

She put her hands on her hips and examined her work, glad to see that the satellite map of the school grounds, including the battlefield, cemetery, and mill, came out better than expected.

Samuel scratched his head under his red cap. "What are you going to do with this?"

She pointed at the map. "It's for my students. We are working on the Lindsey Gillett and London Dumont cases. We're trying to get more students interested in helping out, but it has been slow going so far."

His low whistle filled the empty classroom. "You clear this with Ms. Probst?"

Aubrey frowned. "No, I cleared it with Sheriff Dubois. He thought it was important to get the students talking to see if they have any information he and his men can use." She wiped her hands together. "Last time I checked, he outranks her in this parish."

Samuel shook his head. "Maybe in the parish, but you know how that woman is when it comes to this school. There isn't an article published, a social media post, picture, blog—you name it—that slips by her. Sometimes I think she stays up all night scouring the internet for anything on Waverly."

"That's a terrifying picture."

He nodded. "Scary woman." Samuel inspected the map, squinting as he raised his head to the portions of land along the river. "And what are you going to do with this?"

"I plan to pin the locations of where both Lindsey and Marjorie were last seen, and we know where London was found." She hesitated, still grappling with the image of the young woman at the bottom of the well. "I have access to reports on evidence from when those three girls went missing." She pointed to the broad field at the back of the grounds. "Along the battlefield there."

Samuel followed her finger. "Once you've done that, then what?"

She sighed, knowing it didn't seem like much. "I hope someone comes through this classroom who can tell me more. Perhaps someone who saw something when Lindsey went missing or spoke with London before she took off for those backwoods."

"What about people outside this school?" Samuel kept his gaze on the map. "There might be others who were roaming the grounds when those girls all went missing."

Aubrey stopped and looked at him with an arched eyebrow. "Who? Hunters?"

"We catch hunters here from time to time, but there are others who consider this ground sacred, and despite the efforts of Sara Probst to keep them out, they still come around."

The meaning of his words slowly sank in. "Are you talking about the American Indians who once lived on this land?"

"The Chitimacha are still active around here. They sometimes conduct ceremonies on the land by the old family cemetery. I've caught them a few times, but they never stay long, and no one ever notices when they're here." Samuel turned to her, his dark eyes no longer glinting with friendship. "And you never heard that from me, ya hear?"

She checked the closed classroom door. "Did you tell the police?"

"Hell no." Samuel backed away. "You think I want to lose my job? The only reason I told you is because of this." He waved at the map. "If you go traipsing around these grounds at night, you might run into them."

"When do they hold these ceremonies?"

Samuel removed his cap and held it in both hands. "You'd have to ask them that, but you'll never get close enough to see who they are. They run from strangers."

Aubrey's frustration ate at her. "Could someone from the Chitimacha have done something to those girls?"

Samuel slapped his cap back on. "It doesn't make sense. They've been coming around since I was a boy. But if someone wanted to hurt the school for taking away sacred land …"

Aubrey turned away, feeling sick. "Then abducting girls from this school would do it."

"Now you see why I never said anything to the local boys. They would haul every member of that tribe in for questioning. The Chitimacha community would be in an uproar."

Aubrey pinched her brow, trying to ease the rising tension squeezing her head.

"If someone is trying to bring negative attention to this school, it has to be stopped before another innocent girl is killed."

Samuel went to one of the desks in the room. He gripped the back of the chair and took a moment.

"And how do you propose to do that?"

Aubrey walked up to him. "You must talk to the Chitimacha, quietly. Feel them out."

Samuel avoided her gaze. Anticipation curled Aubrey's toes.

"I've got a nice life in this town," he said, sounding irritated. "I'm not about to jeopardize it for this school. I have no loyalty to this place.

Neither do you. Our blood is all over this land."

His response didn't surprise her, but Aubrey felt compelled to do something. She had to convince him.

"I'm not going to add more blood to those atrocities. What if another girl gets abducted or hurt? Can you live with that? I would never forgive myself for not speaking to Mason."

He faced her, flaunting a sly smile. "Mason? So it's true. Word around town is the sheriff is sweet on you. Do you like him?"

She swept a lock of hair from her face while hiding her grimace.

"No, I'm not sweet on him. I'm helping him with the case. As you should be doing. Don't you want answers?"

He stepped closer. "Answers don't bring back the dead, and they won't do you any good if you end up becoming a target of whoever is killing these girls." He motioned to the map. "They might get wind of what you are doing and want to stop you. You ever consider that?"

She scrubbed her face, tempering her anxiety. "The only person who would be out to stop me is Sara Probst. She's against anything to help the students."

Samuel pointed at her. "That woman will be more than pissed with you. She'll ruin your life like she has ruined so many others."

Aubrey went over his words, a tight knot settling in her queasy stomach. "What lives has Ms. Probst ruined?"

"Ms. LaRoux? I got the pictures you wanted," a shaky voice called from across the classroom.

Aubrey spun around and discovered Cal holding a thick folder in his hand. She wanted to kick herself for forgetting about him. She had to be smarter, more cautious, and stay on her toes.

"Cal." She put on a cheerful smile. "I didn't hear you come in."

Cal came into the room, his wary gaze bouncing back and forth between her and the caretaker. "Hi, Mr. Samuel."

"Mr. Samuel was just telling me about the Chitimacha Indians who used to live on this land. He suggested we do some more digging into the local tribes. It could add something useful to our investigation." She swallowed hard, hoping the young man didn't suspect anything. "What do you think? You're our history buff. Care to take on the challenge?"

Cal came forward and handed her the folder. The rosy color

returned to his cheeks. "Yeah, sure. That would be cool."

Samuel tipped his cap. "Looks like you have work to do. I'll leave you."

Samuel headed along the side of the room.

He had almost reached the door when Aubrey called out, "Don't forget to find out what you can for me. I would appreciate it."

Samuel stopped at the open classroom door. "I'll do what I can. Give me a little time."

The moment the door closed, Cal turned to her. "Why the sudden interest in the Chitimacha Indians?"

She wanted to laugh at his direct interrogation. She should've known he would immediately suspect she was up to something.

Aubrey took the folder to her map. She sat on the edge of the table and looked up at Cal.

It was one of those moments when she had to either invest her trust in her students or keep vital evidence from them.

You know what you must do.

"Mr. Samuel told me that the Chitimacha Indians still meet on the school's land to conduct ceremonies to honor their ancestors. They've been doing it for a while."

"You think someone from the tribe could have taken the girls and hurt London?" Cal sighed and plopped down next to her. "That could be a huge problem."

"I told you this because I don't want to keep anything from you or the others. We have to work together."

Cal lowered his head.

She dipped closer to him. "What is it?"

He raised his gaze and frowned. "There's something I should tell you since we're working together and all."

Aubrey's muscles tensed, preparing for the bad news. "Go on."

Cal scratched his head, his cheeks turning a dark shade of crimson. "Well, we haven't exactly been honest with you. Do you remember that first day you walked into class?"

The burn in the back of Cal's throat traveled to his stomach. He wanted to run away from Jenna's red face. Her shouting did little to alleviate his growing anxiety. The classroom walls closed in, and he feared if he didn't speak up soon, he would never be able to tell his cohorts why he had spilled the beans to Ms. LaRoux.

"She had to know." He pushed Jenna out of his face. "It was time."

He took a breath, relieved the fiery redhead had finally stopped yelling. "If we're going to get anywhere with this investigation, we have to trust her."

Cal analyzed the emotionless faces of Hartley and Bella, praying they would understand.

Hartley stared down at him. "What did you tell her?"

Cal rubbed the smooth surface of his desk. "I told her about what we did to keep others from joining her first period class, how we suspected she was involved with Marjorie's disappearance and Lindsey's, and how London hid Lindsey's note to test her loyalty. The act we put on to keep her from suspecting. And why we took her to the battlefield and mill, seeing if she would crack."

Hartley slapped the side of his head. "Now she can go to Probst and turn us in. You've gotten us all expelled."

Cal raised his head; hope spreading in his chest. "No, she won't do that. She told me a secret. The Chitimacha tribes in the area have been sneaking onto the school grounds to perform rituals or ceremonies."

Hartley rubbed his chin. "That wouldn't explain the girls who went missing in the nineties or even Marjorie. Why would the Chitimacha bother with them?"

"Would you forget about the Indians?" Bella leaned over Cal, a taut expression stretched across her face. "Was she mad at us or what?"

Cal chuckled. "No, she wasn't mad. She was shocked we'd even think she'd hurt Marjorie or Lindsey. Then she was impressed by all our planning."

Jenna shrugged. "Well, that's something."

Hartley pinched his lip between his thumb and forefinger. "It's still too early to say."

Bella glared at him. "Aw, come on. What more do you need to prove that she didn't do it? She didn't hurt Marjorie or Lindsey or London. She's on our side."

"You like her too much," he argued.

Bella got right under Hartley's nose. "We can't keep things from her anymore. If we want to solve Lindsey's disappearance and find out who killed London, we need her help."

"And what if she's a mistake?" he demanded. "It could cost us."

Jenna came up to him, her lips extended into a pensive line. "Lindsey took a chance on us. She befriended us, got to know us, started this group of ours, and only then did she trust us with her secret. Maybe we should do the same with Ms. LaRoux. See what she does with the truth. It's the only way to know for sure if she's on our side."

Hartley backed off, grumbling, "I can't believe you are siding with them."

"I'm not siding," Jenna told him. "I'm keeping my options open."

Cal took it as a sign of victory. He stood, relieved he was no longer the center of everyone's fury.

"That settles it. We are going to be honest with her from now on and share what we know."

Hartley grabbed the collar of Cal's shirt. "If this blows up, I'm taking you down."

Bella removed his hand. "Give it a break, Hartley. You haven't exactly handled this situation like James Bond. Getting caught was a stupid move."

Hartley ran his hands through his hair. "Fine, we work with her, but this wasn't part of my plan. We were brought together by Lindsey because she trusted us with her secret. If Aubrey LaRoux turns on us, we could all end up in big trouble."

Bella smoothed out Cal's wrinkled shirt. "Your plan was to find evidence on Aubrey LaRoux because you were convinced she had something to do with Marjorie and Lindsey's disappearance. But we know it's not her. It can't be. Someone else has been hunting young women at Waverly for years, and we need to find out who before another girl goes missing."

A ubrey focused on maintaining her calm, with her hands folded in her lap as Bella sat on the edge of the classroom desk, carefully laying out her students' plan for getting her to confess to the abduction of Marjorie and Lindsey. Parts were brilliant—manipulating her into taking them to the battlefield and mill, hoping to get her to slip up. And other parts were almost comical—how they cajoled, intimidated, and even paid students off to make them drop her first period class. If she had not understood their good intentions, Aubrey might have been furious, but given the situation, she could not help but feel impressed.

"The reason we did all of it was for Lindsey," Bella explained. "She brought us together. Lindsey made us a group of unlikely friends. It may not seem like it, but all of us …" Her voice faltered. "Even London would do anything for Lindsey."

Aubrey sat motionless, upended by the confession, surveying the faces gathered around her desk, and finding a new appreciation for their cunning.

"Lindsey must be an impressive young woman to bring all of you together."

Cal smiled, bringing a touch of light to his eyes. "She was. I got bullied a lot, mostly by Hartley's teammates or London's friends, but Lindsey stopped all that. She befriended me when no one else would. She told everyone to leave me alone, and when she asked me to hang out with her, Hartley, and London, I didn't know how to react."

"She showed me what a jerk I'd been," Hartley confessed. "Lindsey made me realize I wasn't going to get anywhere in the world if I kept bullying people. She listened to me a lot. She was my best friend."

The young man's palpable sorrow cut into Aubrey.

Jenna fidgeted on her corner of the desk. "I hated everybody until Lindsey. She made me believe that not everyone was an asshole. She was … *is* a good friend."

Bella set her hands on the desk. "We were all influenced and, in some ways, saved by her, but what connected us most was what she shared with us. The secret."

Aubrey leaned forward, her anticipation getting the better of her. "What secret?"

Bella glanced at her friends. "Lindsey said she knew what happened to Marjorie. She came to Waverly to find out the truth. She told all of us the person who killed Marjorie was in this school. Someone who had access to everywhere the students went. Marjorie wrote her a letter right before she disappeared, telling her how afraid she was because she'd discovered something horrible about Waverly's past."

Aubrey went around to the front of her desk, no longer able to sit still. Her stomach was a mass of knots as she considered the ramifications. "Did Lindsey tell you what this secret was?"

Hartley shook his head. "She never got to. She said she was figuring out the pieces of the puzzle, and when she uncovered the killer, Lindsey would let us know, but she shared everything else she learned. Lindsey made us promise to continue the search if anything happened to her."

"And we did," Cal said. "When you showed up days after Lindsey disappeared, and had been a classmate of her sister's, we suspected you."

"I don't blame you." Aubrey went to the window and looked out over the back campus heading to the line of woods. "I would have considered me a prime suspect, too."

Jenna pushed away from the desk, her bright hair catching in the morning sun. "After Hartley read your interview following Marjorie's disappearance, we were pretty much convinced you did it."

Aubrey spun around. "You read that?"

Hartley scratched his head as he came toward her. "When I hacked into the sheriff's server, I found it. What you said sounded damning. Even the lead investigator had you down as a suspect at one point."

She hugged herself and chuckled. "Yeah, for about a minute, until they learned I was in class when Marjorie went missing."

Cal slipped back on the desk and grabbed his knees. "What exactly happened?"

"Yeah," Hartley said. "I read the reports, but I want to hear it from you."

Aubrey leaned against the windowsill and shook her head, memories inundating her. "Funny how some things can be so clear and others a muddy mess, but that day, I remember vividly. I was in biology, bombing a test on DNA. The loudspeaker came on. Marjorie was asked to report to the headmistress's office. Everyone in class snickered, and then they all looked at me. I guess they thought I had gotten her into trouble."

Jenna crept closer. "Why did they think that?"

Aubrey sighed, pushing back against the heaviness in her heart. "Because Marjorie bullied me. There weren't many black girls at Waverly at the time, but I was different because I didn't come from money. I got into the school on a scholarship. Marjorie found out and never let me forget I wasn't quite as good as the others. She harassed me day and night. She even got suspended for two days because she set my dorm room closet on fire. The girl who helped her turned her in, but I got blamed for ratting her out. After that, everyone treated me like an outcast. When Marjorie was called in that morning to see Ms. Probst, everyone assumed it was because of me."

Hartley watched her with his intense blue eyes. "She never made it to the headmistress's office, did she?"

Aubrey gave a curt nod. "Somewhere between leaving her history class in the liberal arts building and Elaine House, she disappeared. The police interviewed everyone, and when they started grilling me about how Marjorie had treated me, I told them how I hated her and was glad she was gone. It was a stupid thing to say, but I was angry. I regret it now."

"I asked Lindsey once why she took all of us under her wing." Bella slowly walked toward Aubrey. "She said her sister had taught her never to be unkind to those who are different. She believed we were all the same."

The sting of tears was not the reaction Aubrey had expected. For years, she had fought to forget about all the cruel and hurtful things Marjorie had done and said, but they had remained with her.

Aubrey wiped her eyes, not wanting her students to see. "I'm glad she listened to her sister."

"We all know what it's like." Bella glanced back at the others gathered around the desk. "What kid can say they were never bullied?"

"But Lindsey tried to change that." Hartley gave a weak smile. "That was just the way she was."

Aubrey smoothed out a crease in her slacks, collecting herself. "She sounds like a special person. I wish I could have known her."

"But do you think she was right?" Cal asked. "Do you think whoever took Marjorie and Lindsey is someone on campus?"

Aubrey turned to her map in the back of the room. "I remember before Marjorie disappeared, she got in trouble for sneaking out of our dorm one night. I was there when she came back the next morning, and the housemother caught her. There was mud all over her shoes. Red mud like we picked up near the river."

Hartley walked to the back of the room, keeping his eyes glued on the map. "Maybe she figured out something about those missing girls from the nineties. It was why we went to the river."

"Could she have figured out who it was?" Jenna asked.

The silence in the room cut through Aubrey.

"That could be why she disappeared," Bella suggested. "She knew too much."

"And so did Lindsey," Hartley added.

Her students turned to her, fear widening their eyes.

Cal stood. "So whoever killed Marjorie is still here."

"That's why they went after London," Bella insisted in a shaky voice. "They must know Lindsey spoke with us. They've probably been watching us all along."

Aubrey's stomach tightened into a ball. "If that's true, any one of you could be next."

Jenna wrapped her arms around her waist. "What do we do?"

Aubrey glimpsed the map with red thumbtacks in places of interest. She studied the pictures of the missing girls below, and the fear in her heart gave way to anger.

"We solve this mystery. We find out who it is and shut them down. We're going to have to explore more of the school grounds."

Cal came up behind her. "And what if the killer comes after us?"

Bella put her arm around his shoulders. "Then the last man standing inherits the legacy of revenge."

"Who said that?"

She grinned. "I did."

The blaring cacophony of the bell silenced Aubrey's wish to get her students back on track. She waited for the quiet to return to her room, saddened that her first period class had come to an end. Aubrey wanted to keep them close, especially now.

"What about the stables?" she asked. "We need to see if there is anything worthwhile."

Jenna clapped her hands together and rubbed them with glee. "Finally, a place I know. I can snoop around. As captain of the riding team, no one will suspect a thing."

"What if something happens to you?" Hartley countered. "We should stick together from now on."

Jenna sneered at him. "I can take care of myself."

"Hartley's right." Aubrey moved closer to the redhead. "If someone knows Lindsey shared her secrets with you, you're a target. We all are. It's dangerous to be alone from here on out. Stick together when you can, and don't go anywhere alone."

Bella returned to her desk. "Why do I feel like I suddenly ended up in a teenage slasher movie?"

Cal followed her. "If this were a movie, no one would touch you. Good-looking people always die. Geeks like us survive."

Bella grabbed her book bag. "Speak for yourself, Geek."

Aubrey smiled at their banter. It was a good sign. They weren't terrified yet, but she suspected they soon would be.

"We can pick this up later." She pointed at Jenna. "If you don't want all of us at the stables, take Hartley with you. I don't want you there alone."

Jenna's mouth slipped open. "And how the hell do I explain him? People are going to ask why he's there. Can't I bring Bella?"

Aubrey shook her head. "Hartley can hit harder."

Bella laughed as she grabbed her book bag. "Wanna bet?"

Hartley bobbed his eyebrows at Jenna. "Tell anyone who asks that you're showing me the hayloft."

Jenna tossed up her hands and stormed to her desk.

Hartley hurried behind her. "It's not a bad idea. We should try it."

When the last of her first period students left, Aubrey made her way to the front of the room.

She had things to do before her next class, but before she reached her desk, a shadow crossed her door.

Sara Probst walked in, wearing another one of her stylish and crisply pressed business suits. Her perfectly coiffed bun didn't have a hair out of place, and her makeup was understated but still highlighted the porcelain appeal of her skin and the curve of her cheekbones.

"Ms. Probst," Aubrey said, trying not to sound disappointed. "What can I do for you?"

Sara closed the door. "I wanted to speak with you about your student John Pucebuquet."

A rush of mild embarrassment overtook Aubrey. She'd forgotten all about her missing student.

"Ah, yes, John. I noticed he has been absent for a few days."

Sara came closer, holding her head high, and keeping her hands folded. "He returned to his home in Covington a few days ago, not feeling well. His mother called me this morning and said John is having surgery next week and will not be back for the next two weeks. She wanted his assignments. If you could please email them to me, I will send them on."

Aubrey weighed the way the woman's gaze inspected the room. She held her breath as she waited for her to spot the map at the back.

Here we go.

When she saw it, Sara stared at first and then slowly walked toward the large map.

Aubrey had an overwhelming desire to rush after her and explain, but then something else took over—anger.

"You didn't come here to tell me about John. You could have sent me an email."

Sara stopped in front of the map, peering up at the red pins positioned throughout the battlefield. "Several students on campus have told me you have been actively recruiting others to join in your search for the truth."

Aubrey leaned against her desk and folded her arms. "Yes, Sheriff Dubois suggested it. He felt it would be easier for me to get through to the students. His men might intimidate them."

Sara turned to her with raised eyebrows. "The sheriff suggested that and never spoke to me about it? How odd."

A nudge of satisfaction ebbed her anger. "Perhaps you should call him and discuss it."

"I won't bother. My school's reputation for excellence in education is more important than ..." She waved at the map.

"It's only my first period class," Aubrey argued, not about to give in. "All my other classes are devoted to history and Waverly's reputation for excellence."

Sara examined her with her wary gaze. "Speaking to students, I wholeheartedly support, but investigating missing girls? This is not in your job description."

"I would have thought anything that would end the nightmare would be beneficial. Besides, it makes the students feel engaged. Getting them involved is helping them cope with their loss."

Sara offered a tolerant smile, but all Aubrey saw was the same loathing she'd detected since her prep school days.

"Ms. LaRoux, I understand your good intentions, and I applaud them, really I do, but this is not what you were hired to do. I suggest you get back to history."

Her condescending tone made Aubrey clench her fists.

"The board has decided to confine all on-campus residents to a dusk curfew. Anyone caught outside of their designated dorms will be suspended without appeal. Additional security measures are to be implemented. We can't have another student getting hurt or disappearing."

"I agree with the extra security, but locking the students away is too extreme." Aubrey raised her voice. "Curfews will only add to their anxiety. We must give them art classes or physical activities to help them through this."

Sara's eyes widened. "One girl is dead and another missing, and you're suggesting volleyball or painting will help them cope? Loss is loss, Ms. LaRoux. You of all people should know that."

Aubrey's fury roared through her system like molten lava. "You're right. I know loss, and perhaps I can understand what these kids are going through better than you."

Sara studied Aubrey with a calculating gaze. "It amazes me that you can't see you're being taken advantage of. These students would milk you for every ounce of kindness and then turn on you when you have no more to give. Lindsey Gillett was a master of that. Up until London was killed, I believed this was a hoax. Something Lindsey concocted to give her the attention she always demanded."

Aubrey pushed away from her desk. "But you didn't feel that way when Marjorie disappeared. You walked around this place like a ghost for weeks. The faculty whispered about how worried they were about you."

Sara glowered at her and then raised her head. "I wanted to know, like everyone else, what happened to her. But Lindsey wasn't like her sister. From the day she arrived, she asked a lot of questions about Marjorie, so when she went missing, I assumed it was a prank."

Sara marched to the door, but then stopped and turned to Aubrey.

"You will cease your investigation activities, stick to teaching history, and follow the outline of the new rules I will be distributing today. If you step out of line again, I will terminate your contract. Do we understand one another?"

Aubrey wanted to tell the stuck-up woman to shove her contract, but then she thought of her students. They were all that mattered now.

"I understand, Ms. Probst," she said, suppressing her outrage.

Sara left the room, quietly closing the door behind her.

The bell sounded for next period, and as the horrible buzzing rocked her classroom, Aubrey slammed her fist into her desk.

There were times when being a teacher was as trying as when she had been a student.

I don't get paid enough for this bullshit.

CHAPTER 18

Hartley admired the setting sun as it stretched its red fingers across the expanse of blue sky. He headed across the freshly cut grass toward the paved path that led to the stables. He'd not planned on tracking down Jenna, but Ms. LaRoux's request for him to stick close still echoed. Hartley didn't want to take any chances, even if Jenna wasn't exactly his favorite person.

The fading sunlight shone on the tin roof as he trekked along the path. It wasn't far from The Quad, but when he glanced to his right and saw the stretch of trees leading to the battlefield, he shuddered. All the details of where and how London had died had traveled the halls of the police station.

Sadness slowed his steps as he thought of her bright smile and funny laugh. He had called it bird laughter because of the way she twittered. Hartley wished he could hear it once more, see her again, and tell her how sorry he was he hadn't protected her against whoever wanted her dead.

I won't let that happen again.

Determined to get to the barn and check on Jenna, he jogged the final few yards to the stable.

Hartley passed beneath the round arch positioned over the wooden gates marking the entrance. Waverly Stables had once been the place he considered the best spot to meet girls. Guys never got into horses. It was a chick thing.

Paddocks constructed of white fences covered the front of the stable grounds. Horses relaxed in the pens, either grazing or rolling in the damp red mud.

He chuckled at seeing a white gelding climb to his feet, a fresh coating of red mud sticking to his coat.

After the paddocks, he arrived at the open shed row, where dozens of cinder block stalls housed the fifteen horses used by the school for riding lessons. The smell of manure and horse curled his nose.

Ugh. No wonder Probst hates this place so much.

The stench and remoteness probably appealed to Jenna. She was one of the best riders in school, had won several competitions for Waverly, but never bragged about her accomplishments. Lindsey was the one who had told him about Jenna's passion for horses. He would never have cared for, nor noticed Jenna before Lindsey. She had opened his eyes to so many things.

When he passed a few of the stalls, he took the time to pat the soft noses of the creatures who came out to greet him. That was when he noticed the quiet. Except for the snorting and pawing of the horses, Hartley didn't pick up any human activity.

Damn glad I came.

He set off down the row of stalls, waving off a passing fly—he hated bugs. The barn's open-plan had stalls facing outward while tack rooms and storage rooms sat at either end. With no sign of Jenna, he hurried to the closest crosswalk to check the other side.

The moment he reached the assembly of doors at the end of the stables, he breathed a sigh of relief. Jenna stood next to a dark bay gelding she had tied to a hitching post. She ran a brush over the horse's coat, talking to him in a high, sweet voice that sounded very un-Jenna.

Hartley rested his shoulder against the corner of the last stall and watched her, amazed by her gentleness. He liked the lean curve of her thighs and the way she wore her black riding boots. He could see her as a dominatrix in those boots, getting off on telling men what to do.

"I always knew you had a soft spot hidden behind all that anger."

Jenna flinched and dropped her brush. "What the hell, Hartley?"

He walked up to her, admiring her ass as she bent over to retrieve her brush.

Not bad.

"I told you we should stick together. I came to check on you and what do I find? You with a horse."

"Manni isn't *a horse*," she argued, imitating him. "He's my horse. We train together every day."

Hartley walked past her. "I bet you spend more time with him than anyone else at this school."

"I prefer horses to people, but you already knew that."

He went to the other side of the stable and peered down the row of stalls. "Who else is here?"

"No one." Jenna set the brush in a bucket. "I like it when the stables are empty. It's peaceful."

"Do you want to get killed? You have to be careful, Jenna."

She tilted her head and smiled. "Wow, never thought I would live to see the day you worried about me."

He approached the horse and patted the animal's sleek neck. "Well, these are strange times."

Jenna untied the horse from the post. "Stop worrying. As you can see, I'm fine. Now you can go."

She walked the horse toward the row of stalls along the back of the barn.

Hartley followed, making sure to stay far back from the animal's hindquarters. "I'm going to hang around and walk with you back to the dorm."

"No, you're not!"

He studied her as she guided the horse. "Ms. LaRoux would want me to."

Hartley counted off the seconds, waiting for Jenna to protest.

"I don't need a babysitter, no matter what Ms. LaRoux says."

He cracked a grin as she escorted the horse into the stall, proud he'd made her see reason.

"What about checking out the hayloft?" he called to her. "We agreed it was worth looking into."

Jenna emerged from the stall holding the halter and lead in her hand. "I already did that. I combed through the loft and most of the tack rooms."

Hartley's grin dropped. "Why didn't you wait for me?"

Jenna came toward him. "I told you before. I don't want people asking why you're here with me."

He shook his head, reining in his disappointment. "Is there anything else we can check out while I'm here?"

Jenna stopped in front of him. Her gaze wandered to a large square shed made of red planking, set away from the stables on a patch of high, grassy ground.

"That's where Mr. Samuel keeps a lot of equipment for the groundskeepers—ATVs and other stuff. But it's locked, and only he has the key."

Hartley stood next to her, eyeing an outside staircase along the back portion of the stables. "Where does that go?"

"Mr. Samuel's office. He keeps the access door above the stairs locked at all times." She headed back toward the hitching post. "Look, I'm fine. So you can go now."

"Jeez, talk about ungrateful." He followed her as she returned to the white bucket where she had dropped her brush. "You won't even let a guy try and help you?"

She picked up the bucket and faced him. "I know how you felt about her—we all did. And what you did with London, or sticking close to me, isn't going to make amends for what happened to Lindsey. Her disappearance wasn't your fault, but you've been acting like everybody's knight in shining armor. You can stop now. Be the guy you were before."

He hesitated and looked away, anxious to hide how much her words hurt and surprised him.

Hartley believed he'd been keeping his grief masked behind his bravado. *Never let anyone see you cry* had repeated in his head since Little League. But how did he return to the outgoing and carefree guy he had been before Lindsey? Knowing her then losing her changed him irrevocably.

Enough of this.

Hartley filled his lungs, expanding his chest and pulling back his shoulders as he confronted her once more.

"I wasn't making amends for anything. I was trying to be a friend." He inched backward, eager to get away. "I'll leave you to finish." He cleared his throat. "Just get back to the dorm soon. They'll be locking everyone in come dusk."

He walked quickly along the shed row, ignoring the horses that nudged his arm, wanting attention.

"Wait, Hartley," Jenna called. "I'm sorry."

He was about to turn around and flash her a winning smile but changed his mind.

If she didn't want his help and felt better slicing him up, then to hell with her. He didn't need someone rubbing his nose in his grief.

Once outside, Hartley felt better. He passed the paddocks and reached the arched gate, glad to be heading for town.

The girls weren't the only ones getting locked up at night. The boys had to be in their dorms in town by sunset. Many complained it put a damper on their social lives, but Hartley had come to embrace it. Being alone in his room gave him time to think and remember Lindsey.

He kicked a few rocks on the path, venting his anger, as he meandered back toward The Quad. He scanned the sky, amazed at how quickly darkness had descended.

Hartley's guilt rose, tightening his chest as he considered going back for Jenna. He didn't want to lose her, too. He would never forgive himself.

He was about to head back to the stables when a high-pitched screech came from the line of trees to his left.

Hartley slowly faced the woods where they had found London. A tingle of dread rose along his spine.

He squinted into the shadows, searching for the source of the sound. "Hello?"

Hartley remained mindful of the dimming daylight.

"Help."

The call sounded weak and very faint. Someone was in trouble.

Hartley took off, sprinting away from the path and heading toward the trees.

He stayed alert for more cries, but the woods were eerily silent.

The moment he broke through the line of trees, darkness engulfed him. His pace slowed to a brisk walk as the smashing of leaves and twigs accompanied him in the thickening woods.

Hartley removed his phone from his back pocket and hit the flashlight.

"Hello?"

He sent the faint beam into the woods, eager to find whoever had called to him.

A rustling to his left elicited a gasp.

He spun the light around, figuring it was an animal, but then caught a glimpse of what looked like a pair of black riding boots.

"Jenna, is that you?"

Crushing branches echoed as the person headed away from him.

Maybe it wasn't Jenna but another student playing a prank.

Or could it be someone else?

The proposition made his mouth go dry. The killer could be watching from the shadows.

Hartley proceeded cautiously. He had to confront whoever was trying to scare him, and then check to see that Jenna was safe.

More rustling rose in front of him, but it sounded closer, making the hairs on his arms stand.

He pointed his phone into the trees, forcing his eyes to adjust to the limited light. He panned the flash as a knot formed in his throat. Hartley became attuned to rapid, shallow breathing echoing throughout the isolated locale.

Stay calm. You can take this asshole.

Something glinted through the trees.

He recalled the defensive moves his old man taught him. Hartley became empowered and decided it was time to turn the tables on his stalker.

Checking the ground, he proceeded slowly, until the snap of a twig made him spin around. Then he heard a quick succession of rapid footsteps.

His heart raced and sweat trickled from his temple to his cheek. Hartley held up his phone and squeezed his free hand into a fist, ready for a fight.

"My hero," a croaky, indistinguishable voice said close by.

Hartley frantically looked behind him. The low light made it impossible to see anything.

He didn't feel brave anymore. This was the asshole who had killed London and taken Lindsey. He sensed it, and confronting them, especially in the woods, wasn't a good idea.

Draw them out into the open.

The strategy would give him a look at his tormentor and a chance to take them on in a fair fight.

He scanned the trees, searching for a way out of the woods. The sun had sunk below the horizon, and the blackness disoriented him. He wasn't sure from which direction he had come.

Hartley decided to hedge his bet and back out. He would either arrive on the battlefield or the grounds of the school. Anything was better than the woods, where someone could hide behind every tree.

He stomped over leaves, twigs, and pine needles, blocking out the sound of all other movement.

He bumped into a tree and cursed, and then a branch slapped his back. Each time something touched him, he tensed.

The darkness outpaced him, and soon he could barely make out the trees with his phone. The panic he'd attempted to control had gained ground. Hartley fought the urge to make a run for it.

Whack.

He froze.

What the hell was that?

"I know your secret—Lindsey's secret."

The strange voice was back, but this time, terror overtook Hartley's desire to challenge the person.

"Who are you?"

Whack.

Hartley recognized the sound of an ax or large knife cutting into a tree.

Shit.

He hurried backward, not caring about branches. Fear propelled him as he scrambled through the woods, slamming into brush and tree trunks.

Hartley should have reached the edge by now. Why couldn't he see the lights from the school?

His heartbeat thundered in his ears as he moved.

Something blocked his way. He kicked a log or stump and was feeling his way around when a shove came from behind.

He went down hard, losing his phone, and the light on the screen died. His cheek grazed against something coarse. A sharp, burning jab shot up from his hip.

Hartley took a moment. His cheek stung like mad, and his hip throbbed, but he could still move, which meant he could run.

He patted the pile of mulch around him for his phone—nothing. The urgency to get away fueled a rush of adrenaline.

Not knowing where to go, he zigzagged around the trees, remembering something from a TV show about never running in a straight line because it made you an easy target.

He saw a far-off light. It had to be the school. Hartley picked up speed.

But when he broke through the wood line and found himself in a clearing, anticipation shattered into deep despair. He was on the battlefield.

He searched the grounds for any shadows or movement.

A pensive breath eked from his lips. He was alone.

Then a rush of sounds swelled behind him. Frantic footsteps, sloshing through leaves, twigs, and mud erupted.

He struggled to see into the woods. Then something shiny glinted in the darkness. Curved and shaped like a semi-circle, it had a sharp edge and came to a point.

It took a few seconds for Hartley to recognize the sickle in the dim light, and when he did, his blood ran cold.

His muscles turned to fire, urging him to run. Hartley sped away from the woods, and no matter how much he wanted to turn around and see where his attacker was, he didn't dare.

He pushed hard, running faster than he ever had, and his confidence grew. He was the best on the track team. He could best this asshole.

Then he heard something that sucked the air from his lungs—the rev of a motor coming to life.

Hartley looked around. The headlights of a four-wheeler were on him.

The rumble of the engine carried throughout the empty field. He wanted to cry out but knew it was pointless. The killer had lured him to the secluded setting to make sure no one would hear his screams.

Hartley kept running, even as the revving engine closed in. The grass around his feet lit up, as the off-road vehicle got closer.

His lungs burned, eating up every breath, but he knew no matter how hard he ran, it wouldn't be enough. He was losing ground.

He remembered the mill and the steep terrain around it. A four-wheeler would not make it through there. If he could get to the edge of the battlefield, he had a chance.

Something nipped at his heels. When he glanced over his shoulder, light blinded him.

Oh, God, no!

Fear gave Hartley a burst of speed, but the light was no longer tailing him. The yellow beams on the high grass shifted as he ran.

Vomit rose from the back of his throat. He tried to veer away, but the vehicle stayed with him.

Then he spotted the edge of the field and surged with hope.

Hartley focused on his breathing as if he were on the track and out to win his heat. It was the only way to keep ahead of his attacker.

The patch of woods that led to the mill got closer. His certainty of escape bolstered his spirit.

The ATV kept turning toward him, but he managed to dash away.

Suddenly, his feet went out from under him, and Hartley flew across the ground.

He landed hard. A shockwave of searing spasms radiated through him. His right leg convulsed with agony. When he looked up, he saw why.

He had slammed into a stone monument dedicated to fallen soldiers.

Hartley clawed at the grass to get back on his feet, but he couldn't move, his leg was injured.

He collapsed, gasping as tears streamed down his cheeks.

Hartley wanted to be anywhere but here—back in his dorm or home with his parents. He vowed never to complain again about his life if God would save him.

The headlights pulled alongside. That was when he spotted the blood—his blood—it was everywhere. He glanced down at his leg and saw the jagged edge of bone sticking up out of his pants leg.

Oh, God!

"Help me," he begged.

The glaring headlamps made it hard to see the figure getting off the all-terrain vehicle. But then light flashed on the sickle.

Brandishing it menacingly, the stranger came closer.

Hartley held up his hands. "No, no, no, no!"

The sickle rose above him, the light reflecting off its sharply honed blade.

Hartley let go of an ear-piercing shriek as the blade came down hard on his neck, and everything went black.

Red and blue flashing lights danced across the parking lot of Waverly Preparatory School, sending eerie streams into the night sky. Aubrey sat on the curb next to Mason's patrol car. Every memory she had of Hartley's smile and playful personality weighed on her heart. She had grown very fond of the young man, and now he was dead.

Something touched her shoulder, and she flinched.

Mason's handsome face hovered over her, his warmth chasing away a small part of her sadness.

"How are you holding up?"

She wiped away tears with her shirtsleeve and sniffled. "I'm not."

"None of us are." He rubbed his face, looking as raw as she felt. "I'm going to put men on campus until we find whoever is doing this."

His bleak tone did not instill much hope in her. "Don't you have any leads?"

Mason held out his hand. Aubrey took it and got up from the curb.

"I want to show you something."

A speck of curiosity broke through her fatigue. Aubrey shook off her grief and followed him to the passenger side of his car.

Mason opened the door and reached inside for a tablet on the front seat.

"We found a few things next to Hartley Gregory's body."

Aubrey braced for more horrible pictures like she had seen of London. She didn't know if she could stomach such images of Hartley, especially after how he'd died.

Mason swiped his finger across the screen, and a photo appeared. He held it up for Aubrey.

A pair of dainty gold earrings with the initials *M* and *C* intertwined sat atop a smooshed pile of weeds. There was no blood, no mangled body parts, and nothing to remind her of Hartley.

"You found earrings?"

He flipped his finger across the tablet. The picture of a blonde-haired, blue-eyed girl materialized.

The photo was the same as the one pinned to Aubrey's map of the school.

"That's Marion Caldwell," she whispered. "She was one of the girls who disappeared in the nineties."

Mason pointed at the girl's earlobe. "Recognize the earrings?"

Aubrey's mouth went dry. "How did Marion's earring end up next to Hartley? He didn't know her. He never knew anything about her until Lindsey came along."

Mason tossed the tablet back onto the car seat. "Whoever killed Hartley wants to connect this crime to those missing girls."

Aubrey's knees trembled. "Why? That was almost thirty years ago."

"Sometimes serial killers leave clues behind, hoping to get caught. Sort of a cry for help."

"Or it could be someone playing a game with us." Aubrey's disgust deepened her voice. "A sick game where they tease us with jewelry while leaving my students' bodies strewn across campus."

Mason nodded. "That is another possibility. We don't have enough to go on yet."

Aubrey gazed out at the flashing lights. "How do we catch this person?"

Mason pushed his brown Stetson back on his head. "I'm working on it, but in the meantime, I want you to consider finding a place to stay in town."

Aubrey sagged against the car. "I can't. I have girls to look after in the dorm. I won't leave them, especially now."

He removed his hat and patted it against his thigh. "Then if you won't go, I'll have to stick as close as I can. I don't want anything to happen to you."

A rush of heat overtook her cold extremities. She should have been devastated, but somehow Mason had a way of erasing all her pain. "Don't you have other official duties to keep you in town?"

He put his hat back on his head. "Nope. This case is my top priority."

She rubbed her arms. "Thank you for saying that, Mason. It makes me hopeful."

The female deputy, Laura, came up to Mason holding out a tablet. "You'd better take a look at this, Sheriff."

"Thanks, Laura."

After his deputy walked away, Mason looked at the report and frowned.

"What is it?" Aubrey demanded.

"They found two different blood types on the monument at the crime scene. One is Hartley's, but the other belongs to someone else."

"I saw blood on that monument when we were looking for clues the other day. We thought it was animal blood."

"It's human. We'll check it against London and Lindsey and see what we come up with."

"And if it's Lindsey's?"

He held the tablet against his chest and paused. "Then it's a good possibility she's not just missing. Perhaps she was chased like Hartley. We found four-wheeler tracks around his body. My team is going through the school equipment shed to check for a match."

Aubrey had grown tired of wasting time. She wanted action. "If they do get a match, then what?"

He took her elbow, guiding her back toward the walkway. "We interview everyone who had access to that equipment."

She stepped on the curb. "We're just going in circles."

"It's procedure. I have to follow the letter of the law, so when I nail this guy, we can get a conviction."

Aubrey's fury burned through her. She wanted to punch someone, destroy something, vent her utter exasperation with playing by the rules.

The killer didn't, why should they?

"Can't you just kill them? I don't want to see whoever murdered London, Hartley, and Lindsey get life in prison. I want them dead."

He brushed a lock of her dark brown hair out of her face. "You don't know how much I would love to do that, too. But I'm the sheriff, and I have to uphold the law."

She raised her face to his, almost afraid to ask her question. "What would you do to me if I killed this person? If I caught and murdered them in cold blood?"

Mason urged her closer to the grand home. "I'd make sure it never comes to that."

Sara Probst marched down the steps of the porch and walked out to meet Aubrey and Mason. Her determined stride and the hard line across her lips held no remorse or grief. She remained the same resilient woman Aubrey had known since first arriving at Waverly as a student.

"Sheriff, have you got anything for me? I have parents calling and wanting answers. They're scared."

Mason took a step away from Aubrey. "They have a right to be scared. Ms. Probst. Their children are in danger."

"And what are your men doing to catch this killer?"

Creases of frustration darkened Mason's brow. "Everything we can. Until we complete our investigation of the scene, I suggest you keep the kids inside. I was telling Ms. LaRoux that I plan to have men stationed around the campus, twenty-four seven."

Sara's glare intensified. "I would prefer to hire private security professionals."

Mason sighed and shook his head. "Ms. Probst, my team can keep everyone safe as well as hired guards."

"The board thinks bodyguards won't get pulled away if something happens in town," Sara asserted with a condescending air. "We will be able to count on them day and night."

Aubrey took in the altercation, recoiling from the hostility charging the air.

"I prefer to have at least a few men on campus," Mason countered. "Professional bodyguards are a good start, but they can't handle an investigation. I want eyes on this school at all times in case anything else happens.

Aubrey felt compelled to appease both parties. "What about the cameras? Wouldn't that help?"

Sara's eyebrows rose. "Cameras on a campus of children under the age of eighteen can lead to legal ramifications my board doesn't wish to address. And camera systems can be hacked into, and privacy violated."

Mason removed his hat and crushed the rim in his hand. "I believe cameras would be welcomed by your board and students, considering the situation. I can set up at a central location for monitoring and put deputies around the classrooms and dorms. I would suggest you close access to outlying areas such as your stables, pool, and track field. I want your students kept together."

Sara stood like stone, interrogating the man with her lethal gaze.

"I guess that will have to do," Sara hissed through her gritted teeth. "Anything else, Sheriff?"

Mason put his hat back on, then grinned. "Yeah, you can open up a few of the guest rooms you have inside your house for my deputies and me. We'll need a place to set up a base while we're here."

Aubrey bit her lower lip, battling to keep her shock from showing.

Sara looked out over the parking lot. "I'll make the arrangements."

She turned on her heels, headed back up to her porch, and then stormed inside the open doors of her home.

"Holy crap," Aubrey muttered. "I didn't think I would live to see anyone speak to her like that."

Mason tipped his hat. "That's why I'm the sheriff, darlin'. Whatever I say goes."

A stiff, cold breeze greeted Aubrey when she stepped from the dorm entrance. She lowered her head and pushed through the wind as she carried her insulated coffee mug and briefcase, not sure if she should even bother with her first period class. Bella, Jenna, and Cal would be too devastated to attend, but she wanted to be there for them, in case they needed her. She hoped they would come because they were the only ones who would understand the whirlwind of guilt, sorrow, anger, and anguish, keeping her up at night.

A few students gathered on benches or huddled close to the buildings to stay out of the brutal wind. They followed her with their gazes, some putting their heads together as if sharing a secret. The behavior added to her paranoia. Since hearing of Hartley's death, she had viewed everyone on campus as a suspect, compounding her sleeplessness.

True to his word, Mason had men stationed all over the campus. Two patrolled The Quad, their guns holstered to their sides. Officer Laura stayed in the dorm lobby. Another remained stationed at the plantation home, monitoring the new security cameras set up at the entrance to each building on campus.

Aubrey approved of the added security but would never feel safe knowing the killer was still at large. She questioned if she ever would again.

At the door to her classroom building, she glanced up at the bullet camera positioned above the entrance—a cold reminder of the danger they were all in.

The halls of the liberal arts building were less crowded than usual.

She approached the white stairs, remembering when Marjorie disappeared and how parents pulled their daughters from the school. With two murders and a possible third on the grounds, it was only a matter of time before parents demanded the school shut down.

She hoped it didn't come to that. Aubrey wanted to find the killer.

The last few days had reawakened old wounds. It seemed the past wasn't behind her, and until the chaos shrouding the school ended, the torment and frustration she'd experienced there would also haunt her students. Aubrey didn't want that for them. She would fight to make sure they avoided the road she had traveled.

Finally rounding the third-floor landing, she balanced her coffee and briefcase and made her way to her classroom.

She walked in the door and stopped when she found the fluorescent lights already on, and a man in blue jeans and a Stetson staring up at her map in the back of the room.

"Mason?"

The sheriff turned to her, holding two cups of coffee.

"I figured you could use this." He then motioned to her insulated mug. "Or maybe not."

"That is very kind." She took the coffee from him. "Thank you. I can use as much caffeine as I can get right now."

He tilted his head, appraising her. "Not sleeping?"

She removed the plastic top and inhaled the bitter aroma of coffee and chicory.

Damn, that's better than mine.

She sipped the coffee and nodded. "How did you know?"

He sat on the table. "There are three times you don't sleep in law enforcement—your first dead body, your first murder investigation, and the first time you shoot a suspect."

The reality of his world swept over her like the icy wind outside.

"And how many of those have you experienced?"

He lifted his coffee to his lips. "All three."

She took a deep breath and had a seat next to him on the table, letting it all sink in.

"I guess I still see you as a small-town sheriff, not some big-city detective."

"A law enforcement officer is a law enforcement officer. It's not where we are that matters, it's how we act you need to worry about."

"And how are you sleeping at night?"

"A lot like you. I won't rest until I catch this guy." He stood and examined her map. "But I have to tell you this is impressive. Makes me jealous I don't have a layout as detailed as this."

Aubrey glanced up at the satellite image of the grounds. "You're welcome to it if it will help."

He pointed to a spot on the far right. "What's there? It never showed up on my maps."

"The graveyard of the family who built Elaine House—The Newberrys. We never went there. There was no evidence to check."

He motioned to the red stickpins. "And these are the sites where evidence was found?"

She stood next to him. "From the cases in the nineties as well as the Marjorie case."

"But not Lindsey Gillett, London Dumont, or Hartley Gregory?"

She set her coffee aside. "I couldn't put anything up. I'm afraid it would make things worse for my students."

He kept his gaze on the map. "You said your students went out there. You found the blood on the monument, but it's not on here."

"I told you, we thought it was animal's blood."

He turned to her, the lines around his mouth deepening. "I got a call this morning. It was Lindsey's blood. DNA was confirmed."

Aubrey covered her mouth. She quickly suppressed her emotions, attempting to appear as if she had it together.

"Then she's dead?"

"I can't say for sure until we have a body." He returned his attention to the map. "My men searched the entire area around the battlefield and the mill." He pointed to the top of the satellite photo. "It was the mill where we ran into problems. It's rickety. The site is filled with debris and dangerous as hell. Surprised it hasn't burned to the ground yet. One match and the place would go up like a tinderbox."

"I kept my students out of there." Aubrey gazed at the map, an idea percolating. "But if someone wanted to hide, make sure no one would find them, wouldn't you go to the most derelict place on this campus and lay low?"

"You have a valid point. Might be time to check out that mill again."

"I wish I could tell you more about when we were there, but the kids kept interrogating me, making it hard to concentrate."

"Interrogating you? Why?"

She folded her arms, blushing. "Since I was here when Marjorie Reynolds vanished, my students thought I could be connected to Lindsey's disappearance. Especially since I showed up soon after she went missing. I can't blame them."

The lines in his brow cut deeper, and then he dropped his hat on the table. "And how did they know you were a suspect in Marjorie's case? I read those interviews. They're in a database ..." He paused and shook his head. "Let me guess. The Gregory boy?"

She stared at him.

He picked up his coffee. "Even if your coming to teach here is coincidental, it doesn't explain why your students suspected you." He pushed his hat aside and sat back down on the table. "Start at the beginning. I want to hear all of this."

She leaned against the table and gripped the edges.

"Well, when I first arrived, they were testing me. They asked a lot of questions about Marjorie's case, how we got along during high school, and convinced me to look into the disappearances. I was trying to get to know them and decided to go along. It wasn't until later, when I wasn't a suspect in London's death, they told me the truth about why they did it."

He waited, watching her with his intense green eyes. "And why did they?"

"Lindsey confided she knew who the killer was. Someone connected to the school. They said she disappeared before finding out who."

Mason rubbed his grizzled chin. "Which may explain why she's missing. The killer knew she figured it out."

"From what I gather, she became close to this group of students. She seemed to take them in like lost puppies and give them a purpose or something. I don't know. They're devoted to her, and the way they speak about her … she seemed like a remarkable young woman." Her grip tightened on the table. "When they find out she's dead, it will devastate them."

"If the killer doesn't take them out first. Your students are being killed off one by one because of what they know."

"But they don't know anything," she argued.

"The killer doesn't know that." He reached for his hat. "I need to interview them."

Subjecting her students to such scrutiny might cause permanent damage—not to mention the furor their parents would create for the school.

"You have to give them time, Mason. Their friends are dead."

Mason stared her down. "You admitted that the killer is someone associated with the school. I need to hear what those kids know. It could point me in a different direction."

A thought struck her. "Or maybe the killer is someone who has access to the school."

Mason's scowl took away the dimple in his chin. "What are you talking about?"

Aubrey rubbed her brow. "Samuel, the head groundskeeper, told me about the Chitimacha Indians coming on the property to perform rituals. I never thought much about it, but with Hartley's murder …"

"You should have told me this before now, Aubrey," Mason told her in a curt tone.

She stood her ground, refusing to be intimidated. "Would it have made any difference?"

"Yes!" He wiped his face. "I could have spoken to the Chitimacha chief here and asked about these rituals for starters. These are the kinds of things that are important to any investigation. You must share everything with me."

The bang of the classroom door carried across the room.

"Everything okay?" Bella asked as she came into the room.

Jenna and Cal waited behind her. The apprehensive way Cal hugged his bag made Aubrey forget about her disagreement with Mason.

Aubrey walked to the front of the class to reassure her students. "Sheriff Dubois and I were discussing our map."

Jenna looked past her to the sheriff. "Sounds more like you were fighting."

The red lingering in Jenna's eyes disturbed Aubrey. The last thing her students needed was more grief. They had suffered a lifetime's worth already.

The sound of Mason's boots rose behind her. Aubrey braced for what he would say, wishing she could have time to prepare her students.

"Ms. LaRoux was just telling me about how you interrogated her when she first arrived at Waverly. She mentioned something about you guys suspecting her of Lindsey Gillett's disappearance."

Bella directed her gaze at Aubrey. "Yes, we suspected her, but when London died, we knew she was innocent."

Mason appeared over Aubrey's shoulder, still carrying his coffee. "You told Ms. LaRoux that Lindsey knew who the killer was. What exactly did she tell you? I need to hear it word for word."

Aubrey felt lower than dirt. Her students would consider what she shared with Mason a betrayal of trust. Whatever progress she had made with them would be wiped out by his blatant disregard for their feelings.

She wanted to turn around and punch him but didn't. Aubrey

stood, taking in the hurt, darting gazes of her students—their distress etched into their smashed lips and clenched fists.

"She said it was someone we knew. Someone we trusted." Bella set her book bag down on a desk. "We never got anything else. Lindsey had been digging into her sister's disappearance for years, and it wasn't until she came to Waverly that she discovered the truth."

Mason scanned their faces. "Which was?"

"She's dead," Jenna abruptly said. "Marjorie didn't run away. Lindsey believed someone took her, and she was killed somewhere on the school grounds."

Aubrey's chest caved as if hit by a blow. "Why didn't you tell me this before?"

Jenna gave a contemptuous toss of her head. "What difference does it make? Whoever did this is after us now. We're getting picked off one by one."

Cal gasped and gripped his bag tighter. "Jenna!"

Mason stepped forward. "I won't let anyone hurt you. I promise."

Jenna's loud snort added to the growing tension in the classroom. "Don't make promises you can't keep, Sheriff. We both know this killer won't rest until all of us are dead."

CHAPTER 20

The rays of light coming through the classroom windows landed on Aubrey's hands as she fidgeted her fingers, displaying her tension.

She sat across her desk from Jenna, Cal, and Bella, searching their downturned faces for some spark of hope, but the oppressive atmosphere in the room only added to her concern.

"I know what happened to Hartley leaves us all deeply sad and not knowing how to express our grief, but—"

"Oh, please." Jenna's irritation saturated the room. "Whoever decapitated Hartley is coming for us. How are we supposed to feel about being hunted?"

Bella slumped as she sat on the corner of Aubrey's desk. "We're not going to get anywhere with you chewing everyone's head off." She paused and grimaced. "Sorry."

Cal remained on his spot of the corner of the desk, keeping his arms folded.

"Why are you getting so bent out of shape, anyway? You hated Hartley."

Jenna stiffened. "I never hated him, but if I had walked back to The Quad with him, stayed with him, and not sent him off angry ..." Tears gathered in her eyes.

Aubrey went around the desk to her side.

"This isn't your fault. What happened to Hartley had nothing to do with what you did or said." She put her hands on her shoulders. "Whoever did this is the asshole here."

Jenna's tears dried, and a slight grin crossed her lips. "Did you just say asshole?"

Aubrey let her go, glad to see her smile. "Yes, I did. And I meant it. I would love to get my hands around the neck of the asshole who's doing this."

Jenna wiped her face with the sleeve of her gray shirt. "Yeah, me too."

Bella put her arm around Jenna. "See, you have friends. You always go on and on about how nobody cares about you." Bella gestured to Aubrey. "But we care, so stop being such a bitch to everyone."

Jenna sniffled and snickered at the same time. "Can't help it. And it will probably get worse now. I get extremely bitchy when I can't ride. They've banned students from the stables."

"That sucks," Bella said. "What will you do with all your spare time?"

Bella's intervention seemed to appease Jenna, and for that, Aubrey was grateful. She might not have known the kids for long, but she had grown extremely fond of them.

Cal turned toward the map of the school grounds. "I think we should return to the mill. The sheriff admitted his men hadn't thoroughly searched there. Maybe we can get more answers about who is doing this."

Aubrey approached him, her lips smashed together. "How do you know Sheriff Dubois said that?"

Crimson tinged his cheeks. "We were all listening at the door while you two were in here."

Aubrey rolled her eyes. "Cal, that's not appropriate."

"To hell with appropriate," Jenna said. "It's the only way any of us learn jack these days."

Aubrey glanced over her shoulder, eager to scold them, but understanding their position.

"So can we?" Cal asked.

Aubrey faced him, examining his hopeful eyes. "What?"

"Go to the mill."

She balked at the suggestion. Traipsing through areas where students died would be emotionally challenging for everyone. It also wasn't the smartest thing to do in the middle of a murder investigation.

"I don't think Sheriff Dubois wants any of us leaving the safe areas of the school. He's trying to protect us."

"Invite him to go along," Bella suggested. "He likes you. I bet he'd jump at the chance to spend time with you."

Aubrey put her hands on her hips. "Where did you get that idea?"

Jenna came forward, strutting like her old rebellious self. "You two are so obvious. You were all over each other when you were alone in here. Surprised you didn't have sex on the back table."

Aubrey's cheeks burned. "That remark was uncalled for."

Cal walked to the back of the classroom. "Jenna, you have all the subtlety of an eighteen-wheeler."

"Yeah, nice one," Bella added.

Aubrey put her hands to her cheeks, praying the redness had faded. "Whatever you think is going on between the sheriff and myself, I can assure you—"

"What's this?" Cal called from the back of the room.

Aubrey wheeled around to find Cal pointing to something at the very top of the investigation map. Intrigued, she headed to the back of the room, fixated on the spot next to the river.

Once she got close enough, she squinted at the map. "What am I looking at?"

Jenna and Bella joined them at the back of the room.

"There." Cal kept pointing. "Next to the mill. By the river. There's something there. Something we never saw when we were there. It looks like a structure. A shed perhaps."

A funny tingle rose in Aubrey's chest. She concentrated on the map, and then a white speck, a small outbuilding took shape. It remained hidden behind the mill ruins and piles of debris. From above, it was easy to make out.

"Why didn't I notice that before?"

Cal climbed on the table and put his nose to the top portion of the map. "I knew we had missed something there."

She waited as he examined the spot. Jenna and Bella stood next to her, craning their necks to get a better view.

"We were here." Cal pointed to the front entrance of the mill. "But this is on the back, along the river. Unless you went looking for this building, you would never have seen it from the front of the ruins."

"A great place for someone to hide," Bella suggested.

Jenna nodded. "Or put a body."

Cal glanced down at her. "Does the sheriff know about this?"

In a determined stride, Aubrey headed for her desk. She rummaged her phone from her briefcase. "He'll know about it now."

Aubrey's hair whipped around her face, making it difficult to see the paved walkway ahead. She wished she'd brought more than her sweater to stave off the cold as they trekked to the mill. The dull, dark sky appeared foreboding, and she prayed they would avoid getting drenched. Wet wasn't a good look for her, especially since she had already added a coat of mascara and a touch of lipstick before heading out to meet Mason.

"Thank you for letting us tag along," she said as they traversed the manicured green grass, heading to the line of trees. "I know it's not procedure, but I feared if you turned them down, my students might come on their own."

Mason walked next to her, letting his two officers take point. "When a student spots something we have missed, it seems only fair. But if we find anything, you and the kids are to return to the school at once. Understood?"

She liked the way his voice got deeper when he took charge. "Yes, sir."

He rocked his hat back on his head as they walked. "You're going to be a handful, I can tell."

She shot him a sly smile. "Would you want me any other way?"

"I'm sorry I was an ass before," he whispered to her.

Aubrey nervously tucked a curl of hair behind her ear. "Just don't do it again."

Jenna leaned in closer to them. "You two should get a room."

"Jenna!" Aubrey wanted to fall into a hole and die. "You shouldn't say such things."

Mason chuckled. "You know she's right."

He walked ahead, leaving a stunned Aubrey to deal with her students.

"I like him," Bella said, watching the sheriff speak with his deputies. "He's good for you."

"Yeah, but would you want to date a cop?" Cal asked. "Think of all the late nights worrying about him."

Jenna nudged Aubrey's elbow. "Think of all the speeding tickets you could get out of."

Cal frowned at her. "Only you would think that way."

Bella kept her eye on the three men ahead of them. "Lindsey would have said the same thing. Remember how she was always figuring out ways to get out of stuff."

Jenna laughed. "Like the time The Prober tried to keep her in detention for a week."

Aubrey enjoyed their banter. "Who's The Prober?"

"Probst," Cal explained. "We've got tons of names for her. Everyone on campus hates her. Lindsey more than anyone. She was always coming up with new names for Ms. Probst."

An inkling of curiosity came alive in her. "She ever tell you guys why she hated Probst so much?"

Jenna pulled her jacket closer. "Lindsey worked for the old bag in her office. You know filing papers and stuff. When Lindsey first came here, she was a real ass-kisser to Probst. Everyone teased her about it, then one day, she quit. That's when we all befriended her, or she befriended us."

Cal pulled his phone from his pocket. "Probst had it out for Lindsey after that. She put Lindsey in detention all the time." He held up his phone to Aubrey. "Here's a pic I got when she was playing around during one of her detentions. Cool, huh?"

Aubrey examined the photo of a brunette with a vibrant smile, hanging out a third-story window and waving wildly. Her effervescent personality leaped from the picture.

She smiled, hiding the sting of Lindsey's death from her students.

"She seems like quite a character."

Cal grinned as he pocketed the phone. "Lindsey was the best."

"Remember that time she set off the fire alarm in the dorm?" Jenna asked.

Bella chuckled. "It was the night before our big achievement exams for the state, and she kept everyone up all night pulling the fire alarm. Probst was ballistic."

Aubrey glanced ahead, checking out the line of trees. "What did Ms. Probst do to her?"

"Nothing," Jenna told her. "No one ratted Lindsey out. Everyone liked her too much. Probst spent weeks trying to figure out who it was, but no one rolled over. They enjoyed seeing The Prober having her meltdowns in assembly. The woman would rant for hours about finding the culprit. The more she spoke, the more everyone became determined to protect Lindsey."

A ripple of anger moved through Aubrey. Her students deserved better.

"Ms. Probst was the same way when I attended Waverly. I was hoping things had changed."

Jenna's bold laughter reverberated through the nearby trees. "The only way things will change is if someone takes her place."

Cal pointed at Aubrey. "You should apply for her job. Think how much better Waverly would be with you in charge."

Aubrey shook her head. "The board determines who lives in Elaine House at Waverly, and they will never choose me."

Bella hooked her arm. "You never know until you try, Ms. LaRoux."

The shadows of the trees covered them as they stepped under the green canopy.

Mason returned to Aubrey's side. "Everyone stick together. No wandering off."

The woods felt more ominous than that first time she combed through them with Mason—the day they had found London. The image of the dead girl was still fresh in her mind, heightening her apprehension.

Her students fell silent as they stepped over pine needles and downed branches. Aubrey prayed to avoid the trapping pit; she didn't want her students to see where their friend had died.

The trees thinned, and the gray skies reappeared, but as the grass got taller, and the expanse of the battlefield came into view, her dread escalated. Aubrey would do everything to avoid the monument where Hartley and Lindsey had lost their lives.

"We'll stay on the western portion of the field," Mason said loud enough for her students to hear. "It's a shorter route to the mill."

No one argued, not even Cal. Aubrey figured they already knew where Hartley had died and had little interest in seeing the monument again.

A few specks of rain lighted on her cheek, but the deluge stayed away. Aubrey was thankful for that, but when the rafters of the old mill appeared over a cluster of trees, she dreaded what may lie ahead.

She studied the structure, or what was left of it, as their party got closer. The remote location and the loud churning of the river as it broached the bend right by the mill would allow anyone to hide without fear of being found. But what type of person would take the lives of teenagers on the cusp of adulthood? What secret had Lindsey discovered that was worth killing for?

Aubrey stuck close to Mason as they passed through the trees. When the area opened, the remains of the brick mill rose in front of them. Mason paused and eyed the impressive single smokestack.

"I don't understand why the school has left this here. Huge liability if you ask me."

"But historically significant," Cal told him. "There are only a handful of these old sugar mills left in the country. If it were up to me, I'd restore the place and use it as a museum."

Mason peered down at Cal. "What else would you do?"

Cal stared at the wall where a shadow of the press's steam wheel appeared in the gaps. "I'd save as much of the past as I could. The battlefield, the dock, all of it."

Mason unclipped the strap securing his gun to his belt. "We'd better make sure no one is here."

Cal inspected the holstered gun. "Impressive 9mm Glock."

Mason gave him a second look. "You know guns?"

Cal raised his gaze to the smokestack. "Read about them on the internet."

Mason smiled at Aubrey. "You four stay behind me."

Bella tapped his sleeve. "You can't get to the back wall from this side. You have to go back along the dock next to the river. There's too much debris in the front."

Mason slipped his gun in his holster. "How do you know that?"

Bella lowered her gaze. "Hartley told me last time we were here. We wanted to come back and check out the other side, but …"

"We planned on coming here and searching for Lindsey," Cal admitted.

Mason approached the piles of fallen bricks outside the main building. Tall weeds obliterated the foundation while creeping ivy vines covered most of what remained of the wall.

"That might have been dangerous for all of you."

Cal passed one of the iron sugar melting kettle pots. "She's worth it. We would do anything for her."

Mason gave Aubrey a sad smile.

Aubrey stayed behind her students as Mason led them through the maze of discarded equipment, debris piles, and upended sugar kettles. Old wooden hammers, broken glass, and an assortment of metal littered the ground or poked up out of thick patches of shrubs and weeds. The air was stale as if the old age of the building permeated the land.

She passed a few of the holes where windows had been, or broken gaps in the wall and peeked inside to get a better look at the huge press. Old wooden beams from the arched roof that had covered the press lay broken on the deteriorating stone floor. Birds had made nests in patches along the inside portions of the wall. Straw, twigs, and even pieces of trash cluttered the intact parts of the roof and eaves.

I can't believe this is still here.

Mason stopped at the edge of the derelict building. He glanced back at Jenna, and she pointed at the ruins toward the river.

Mason waved his deputies ahead.

The two officers skirted the shadows outside the ruins and then disappeared behind a wall of ivy.

Aubrey followed as Mason slowly walked where his men had gone. The crunch of broken glass and brick chunks beneath her tennis shoes elicited a grimace. They weren't going to be able to keep quiet in a place with so much trash covering the ground.

Mason reached the thick clump of ivy hanging from the corner of the building. He raised his gun and carefully checked around the corner, reminding her of their dangerous situation.

If The Prober ever finds out, I'll get an earful.

When they broached the corner, the essence of the sweet freshwater from the river chased away the mustiness. The breeze picked up, and Aubrey got a good look at the eddies surging through the bend.

The mill butted against the river's edge and large rocks had been placed along the shore to keep the strong currents from eroding the land. Piers left over from when the dock used to transport sugar jutted from the water. White herons and a single pelican rested on the perches, eyeing the humans as they snuck around the back of the building.

"Sheriff?" A man's husky voice sent the heron flying from its roost. "We've got something."

Mason hurried around to the back, leaving Aubrey and her students peering into the swift river.

Cal broke away. She just missed snagging the back of his shirt.

"Dammit, Cal."

She went after him. Jenna and Bella stayed right with her.

The other side of the ruined building was almost impassable. The entire wall had given way on this side, and the small patch between the ruins and the dense forest next to it remained impassible due to the fallen bricks and timbers.

Mason and his men stood to the side of the rubble, inspecting a white shed built partly into the brush, their guns at the ready.

Made of old wood that appeared reused from another structure, the construction was crude with gaps between the planks, allowing light inside. The roof was a gray tarp, and the rickety building stood a few feet off the ground. Bricks from the mill provided the base while a shiny padlock secured the flimsy door.

Mason motioned to her. "Get them back."

Aubrey pulled her students closer while Mason and one of his deputies put their shoulders into the door.

The wood gave way along with part of the frame.

The afternoon light shone inside the shed, which did not appear very deep. Aubrey struggled to get a good look at the contents and glimpsed something shiny for a moment.

Mason holstered his gun and donned a pair of plastic gloves given to him by a deputy. He leaned into the shed, and the top part of his torso became drenched in darkness.

When he stepped out, he had a sickle in his hand.

A cold swath of horror rushed through Aubrey.

Mason glanced back at her, then handed the tool to one of his men. He walked over, herding her students around the side of the old mill.

"It's time to get you guys out of here."

"What? What's in there?" Jenna asked with her usual snark.

The shove Mason gave Aubrey felt more fearful than forceful. His lips disappeared into a thin line—something was wrong.

"We have to get back," she said to her students. "We've been gone long enough."

Mason led the way, guiding her and the students through the debris field surrounding the mill. His long stride worried her more than the way his jaw muscles clenched as he moved.

They were almost to the trees when she came alongside him, eager to find out what had troubled him.

Aubrey made sure Bella, Cal, and Jenna were out of earshot when she asked, "What did you find?"

He turned his narrowed gaze to her. "Tools. Most were new, and one fit the description of the murder weapon used against Hartley Gregory."

Aubrey almost stumbled. "Are you sure?"

Mason focused on the trees ahead. "We will be as soon as we get everything to the lab."

Aubrey wiped the few sprinkles of rain that had gathered on her brow. "And if it is the murder weapon?"

Mason removed his Glock from his holster and checked the safety. "Then we're one step closer to finding our killer."

The outline of the square school buildings shone against the gray sky as Aubrey, Mason, and her students emerged from the woods at the edge of the manicured grounds. The rain held off, but the atmosphere appeared more threatening than before they set out for the mill.

A clap of thunder rolled through the black skies. Aubrey picked up her pace, hoping to get her students back to The Quad before the heavens opened.

"Can we check on my horse at the stables?"

Jenna's request rustled a stir of annoyance in Aubrey. "Of course not. The stables are off-limits."

"But I haven't seen him since yesterday." She veered away from the group. "It will take two minutes."

Aubrey hooked her arm. "It's about to rain, and we need to head back. We've been gone too long, already."

Jenna shirked off her grip. "What difference will another few minutes make? I want to see my horse."

Her whiney voice wasn't like Jenna. Perhaps the stress of the last few days had finally weakened the walls the young woman used to keep everyone out.

Bella tapped Aubrey's elbow. "Jenna misses her daily ride. It's all she talks about. I don't mind if we take a detour."

Aubrey looked at the sky. "No. We need to get back."

Mason held up his hand. "I'll take her to the stables and then meet you at the classroom." He motioned ahead. "Get the others out of here before you get drenched."

The offer was unexpected but struck Aubrey as unusually kind. In the middle of a murder investigation, and after discovering damning evidence, the man was willing to take a few moments to let a frightened young woman visit her horse.

She wanted to be mad at Jenna and him but couldn't find the strength. "Don't take too long."

Mason jogged to Jenna. "Let's go."

Aubrey headed toward The Quad but kept her sights on Jenna and Mason as they headed to the walkway that led to the stables.

"He's a nice guy," Bella said next to her. "Are you going to date him?"

Aubrey noted her crafty smile. "I think he has other things on his mind right now."

Cal lolled his head to the side and grinned. "The only thing he has on his mind is you. You can tell the way he looks at you."

Another round of thunder roared through the sky. Aubrey broke into a brisk walk.

"Forget about the sheriff and me. Let's get inside."

"You're avoiding my question," Bella pointed out.

Whatever fate had in store for her and Mason, Aubrey didn't need her prying students making her more uncomfortable than she already was with him.

Small drops of rain landed on her sweater, and she picked up her pace. "Hurry up, guys, before we get caught in the storm."

CHAPTER 21

Jenna ran beneath the shelter of the metal roof, glad she'd avoided the worst of the rain. The smell of horses, manure, and sawdust filled her nose, and she drank in the aroma. One day without her horse was torture; two was agony. She was grateful to the handsome sheriff for her reprieve. All she needed was a few minutes with her beloved gelding Manni, and she could head back to class.

Mason ducked under the roofline behind her, a few raindrops dotting the shoulders of his tan shirt. "You want to tell me why you had to come here?"

Jenna waved down the shed row to the horses popping their heads out to see who had come to visit the empty stables. "My life is here. I hope to get a scholarship to ride in college. My riding teacher thinks I can."

Mason covered his nose. "Sounds great."

She laughed at his smooshed face. "Give it a few minutes. You will acclimate to the smell."

He checked the sky. "We don't have a few minutes. See to your horse, and then we need to head back."

Jenna didn't let his deep, threatening voice bother her. She'd seen how gentle and attentive he was with Ms. LaRoux, and knew he had a softer side behind the professional law enforcement exterior he exuded.

"You like Ms. LaRoux, don't you?"

A hint of aggravation darkened the green in his eyes. "Ms. LaRoux is your teacher and someone I'm trying to protect during this investigation." He pointed at her. "I'm also trying to protect you."

Jenna didn't buy his tough-guy bravado. She headed down the aisle.

"Every time you look at her, it's like you're seeing a favorite movie or a beautiful picture."

Mason scowled at her. "You're exaggerating."

"No, I'm not." She glanced back at him. "You're doing it now."

Mason wiped his face. "Where's your horse?"

Jenna nodded to the crossway that led to the other side of the stables. "Just around the corner."

A tinkle, sounding like fingers drumming the tin roof, filled the stables. Thunder shook the stall doors, and a few of the horses nervously pawed the sawdust-covered floor.

"Whatever your intentions with Ms. LaRoux, tread softly. She's a nice person and deserves a man who sees all of her, not just the pretty outside."

Mason sucked in a breath, expanding his sizable chest as he approached her. "I appreciate the advice. Now hurry up and check on your horse."

Jenna was about to turn away when the crackle of the sheriff's walkie spooked a few of the horses.

"Sheriff? You there?"

The animals shied back inside their stalls as Mason reached for the radio on his belt. "Dubois, here. Go ahead."

A voice came over the speaker. "This is Jones. We have a suspect for questioning. He's at Elaine House."

Mason lowered the walkie from his mouth. "Damn."

Jenna waved to the walkie. "Don't worry about me. I can get back on my own."

Mason shook his head. "Not going to happen. I'm not leaving."

"Sheriff, are you on your way?" squawked from the speaker.

"You don't need to stay," Jenna said. "I will only take five minutes. Promise."

Mason glared at her and clenched his jaw, not looking as if he believed a word. He pressed the button on his walkie. "Jones, send one of our people to the stables right away. I want someone with Jenna Marchand before I leave."

"Roger that, Sheriff."

He clipped the walkie to his side. "My officer will be here in five minutes." Mason pointed at her and twisted his lips in a menacing way. "If you ditch my guy, I will arrest you."

Jenna met his threatening frown with an impudent grin. "Yes, Sheriff."

He furrowed his brow, appearing as if he wanted to add more, but then directed his attention to the sky. "And you're right, Jenna. I do like Ms. LaRoux, but let's keep that between us."

Jenna was glad he'd admitted his feelings for Ms. LaRoux. She would like something good to come out of the horror.

Irritated she would not be left alone to visit with Manni, Jenna headed toward the horse's stall on the other side of the barn. She listened to the comforting tap of the increasing rain and shut out the thunk of the sheriff's boots on the sawdust-covered walkway. Her mood lifted, glad she could stay in her favorite place, surrounded by the horses she loved, and forget about the crumbling world outside.

Aubrey paced in front of the window that overlooked the path to the stables. The knots in her stomach twisted tighter as the rain beat down. There was no sign of Jenna returning with Mason. Her mind immediately went to the worst-case scenario, even though she knew the young woman was safer with the sheriff than anyone. But still, the bitter taste in her mouth only intensified with every passing minute.

"Maybe they decided to wait for the rain to stop," Bella suggested.

Aubrey wanted to agree with her, but until Jenna was back safely, she would worry.

"Sheriff Dubois isn't going to let a little rain slow him down." She stepped from the window, attempting to appear calm. "I don't want Jenna to take up too much of his time. It was kind of him to take you guys to the mill."

Cal stood from his desk and went to the window. "What did they find in that shed? I know he told you."

Aubrey's mouth went dry as she struggled to come up with a lie.

Then Cal pointed out the window. "There's the sheriff, running in the rain."

Aubrey quickly joined him and followed his gaze.

Mason's figure cutting across the grassy field behind the building stood out in the gloomy afternoon light.

Her stomach cinched tighter when Aubrey discovered Jenna wasn't with him.

"Stay here." She walked to the door. "I'll be back."

Aubrey headed toward the stairs, her heart galloping. Her rational mind told her everything was okay. Mason wouldn't have left Jenna alone if he felt she was in danger.

She ran down the staircase, thankful there were no students to block her way.

Once outside, Aubrey inspected the rain but didn't care what it did to her hair. She followed the path that led to Elaine House, where the police had set up their headquarters.

The rain came down harder as she approached the back of the grand home. Her hair flattened against her face, and her damp clothes clung to her, but Aubrey pushed on.

She followed the path to the front of the home, and as she was about to climb the porch steps, she spotted Mason, jogging through the downpour.

"Where's Jenna?" she shouted over the rain.

He wrapped his arm around her waist and took her up the steps, two at a time.

They stopped beneath the shelter of the wide porch. The wind picked up, bringing the white rocking chairs to life.

Mason examined her wet clothes. "What are you doing out in this?"

Aubrey pushed her wet hair from her face. "Where's Jenna?"

"She's fine. I had one of my deputies stay with her at the stables. I had to get back here."

Aubrey was about to ask why when an officer with bulging biceps and short-cropped dark hair came through the oak doors to the home and scrambled to Mason's side.

"Sheriff, we were about to load him into a car to take to the station."

Mason stepped back from Aubrey. "I'll ride with you."

Aubrey opened her mouth to ask what was happening when a shadow crossed the house's open door.

Samuel stood with the female deputy, Laura, without handcuffs. The tightness in his jaw and shoulders conveyed a man overcome with anxiety.

"Mr. Samuel?"

Aubrey lunged, about to go to Samuel, but Mason put his arm in front of her.

"No, Aubrey. We are taking him to the station."

She pushed him away. "Why? He hasn't done anything."

Mason escorted her to the side of the porch as the officers guided Samuel onto the porch.

"After Hartley died, I discovered he was the only person with a key to where the ATVs are stored. After hearing he has information about the Chitimacha tribe coming onto the property, and uncovering what was hidden in that shed, I have enough to take him to the station for questioning."

She gripped Mason's arm, a lump forming in her throat. "Is that necessary? I've known the man since I went to school here. He's loved by the kids and wouldn't hurt anyone."

Mason put his hand over hers. "I can't rule out any suspect because of how your—"

"He's right to bring me in." Samuel stood at the edge of the porch, staring at Aubrey with wide, horror-filled eyes. "But the killer is still here, and every one of your students is in danger. You have to protect them."

Mason left her side and walked up to his suspect. "Mr. Collins, please. We'll talk at the station."

He motioned for his deputy to see Samuel to the white cruiser waiting by the curb in the parking lot.

Aubrey watched as Samuel jogged across the parking lot to the waiting patrol car, avoiding puddles along the way.

She turned and studied the sheriff's profile, attempting to read his thoughts.

"You don't believe he did it, do you?"

Mason slapped his gun belt. "I think he knows who did. People are already whispering about him being involved in the killings—that's why I'm taking him in for questioning. I have to shut down the gossip. Maybe he will open up away from the place."

Aubrey's hands trembled as she remembered Samuel's warning about the killer. "Are you sure Jenna is all right? Perhaps we should head to the stables and get her."

Mason placed his hands over hers. "She's with one of my guys, probably making her way back here as we speak."

Aubrey spotted the walkie clipped to his belt. "Can you check for me? I need to hear she is okay."

A shadow darkened Mason's gaze. "What is it? This isn't like you."

She pulled her hands away from his. "You don't know me or what I'm like when I'm worried about one of my students. Now call and check on Jenna, please."

Mason sighed as he unclipped his walkie.

He pressed the red *send* button on the device. "Baxter, this is Sheriff Dubois. What is your ETA with Jenna Marchand? Come back."

Mason released the button, and static filled the speaker.

Aubrey wanted to yank the walkie from his hand but refrained.

"Baxter, come back," Mason repeated with more urgency.

Again, nothing but static crackled through the air.

"These damned things are always going out in bad weather." He secured the walkie to his belt. "I'm sure she's fine."

Aubrey's trembling grew more intense, and her teeth chattered as she spoke. "What if she's not?"

Mason held up his hand, urging calm. "Officer Baxter probably brought her back to your classroom by now."

"I have to know for sure. We have to find her," Aubrey muttered. "She could be at the mercy of this killer."

Mason gripped her arms. "You have to trust me. Jenna's with one of my deputies. She's safe."

Bolstered by his presence, Aubrey took a breath and her anxiety receded.

"Go back and check your classroom," he ordered. "If Jenna's not there, she may have gone to her dorm to change."

Aubrey nodded. "And if she's not at either place?"

Mason didn't let her go, and she was grateful. Having him in her life the past few days had kept her together. He had become more than the flirty sheriff; he'd turned into a friend.

When he released his grip and stepped away, a cold draft enveloped her.

Mason adjusted his hat. "Right now, I have to go with Mr. Collins, but I will send a car to the stables if that will make you feel better."

His reassurance bolstered her. "It will. Thank you."

He was about to step back out into the rain, and a stab of dread went through Aubrey's chest.

"Be careful."

Mason flashed her a radiant smile. "Not to worry, darlin'. I'll be back."

He descended the steps while rain pelted his hat, and puddles of water splashed his black cowboy boots.

Aubrey's gaze stayed on him as he raced across the sidewalk and around to the passenger side of the patrol car. She wanted to wait for the vehicle to pull away, but her concern for Jenna nudged her from her spot on the porch.

The rain pelted her face, and her water-logged tennis shoes squeaked on the cement as she ran back toward The Quad. Worry for her students, and her school, beleaguered her every step. But what terrified her most was wondering if she could return to the life she knew before setting foot on Waverly's campus.

I'm afraid this is your new normal.

A throbbing startled Jenna awake. She gasped, and a coppery taste filled her mouth. Flickering images of the officer falling to the ground, and then running past horse stalls crowded her head. A sharp, burning jolt ran from her shoulder and down her back. The discomfort helped her focus, sweeping aside the fog muddying her thoughts. And when her eyes adjusted, she found everything drowning in darkness.

Panic twisted her insides. She could not see where she was but knew she was pinned against a wall and sitting on a floor. A thin line of light shone beneath what she guessed was a door. Jenna concentrated on the brightness, breathing in and out to quell the bile rising in her throat.

A familiar scent engulfed her—earthy leather, fresh saddle soap, pungent horse sweat, and the slightest hint of manure. A tack room—it had to be. She was still in the stables.

Her frightening dream repeated, and the more she went through the snapshots, the more real the images became.

I was running. Someone was in the stables, and I was running from them.

Anxiety exploded in her chest. She struggled to get up, but her feet and hands would not cooperate. Something cut into her wrists and burned against her flesh.

She put her wrists to her face. Smooth, polyester rope rubbed against her cheek, stinking of rotted fish. She ran her fingers over her ankles, examining the same material.

Okay. Think. How do you get out of here?

She pressed her sore shoulder into the wall. Then she rocked back and bumped against the wood, hoping to alert someone outside.

Every time her shoulder met the wood, an electric shock went down her back, but it didn't stop her. Someone had to be out there. The sheriff had promised to send someone to get her. She had to try.

The door to the tack room flung open, and a high beam from a flashlight blinded her. Jenna instinctively put her hands to her face, but the binding on her wrists kept her from blocking out the glare.

"I've got you now."

The voice was cold, did not sound male or female, just flat and nondescript.

The panic Jenna had subdued returned, triggering a violent trembling in her muscles.

Jena lowered her hands and shouted into the light. "Who are you? What do you want?"

The flashlight went out. All Jenna could see was a fuzzy, incomplete shadow.

Rain, pouring on the tin roof, rose in the background. The damp smell wafted into the tack room, and she filled her lungs, hoping to clear her head.

Jenna hugged the wall, pushing her sore shoulder into the wood to help get to her feet.

She ignored the wrenching pain, and then the shadow filled the door.

Jenna was about to make her move and rush her attacker, using the wall as leverage when something flew into her face.

She slapped at the object and then felt it slip over her head and cinch around her neck.

No!

A rope pressed into her flesh. The dark figure in the doorway backed away, letting in the gray light. Then a hard tug sent her to the ground.

She gagged and struggled, wiggling as best she could to get enough slack to breathe.

Another hard yank dragged her out of the tack room.

Her eyes bulged as she fought with everything she could to get free.

The rope coiled tighter, burning her skin, and bringing tears to her eyes.

Jenna lay with her cheek in the sawdust covering the stable floor. The tension in the rope let up, and she sucked in a smidgen of air, hungrily gasping.

Then another yank tightened the noose around her neck.

A fire burned in Jenna's lungs, and black spots appeared before her eyes. She struggled to get free of her bindings, but the rope on her wrists and ankles held no matter how hard she fought.

Another moment of slack left her gagging as vomit rose in her throat, cutting off her chance to breathe.

She could barely make out anything around her. Her vision went in and out.

Then she heard a familiar sound—the long snort of a horse.

An object came into focus close to her face. A horse's hoof was inches away. She concentrated on raising her gaze to see the white sock and the dark bay color that rose from the ankle.

She knew that sock. She blinked a few times, attempting to see the rest of the horse.

Jenna knew every inch of the dark bay towering over her. It was her Manni.

She croaked, trying to call to her horse, but all that came out of her mouth was a pitiful croak.

A figure covered in a black robe appeared next to Manni's neck, seeming intent on her horse.

Jenna opened her mouth to scream, but her throat hurt too much to make a sound.

She struggled to sit up, anything to get off the ground, but she was dizzy and weak. Everything went sideways, but she kept raising her head. Shooting currents of pain traveled to her fingers, but Jenna worked through it. She had to know who was torturing her.

Jenna got her shoulder off the ground, and then she saw it. The thick rope serving as her noose had been looped around Manni's muscular neck and secured with a strong knot.

The black figure stepped back. "Consider this your last ride," her attacker said in a demonic hiss. "And your secret will die with you."

Jenna opened her mouth, forcing a squawk from her bruised throat.

The robed figure raised a hand into the air and slapped Manni's neck, spooking the horse. Manni's shoes clopped on the cement beneath the shavings under the stable's roof, and then he dashed into the rain, letting droplets dot his dark coat.

The sound of his galloping footfalls reverberated throughout the barn.

Jenna looked on in terror as the coiled rope connecting her to Manni quickly unwound. She squirmed against her restraints, frantic to get free, but as the last few feet of line pulled tight, she closed her eyes and braced for the agony to come.

The sudden powerful tug sent her flying into the air as a white-hot stabbing shot through her neck. Bones cracked, and her feet became instantly numb. The inferno in her chest spread across her body. She hit the mud and rocks outside the paddock area, and the skin along her cheek sliced open.

Jenna used the last dregs of consciousness to pray. Her body bounced hard on the ground, twisting and turning at odd angles as her horse dragged her. She was relieved there was no more suffering, and even the frenzy for air had lessened.

A calm took over her being as a tunnel of black slowly collapsed the lights of the stables.

At least I'll die with Manni.

Adrenaline poured through Aubrey, tensing her muscles as she waited for the dorm elevator to open. The car plodded, and every floor passed felt like a century to her. Worry caused a flurry of horrible images to awaken in her mind—all centered around Jenna.

The young woman had not been in the classroom when she returned. Aubrey had waited, shivering in her wet clothes as Cal and Bella repeatedly called the girl's phone. She did not wait to contact Mason, but rushed to the dorms, anxious to see if Jenna had returned to her room.

She attempted to soothe the terror snaking through her with rationalizations about being wet and cold, but in her heart, Aubrey knew something was wrong.

The elevator door opened on Jenna's floor. Aubrey darted out, flinching every time the fluorescent lights overhead flickered in time with a crack of thunder.

The quiet was a far cry from the constant hum of conversation, music, and ruckus from the young women. The empty dorm reminded her of a tomb.

Stop that.

Jenna's door, decorated with photos of a sleek bay horse with bulging neck muscles, cropped up on the right. Aubrey had not even come to a halt when she began banging on the door.

"Jenna, are you in there?"

She waited, listening to her rapid breathing.

Nothing.

Aubrey knocked harder with her closed fist.

"Jenna? Jenna, answer me!"

Aubrey didn't wait for a reply but pulled out the keychain, and Mason's business card she'd stuffed into her pocket before running out of her classroom.

She trembled as she shoved the master key into the lock. Reason told her the young woman wasn't inside. Jenna would have come to the door, smirked at her, or complained about her lack of privacy. The eerie silence wasn't like the uppity teen.

It took a moment of fighting with the key, but the door eventually gave way, and Aubrey bounded inside.

Photos, like those on the door, crammed the room with a collage of different shots of a horse running and grazing in a field taking center stage. Above was a paper banner, rendered by an artistic hand, with *Manni* spelled out in an array of dark and light blue colors.

Aubrey marveled at clothes strewn over the small desk and chair, while books sat next to a hot plate, and wet towels hung from pulls attached to a dresser built into the wall. The neatly made bed stood out from the chaos.

The pictures of the horse implored Aubrey to do something. Jenna had gone to the stables out of concern for her horse, and Aubrey feared that might have been a lethal mistake.

Aubrey wrestled her cell phone out of her back pocket, and then she retrieved Mason's card. Her hands shook as she dialed.

She stood in the room, cold and dreading their next move.

She waited for Mason to pick up, but instead, his phone rolled over to voicemail.

Aubrey didn't bother to leave a message. She needed help to find Jenna, and she needed it now.

Cal's fingers flew across the keys as a wave of numbers and letters scrolled across his laptop screen, leaving Bella in awe. She wasn't sure what she was looking at but became convinced the geek could do what he said. She didn't care about the ramifications of their illegal activity. Bella needed answers, and Cal's hacking talent was her only option.

"You do know that if they could trace Hartley, they can catch me," Cal said with a measure of apprehension. "I don't have the right equipment to do this from a school classroom."

"We have a killer up our ass, Jenna is MIA, and you're worried about getting caught? Dude, you need to get some perspective."

Cal frowned and went back to his computer. "Ms. LaRoux did seem pretty panicked when she ran out of here."

The screen changed, and a header with *St. Mary Parish Sheriff's Department, Franklin Division Main Terminal* appeared.

"What are we looking for?" Cal demanded.

Bella scanned a list of options that popped up. "We need something to give us a hint about what the police know. They found something in that shed. What was it?"

"Let's start with the obvious." Cal clicked on *Recent Reports*.

Jenna read over his shoulder as digital pages swept past.

"Wait," she said when a name caught her attention. "This is a request for questioning on a Samuel Collins." She got closer to the screen. "Is that our Mr. Samuel?"

Cal pointed at a typed summary at the bottom. "Look. It says, 'for questioning about the Waverly murder cases, regarding knowledge of outside persons using the campus as a meeting place.' What the hell?"

Bella gleaned the document a second time. She stood up, tapping her lips with tingling fingers.

"So, they think Mr. Samuel knows something and they want to question him."

Bella put her hand on his shoulder, checking the screen. "Pull up that menu again."

Cal clicked the left side of the screen, and the menu reappeared.

Bella scrolled through the contents, and then one jumped out. "There." She pointed at the word, *Camera*. "Click on that."

"It's probably just security stuff," Cal insisted.

Bella waited as he maneuvered into the camera system. "Could be, but all precincts have holding cells and interrogation rooms that are equipped with cameras. If they have Mr. Samuel in one, we might be able to find him and get an idea of what the officers are thinking."

The page on the screen opened into an array of two dozen boxes. Each box had a small live image from somewhere in the precinct with a number labeling the camera in the top right corner.

Bella leaned forward, searching every tiny image. "Look for anything with Mr. Samuel in it."

Cal's head was right next to hers as they scanned the screen.

"Got it," Cal shouted and then pointed at the box labeled, *18*.

He clicked on the camera. The image changed.

A room, no bigger than Bella's dorm, cropped up on the screen.

White walls, gray floors, and harsh fluorescent lighting presented a gloomy picture. Two men sat across from each other at a table in the center of the room. Despite the grainy quality, Bella could make out the handsome sheriff and Samuel.

"Shit. We hit the mother lode."

Cal squinted at the screen. "Why Mr. Samuel? He's never done anything."

Bella ignored Cal's whining. "Can you get audio?"

Cal clicked on the audio icon button.

The men's deep voices boomed from the small speaker.

"We found the shed by the mill, and the contents inside are being analyzed by our lab." The sheriff folded his hands on the table. "You want to tell me why you never said anything about that shed?"

Bella observed how Samuel squirmed. To her, he looked guilty as sin.

"They pay me to keep quiet about the rituals they perform on the land," Samuel told him. "They don't do no harm. They just go there twice a year for the summer and winter equinox and pay tribute to their ancestors."

The sheriff picked up a pen and reached for a manila folder next to him. "And who is your contact with the Chitimacha?"

Samuel rocked back in his chair. "I can't tell you that."

The sheriff tapped the pen on the table. The tension in the room came through the screen.

"Mr. Collins, three students have died on that campus in the past few days. I could hold you here as a suspect unless you cooperate."

"Three?" Cal asked, glancing up at Bella.

A horrible weight pressed down on Bella's chest. Tears gathered in her eyes as she thought of her friend and her effervescent personality.

"Lindsey makes three," she said, stifling her grief. "There must be evidence that she's dead."

Cal turned away, facing the screen.

She wanted to touch him, console him, but if she did, they would both end up wallowing in their misery. Later, when they caught the killer, she would cry. Until then, Bella would summon her anger to keep her sorrow at bay.

"Lindsey's dead?"

Cal sounded so frail.

Bella slapped his back to keep him from falling apart. "Don't think about it. We must pay attention to what is being said in that room. Focus only on that."

Cal sniffled, and his shoulders stiffened.

Bella was grateful he understood. She couldn't do this alone.

"How many years have the Chitimacha been coming to the Waverly property to perform their rights?" the sheriff asked.

Samuel didn't hesitate. "Since before my father was a caretaker at the school. My old man said it was something we owed them, and it was my duty to carry on the tradition."

The sheriff leaned across the table. "Mr. Collins, one of those people you allowed on the property could be a killer."

Samuel's gravelly laugh came through the speaker. "Sheriff, do you know the history of the Chitimacha in this area? They've been fighting inside that tribe for decades. If you go around questioning the chiefs, you gonna have more than problems at Waverly school to contend with."

The sheriff leaned back. "What kind of problems?"

Samuel shook his head. "You're new here, and I'm not the one to explain it. You best get to know the area you're sheriff over if you want to keep the peace. There's a whole lot more to this place than meets the eye."

Bella arched away from the screen. "What is he talking about?"

"Got me." Cal tapped the mouse pad. "I never heard of any infighting with the Chitimacha."

"That Mr. Samuel has been letting people on the property is creepy." Bella hugged herself. "Maybe Lindsey was wrong, and it isn't someone in the school that killed her sister. One of the people Mr. Samuel let on the property could have done it."

"She sounded pretty convinced when she told us." Cal sharpened the picture on his screen. "But this would also explain what happened to those girls from the nineties."

The sheriff stood and picked up his folder from the table.

"Why don't we take a break? I suggest you reconsider what you want to share with me, Mr. Collins. If another student dies at Waverly, I will throw you in a cell and hold you as an accessory."

Samuel rested his folded hands on the table, appearing collected. "Threatening me won't get you anywhere."

Mason walked toward the door, and a buzzer sounded.

Bella waited for the door to the interrogation room to close before she turned to Cal.

"We need to find out what Mr. Samuel knows."

He waved at his computer screen, which showed Mr. Samuel still seated at the table.

"If the sheriff didn't get anything, how do you expect us to?"

Bella glanced at the cloudy sky. The rain still poured, battering the classroom windows.

"We need to find Ms. LaRoux. She has to hear about what we've found."

Cal lowered his laptop screen. "I'm going to do some more digging into the Chitimacha. See if I can find anything about what Mr. Samuel was referring to."

Bella patted his shoulder. "Just don't wander off like Jenna. Not sure Ms. LaRoux would survive it."

Cal reached for his book bag. "You think Jenna is okay?"

Bella went back to her desk, hiding her apprehension. "Sure. You know Jenna." She attempted to sound upbeat. "You can't get rid of her, no matter how hard you try."

Aubrey climbed the steps of Elaine House, shaking and cold with fear. Her phone in her hand, she skidded on the slippery porch to the front door. She banged on the leaded glass, hollering over the rain.

"Help. Help me, please."

The shadow on the other side of the door had her chest swelling with hope. Until that moment, she had felt like the only person on the empty campus.

The door opened, and Laura, her pistol in her hand, stood at the ready, the chilling glint of resolve in her pale blue eyes.

"My student, Jenna Marchand." Aubrey paused to catch her breath. "I can't find her. She's not in my classroom, or in—"

"Calm down, ma'am." Laura returned her gun to her hip holster. "One of our cars just came back from there. No one was at the stables. She must be around here. Have you—"

"My student is in danger," Aubrey snapped. "If she isn't at the stables, then—"

"I was with her."

An officer dressed in a damp, wrinkled uniform trudged up the steps, holding his head.

He wasn't thick and muscular like the other men she'd seen working with Mason. This man appeared younger and had a wiry build. Aubrey immediately sensed he was in trouble by his unsteady gait and the glassy look in his eyes.

She rushed over and guided him to one of the rocking chairs on the porch.

The deputy sat down and leaned forward, placing his head between his knees.

Laura checked the back of his head and moved aside his dark hair, exposing a large bump.

Aubrey knelt in front of him, desperate for answers. "What happened?"

"The sheriff sent me to walk her back to the school," he said, sounding shaky. "I was with her, talking about her horse, but then someone clobbered me from behind."

Aubrey read his name tag. "You're Deputy Baxter. Mason tried to get you on the walkie."

"I woke up and the girl was gone, so was her horse." Baxter sat up. "I got back here as fast as I could."

Laura checked his eyes. "Can you remember who hit you?"

He rested against the rocker. "No. I got nothing."

Aubrey leaned against the arm of the chair. "I can't find Jenna anywhere. I've looked all over."

Deputy Baxter glanced at Laura. "Call Sheriff Dubois. Let him know what happened and that Jenna Marchand is missing."

Laura retrieved her phone from her pocket. While she made the call, Aubrey backed away from Baxter's rocker, overcome with a sickening feeling.

Aubrey bounded down the steps and back into the rain.

"Ms. LaRoux, wait," Laura called from the porch.

Aubrey didn't notice the drops on her face, or shiver when the cold wind blew through her wet clothes. All she could think of was Jenna.

The moment Aubrey hit the sidewalk, she broke into a run, heading back to The Quad.

Fatigue ached in every muscle, but fear kept her going. The constant state of fright, the sleepless nights, the worry, and devastation over losing her students made those last steps brutal.

She took a break beneath a blooming crepe myrtle planted along the edge of the pond. The tree's pink buds brought a touch of color to the gray and gloomy atmosphere. Not a single student was in The Quad, having stayed inside to avoid the rain. Then a bolt of lightning ripped through the sky, and she saw the reflection in the silver sculpture rising from the water.

An unfamiliar sound cut through the air—the nervous snort of a horse.

Aubrey spotted the animal, hiding behind the sagging branches of another pink crape myrtle. The animal's dark bay color shone from behind the gaps in the branches.

"What's a horse doing here?" Laura demanded, as she stopped next to Aubrey and caught her breath.

Aubrey slowly went around the fountain to the animal. "Maybe it got spooked from the storm and bolted from the stables."

The animal nervously rocked back and forth on its front legs, almost as if caught on something.

Aubrey eased around the pond, making sure not to startle the creature. She held out her hand, offering to comfort the tall, sleek bay.

Frothy sweat covered its neck, and its nostrils flared as if recovering from a hard run. The closer Aubrey got, the more familiarity nudged at her. She had seen the horse before.

It wasn't until she was within a few feet of the creature that she spotted the mud over its flanks and legs. The blue halter on its head struck a chord.

"Manni?"

The horse turned to her, and then she saw the rope tied around his neck.

"You know this horse?" Laura asked.

Aubrey held out her hand, softly cooing to the skittish creature.

"It's Jenna's horse. She has pictures of him all over her room."

The horse snorted and then took a step closer.

Something on the ground behind the animal came into view as he approached Aubrey.

She couldn't make out the object at first and thought the animal was dragging a post or something used to secure it. But then the bright red of a young woman's hair dropped Aubrey to her knees.

"Oh God."

Laura ran out from behind Aubrey and went to Jenna's lifeless body.

Her head was at a ninety-degree angle to the side, and her neck had stretched out, allowing her chin to rest below her shoulder. The rope around her neck had cut into her skin, leaving blood oozing onto the top of her school uniform. Her blue and purple skin almost matched her pants' color, which had a layer of fresh mud and grass stains. It indicated the horse had dragged her quite a distance, while her swollen lips, bulging eyes, and the numerous cuts and scrapes on her face testified to her agonizing end.

"Code three, code three," Laura yelled into her walkie. "I've got a dead girl in The Quad and need backup immediately."

Time stood still for Aubrey. She wanted to run to help Jenna, but her legs would not move. She remained in the soft ground, watching as the officer pulled out a knife from her gun belt and cut the rope securing Jenna to her horse.

Dizziness overtook Aubrey as the dutiful deputy went to Jenna's side and checked for signs of life.

When she lowered her head and pushed her blue St. Mary Parish SD cap back, the remnants of Aubrey's strength left her.

The ground came up to meet her, and she eyed the grassy patch, almost glad to lie down and forget. But as she came to rest, the horror of what Jenna had endured made her cry out and hold herself, shredded by the death of the girl who had loved horses more than anything else in the world.

Aubrey hugged her knees as she sat on the porch steps of Elaine House, fighting like hell to hold it together. Her shaking had lessened, her nausea had subsided, but the massive hole in her chest remained as excruciating as the first moment she'd seen Jenna's swollen and battered face.

Until the end of her days, Aubrey would never get over the image of Jenna's twisted and mangled body. She wanted to wrap her hands around the neck of the son of a bitch who had hurt that poor girl, tortured her in such a way, and squeeze the living shit out of them until she witnessed their eyes popping out.

Aubrey had never experienced such rage. She had come close after her parents died, wanting to kill the drunk driver who had taken them, but what surged through her veins now was beyond compare.

"How are you holding up?"

Mason's deep smoky voice brought her out of her maniacal rage.

"Please tell me you have a suspect. Someone I can kill."

He had a seat next to her. Mason removed his Stetson and set it on the side of the steps. He held out a plastic evidence bag. A delicate piece made of a gold chain had a plaque in the center with writing carved deep into the metal.

"What's that?"

He handed it to her. "A bracelet found tied to the rope around the horse's neck."

She fingered the loops of the chain through the plastic. "Just like the earrings and the necklace."

Mason tapped the bag. "Read the name."

She positioned the bracelet to get a better view of the plaque. "Marjorie." She gasped. "This belonged to Marjorie Reynolds?"

He took the bag from her hand. "It was a gift from her father and listed as missing from her things after she disappeared."

"With jewelry coming from the different missing girls, we can be confident our killer was involved in all the murders, even the ones in the nineties."

"Yep, looks that way." He picked up his hat. "That's why I'm about to do something drastic."

She watched him stand and asked, "What's that?"

The tap of heels coming onto the porch rose behind Aubrey. She knew that sound all too well, having dreaded it in high school.

She shifted around and raised her gaze to the entrance of the grand home.

Sara Probst stood on the porch, focusing her attention on the black coroner's van.

"This is what becomes of your extracurricular activities, Ms. LaRoux. Your meddling has awakened something evil in my school."

"That's ridiculous," Mason snapped. "You can't blame Aubrey for what's happening."

"Then tell me you have something, Sheriff. Give me someone to blame." She walked up to Mason in her usual determined strut. "If you can't catch this lunatic, call someone who can."

Mason returned his hat to his head and flexed his shoulders, presenting an intimidating image. "Ms. Probst, I have FBI coming from New Orleans in the morning to help with the case, but if anyone is going to catch this maniac, it's my team."

She moved closer, driving her heels into the wood, adding to the outrage she exuded. "I appreciate your bravado."

She had the same condescending tone that had haunted Aubrey's nightmares in high school.

"But you haven't been at this job for long, and perhaps you need to admit you are out of your league. Hand this off to more experienced people."

Mason's jaw muscles quivered, but he kept up his cordial smile. "No one can handle this situation better than me. As Sheriff of St. Mary Parish and all its subsidiaries, I think it best if you close Waverly, Ms. Probst. It's the only way to ensure your students will be safe."

"Close Waverly!" Sara's high-pitched reply jarred Aubrey's ears. "Are you mad? I can't just shut down this school. We have over two hundred students here from all over the state and—"

Mason closed the gap between them with one long stride. "How long do you think it will take for the news outlets to pick up what's going on here? By morning, you will have parents descending on this place and demanding to remove their children. Do you want to be proactive and save some of your reputation, Ms. Probst, or do you want to be ripped apart in the media as the woman who refused to close the school and keep her students safe from a killer?"

Aubrey had just found her new hero. Mason exhibited all the courage she lacked in standing up to the head of the school.

She held her breath; her gaze pinned on Sara. The circumstances may have been horrible, but for Aubrey, this was a long-awaited day of reckoning for Sara Probst.

"I am never intimidated, Sheriff." Sara straightened her short gray jacket. "I will call the board and ask for their advice on the matter."

Mason tilted his head to her. "That's fine, ma'am. Just make sure you tell them I'm suggesting this before I'm left with no alternative than to demand it."

Sara's small eyes burned into Mason, radiating more contempt than Aubrey had ever seen from the woman.

She worried Mason had just made a powerful enemy. Sara Probst's ties ran deep in St. Mary Parish, and across many political and educational communities in Louisiana.

Sara spun around and retreated into her home.

Mason came back to Aubrey and offered her a hand. He helped her from the step. Once she was on her feet, he tugged at the collar of her blue St. Mary Parish SD jacket.

"You need to get out of those wet clothes, and then I want you to pack. You're coming to stay with me."

She put her hand on his chest, her heart thumping like a rabbit on the run. "Mason, I can't leave. I have my students in the dorm to look after. And then there is Cal and Bella. I can't abandon them."

A stretcher loaded with a black body bag came around the side of the house, following the walkway.

The creak of one bent wheel on the gurney carried across the grounds. The horrible sound made the deputies, students, and faculty go quiet. Stillness filled the parking lot as Jenna's body rolled into the back of the coroner's van.

When the slam of the loading doors echoed, Aubrey closed her eyes and shuddered.

"I want you out of here," Mason grumbled under his breath.

"And I want to protect my kids."

"Sheriff?"

A man dressed in white coveralls stood at the bottom of the porch and waved an iPad at Mason.

"I need you to sign for the body."

Mason gripped her arm and moved her a few steps to the side, out of earshot.

"Stay here. We aren't finished with this conversation."

He left her side and trotted down the steps before she could get a word in.

Aubrey went after him but stopped at the bottom of the steps. It wasn't the time or place. Later, when they were alone, she would turn down his offer.

"Is it true, Ms. LaRoux?"

A sniffle came from behind her.

Cal and Bella waited on the sidewalk by the bulletin board, holding hands. Their pale faces and vacant gazes made them look as if the world had fallen out from under them.

Cal's trembling lower lip strengthened Aubrey's resolve to stay with her students.

She put her arms around Bella and Cal, holding them close, and subduing her tears.

"They said she was dragged behind Manni," Bella muttered between trembling lips.

Aubrey didn't confirm anything. She didn't want them to know the horrific details.

"I want you two to contact your parents and tell them to come and get you. The school is going to close."

Cal pulled away. "Close? But how will we catch the killer?"

Bella stood next to him, raising her chin. "I'm not going anywhere. We need to finish this for our friends."

Aubrey gripped Cal's hand and then Bella's. "You guys are on this killer's list. You can't stay. You have to get far away from this school."

"And then what?" Bella's composed expression didn't come across like a rattled teenager. "It doesn't matter if we are at school or home. Whoever killed those girls and murdered our friends means to finish until no one else knows his secrets."

Aubrey studied Bella's wide stance and set jaw. "What makes you say that?"

Cal came forward; the emotion she'd seen from him had evaporated as he stared her directly in the eye. "I hacked into the Sheriff Department's operations center. Bella and I watched Sheriff Dubois interview Mr. Samuel. The sheriff thinks Mr. Samuel let someone on the property that killed London. Hartley, Jenna, and Lindsey."

Aubrey's chest heaved. "Lindsey?"

Bella tipped her head slightly. "We overheard the sheriff talking about Lindsey's death. The blood we found at the monument was hers, wasn't it?"

At times, Aubrey believed her students were capable young adults, but Bella's quaking voice reminded her that on the inside, they were still kids.

She decided not to sugarcoat what she knew. "Yes, what we found there was Lindsey's blood."

"Where's her body?" Cal inched closer, not appearing fazed by the news. "We've found everyone else killed recently, but not her."

His reaction flustered Aubrey. "There's a lot of ground to cover. It might take time to find her."

"That's why I want to stay," Cal said. "I won't leave until we have answers. Even if it puts me in danger, I don't care. We were friends, and I owe her closure."

His resolve impressed her, but still, Aubrey feared for his safety. She felt certain his parents would not leave him in harm's way.

"Why don't we talk about this some more later? We can get together before you have to return to town."

Aubrey ached for coffee and perhaps a shot of something more substantial, but she could not risk clouding her judgment. She had to stay sharp and awake to watch over her students through the long night ahead.

Cal slipped his hands into his pockets. "I won't be going back to the dorm in town. An officer told me they have a place in the house for me to sleep tonight. The sheriff wants me close by."

That set off an unsettling wave in Aubrey's stomach.

"Here? He never mentioned that to me."

"It's all good, Ms. LaRoux." Cal smiled for her, despite the emptiness dulling his eyes. "I'd prefer to stay on campus. I can help with the investigation by doing some research."

Aubrey was thankful for his brave face but still worried that the past few days had been too much.

"Why don't you leave the investigating to the sheriff from now on?" She put a steadying hand on his shoulder. "I want to make sure nothing happens to you."

Cal stepped out from under her hand. "Geeks don't die. In the movies, they always crack the case."

"What are you talking about?" Bella rolled her eyes. "Everyone dies in the movies."

The return of their playful banter lifted her concern, but the subject reignited the churning that had plagued Aubrey's stomach since finding London. A jolt of unrelenting terror ripped through her.

Please let this not end like the movies.

CHAPTER 25

Aubrey stood at the window in the common room and admired the afternoon sun coming through the dark clouds. The way the gray evaporated into glorious streams of red and pink lifted the sadness pressing on her heart.

She turned from the window, her emotions a mass of chaos. She teetered between bouts of weeping and bellowing with outrage. How had such a diabolical person, who reveled in taking innocent lives, survived for so many years undetected? It was enough to threaten her faith in a benevolent God.

The Waverly hues of blue and gray, the comfy sofas, the plethora of posters about school spirit, and the array of books and fashion magazines, broke her heart. The room represented the world as it should be for the students at the school. Not the bloody, disfigured corpses, or body bags.

With classes canceled, the common area should have been awash in girls gossiping and laughing, but everyone had retreated to their rooms—probably packing for their anticipated departure.

Aubrey flopped onto a sofa and moaned. Her fatigue finally won out against the gallons of coffee she'd consumed. She rested her head and closed her eyes, questioning if she would ever find the energy to get up from that sofa again.

"There you are."

The smooth deep voice wrapped around her like a favorite blanket. She relished the sensation before opening her eyes.

"You found me," she said to Mason, who stood over her, his hand on his gun belt.

He wasn't wearing his hat but still had on the same damp, wrinkled clothes. A dark shadow of stubble had appeared on his jaw, adding an edgy quality to his good looks.

"Everything all right?"

"Fine. I have an officer sitting with Cal and Bella at the house. They are researching his computer. Clever guy, Cal."

"Did he tell you he hacked into your system and watched you interrogate Mr. Samuel?"

His eyebrows went up. "Remind me to hire him when this is over. He can debug our system."

He sat next to her and moaned almost as loud as she had.

"Damn, this feels good." He stretched out, folding his hands over his stomach and crossing his long legs. "I can't remember the last time I sat on anything this fluffy and comfortable."

"Ah, yes. We hide all the fluffy furniture in the girls' dorm."

She chuckled and then felt guilty. Aubrey questioned if she would ever be able to enjoy herself again without thinking of her students.

He sighed and then clasped her hand.

"Please consider relocating to my home. I have an alarm, a large dog named Max, and a whole lot of whiskey."

She squeezed his hand. "The whiskey sounds tempting. You never mentioned you had a dog."

He turned his head to her. "I never mentioned a lot of things about myself."

Aubrey drew up her knees and got comfortable on her side while gazing into his alluring eyes.

"So tell me? Who is Mason Dubois?"

He sat up. "That's a loaded question."

"We have been through so much together, but I still know so little about you."

He scratched his head. "Well, I'm the sheriff."

She liked how his brow crumpled when he was perplexed. "I got that part."

"You know I was a detective in New Orleans. I'm originally from a small town in Texas called Dripping Springs. I have a sister, Ella. Two nieces named Lisa and Winnie. My small house has a huge mortgage, but my truck is paid for. I'm proud of that."

"Yes, that's a big accomplishment." She smiled. "Go on."

"Let's see." He let go of her hand. "I've never been married. Never come close. I like to jog through the town naked early in the morning."

Aubrey chuckled, a full-on belly laugh that lifted her heartache, if only for a moment.

He touched her cheek. "I like your laugh."

She pulled herself up on the sofa. "Yeah, well, then why do I feel so guilty for doing it."

"Give yourself time. It doesn't go away overnight, but the sinking feeling lessens eventually."

"How do you do this day in and out? How do you deal with all the death?"

Mason eased in closer and slipped his arm around her shoulder. Aubrey wanted to pull away, but his warmth was too much to resist. She melted into his broad chest and let his musky smell wash over her.

"I used to let it get to me when I worked in New Orleans. Ate me up most of the time, but there was an Iraq War veteran on the force who gave me some perspective. 'Save who you can and fight for the ones you can't,' he told me." He let out a long slow breath. "It sounds cold, but it gave me focus."

"Focus?" Aubrey rested her head against his shoulder. "Perhaps that was what I've lacked in my life. I finished my master's and thought, okay, I'll be a teacher. But after almost three years, I became disillusioned. I believed coming back to Waverly would give me the focus I lacked."

"And has it?"

She considered the question and then pushed away from him. "Yes. I no longer question if teaching is what I want to do, but I want to be more than a teacher. When I came to this school and saw my students' faces, I saw myself. The me I was ten years ago." She rubbed her face, her nerves raw. "When Sara Probst blamed me for what is happening, I almost agreed with her, but now I realize it isn't me who needs to change—it's her. She's the reason every student and I feel so lost. She's never guided anyone toward the right path. If anything, she's pushed them away with all her criticism and disdain."

Mason sat up and rested his hands on his knees. "I doubt you will have to worry about her much longer. Parents will be taking their kids out of this school tomorrow and damning Sara Probst for these murders."

"But it's not her fault."

Mason patted her thigh. "Of course not, but hiding a secret for years doesn't make it go away. The past has come back to bite her in the ass." He stood. "This school will need your help getting rebuilt when this is over."

"I'm not sure I'll have a job at this school when this is over."

"You've helped with this murder investigation, which makes you an asset to this place."

She stood next to him. "I haven't helped because the killer is still out there."

"I'll find him, don't worry," Mason whispered. "I want this guy. I want to make sure he pays."

She put her hand on his chest, struggling to find the words to express her gratitude.

He put his hand over hers. "When this is over, I hope we can spend some time together and get to know each other better."

Her toes tingled. "Sure thing, Sheriff."

"And no backing out." He let her go. "I'll arrest you if you do."

He gave her a small smile, just enough to deepen the dimple in his chin, and then he headed toward the dorm entrance.

After Mason waved to the officer stationed outside, Aubrey hugged herself.

Elation warmed her bones, but then she became upset that she could feel something wonderful when the world around her was falling apart.

A zing of enthusiasm cruised through Cal as his fingers flew across the keys of his laptop. He worked at the desk the officer had assigned him in Elaine House, digging out the nooks and crannies of the plantation's history. It was his contribution to the investigation. Even as Cal sat in the large study—the sheriff had designated it their control room—the buzz of the other officers felt comforting. He was part of the team, even if he was still in high school.

A lock of Bella's soft brown hair landed on his keys. He trembled, and his hands stopped moving.

"What is it?" Bella asked, crouched next to his laptop.

He hesitated, not sure what to do. Did he touch her hair, or ask her to move? He pointed at the offensive curl. "That's in my way."

Bella chuckled and eased back from him. "You need to get some social skills."

He went back to his work. "I don't need to get along with people. Everything I need is on the internet."

"You can't date the internet."

A wave of nausea overtook him. "Please. I just ate."

Bella took a seat on the chair next to the desk. "Have you ever been on a date?"

Her questions had gone from distracting to annoying. "Do you want me to find out what's going on around here or not?"

Bella smugly smiled. "I'll take that as a no."

He slapped the keyboard. "Stop it!" He glanced at the two deputies monitoring the security camera screens. "Now is not the time to talk about this. Not when ..." His voice trailed off as he thought of his friends.

Bella put her hand over his on the keypad. "It's okay. I miss them, too." She removed her hand and pulled away. "But we can still help them. We can catch this killer."

Cal gleaned the information on his computer screen.

The database he had logged into didn't offer much about the history of Waverly. It was the same stuff he'd found on several other sites. He needed more detailed accounts of what had gone on related to the Chitimacha Indians and when they had owned the land. In his gut, Cal felt that was the key.

"I need to go to a better source."

Bella glanced at the computer screen. "What's wrong with the Hallowed Historical Society link?"

"The only information here is the same thing everyone else has. Most of these sites draw their data from one source. That's why so many repeat the same thing. I need something older, not found on the internet."

"Like in a library?" Bella suggested.

Cal examined her heart-shaped face. If he ever had a type, Bella was it. But how did he let her know he liked her? She'd probably laugh in his face. The others had, and those humiliating experiences had taught him to avoid girls at all costs.

"Yeah, a library."

Bella turned to the window and glanced across The Quad. "What about our library? Are there any records there you can use?"

Cal followed her gaze to the one-story, red brick building. The wolf etched into the glass on the entrance doors called to him.

"There's a room that houses a private collection right behind Mrs. Gibson's desk."

Bella turned to him. "You ever been in there?"

Cal sat back in his chair, remembering the day Mrs. Gibson had showed him the locked door.

"No, she told me about it, though. Said they have archives from the property—old maps and a few books about the house and plantation. I even heard about the sophisticated fire system installed during the summer to protect all the records. She's obsessed with keeping the records safe."

Bella glanced at the officers, who were drinking coffee and watching the monitors. "You need to get in there."

Cal shrank in his chair. "Are you crazy? I'll get expelled."

Bella motioned to the two deputies sitting at the monitors. "Not if one of them takes you there."

His toes curled in his shoes. "They won't let me out of this house. You heard the sheriff. We're both to stay here."

Bella slyly smiled and blinked, flashing a glimpse of her purple glitter eye shadow.

"What if I ask them to? Say you found something uber-important for the case. Then you could go to the library and check out the archives. If there is nothing, you could come right back."

"Are you crazy? They won't go for that."

"I can talk them into it," she countered in a cocky tone. "But you're going to have to help me make it sound convincing."

Even if he wanted to believe she was right, Cal couldn't ignore the other problems standing in their way. "The library is closed. I watched Mrs. Gibson lock it up after they found Jenna."

Bella motioned toward the men at their station. "They've got keys to the whole place, so you can waltz in there and get what you need."

Cal's lower lip trembled. "You make it sound so easy. I'm not like you, Bella. I can't sneak into places and steal—"

"What stealing? You're going in to get vital information accompanied by a deputy. Come on, Geek. We need to know what's there. Don't you want to fight back against whoever is doing this? Hartley, Jenna, and London would have done it for you. So would Lindsey."

His willpower dwindled at the mention of Lindsey. She had done so much for him, given him friendship and confidence he never had before. He owed her, no matter the cost.

"What do you want me to say?"

Bella tugged at her purple sock as she leaned away from her chair, analyzing the officers behind him. "Tell them a vital clue is in the library archives. You think it could crack the case wide open."

"You've watched way too many cop shows," he whispered, moving closer to her. "No one talks like that."

She puckered her lips. "Just let me handle it. How long will you need in the archive room?"

Cal combed his hand through his hair, running through what he knew about the library.

"I have no idea. I'm not sure I can even get in the archive room. It's accessed by a code that only Mrs. Gibson knows."

Bella glanced over his shoulder to the deputies on the other side of the study. The computer monitors in front of them showed different locations around the school.

"I will bet any amount of money Mrs. Gibson keeps the code in her desk."

He nodded, thinking that sounded reasonable. Mrs. Gibson was rather forgetful. "And what if her desk is locked? Do I ask the officer to break it open for me?"

"Jeez, Cal, have you never broken into anything before?"

Her incredulity made Cal wish he were more of a badass. His life was reading, studying, and researching history, but now he regretted not picking up a few vices that might impress a girl like Bella.

"I've been busy," was all he could think to say.

Bella shook her head. "Look, when you get in the library, act like you know how to get the code to the room. When the deputy isn't looking, use something hard to break the lock on Mrs. Gibson's desk. Can you do that?"

Cal felt like he should take notes. "How do I get him not to watch me?"

She gripped the sides of Cal's face, and his senses exploded. He picked up the whiff of jasmine coming from her hair, noticed her full purple-painted lips, and the creaminess of her skin.

"Jeez, Cal, I don't know. Maybe you should talk about history." Bella snorted and let go of him. "That usually makes everyone stay far away from you. Would you stop worrying? The guy won't care what you do as long as you're quick about it."

He looked away, afraid to let her see red creep up his face. "There's a camera at the entrance. What if the deputy watching the monitors sees me rifling through her desk?"

Bella stood from her chair and unbuttoned the top button on her blouse. "I'll stay here and distract him. Now, are you ready?"

Cal gathered his book bag from the floor as Bella strutted away from his desk. He wished he had half her courage. Imagine the historian he would make then.

This is your chance.

If he could pull this off, maybe things would change for him. He had always craved adventure but was too afraid to try. Cal vowed not to let fear hold him back anymore.

CHAPTER 26

Cal stood under the portico of the library entrance, his heart in his throat as Deputy Kennedy slipped the key into the lock at the base of the door. The click of the bolt easing back should have relaxed Cal—he was one step closer to the archive room—but the intimidating officer, and the way he kept scrutinizing Cal's every move, intensified the butterflies in his stomach.

Bella had presented their case to the two officers, and a flabbergasted Cal could hardly believe their luck when Deputy Kennedy volunteered for the task. But as the wet cold seeped into Cal's loafers, he reconsidered his trek in the rain. Cal wasn't cut out for this. Sure, he had an officer with him, but suddenly being away from the safety of Elaine House made him reconsider how badly he needed those archives.

"There you go," Officer Kennedy said after he pushed open the outer library door.

Cal's hands shook. "Ah, thanks."

He walked into the boxy alcove with wooden benches along the side and fliers of upcoming library events taped to the walls.

The officer followed him inside and then went to the double glass doors at the end of the short entryway.

Cal gulped as the man turned the key in the lock.

"You can just wait here, if you want?" Cal's voice cracked as he spoke. "I won't be long."

The deputy scanned the open view of the check-in desk from the entryway.

"Stay where I can see you." Deputy Kennedy took a seat on one of the benches. "Holler if you need me."

"I sure will," Cal said as he opened one of the doors.

He was thrilled when the man took out his phone and started scrolling.

That will keep him occupied.

The whoosh of the door closing brought a sigh of relief, and Cal took in the dark, silent library.

The freedom of having the entire library to himself was intoxicating. A dream come true for any book nerd.

The gray light filtered through the entrance and illuminated a vast collection of tall metal bookcases and large tables, venturing out on either side. In front was Mrs. Gibson's large oak desk, surrounded by shelves where students returned books. Behind the check-in area was the solid door to the archives room.

He took a step, anxious to get what he needed, and then noticed his watery print on the soft blue carpet. Then the essence of books, musty but tinged with a fresh earthiness, overtook him. The aroma plump with the promise of knowledge always soothed his curiosity and craving for exploration. It was the only place he ever felt at home.

He browsed a few titles of books left on the shelves behind the desk—geography, philosophy, and a few references on current events.

Cal glimpsed the bullet camera positioned over the entrance and pointed at the check-in desk.

I hope you are right, Bella.

He scurried to the archives door and examined the button lock in the silver handle.

Invigorated, Cal turned to the desk and set down his book bag. He pulled at the top drawer, expecting to find it locked, but to his amazement, it slid right open.

Sweat dripped down his back beneath his shirt as he checked on the deputy seated in the glassed-in entrance—he was still on his phone.

Cal trembled as he looked through the drawer—pens, blank writing pads, keys, and an assortment of pamphlets touting library rules.

Mrs. Gibson loves her rules.

He spied a single slip of paper taped inside the back of the drawer.

He leaned closer, but it was too dark to make out the scribble.

Cal wrestled his phone from his bag and shined his flashlight on the paper.

"Bingo. Seven, nine, four, three, five."

Cal scrawled the numbers across his palm.

Pride welled in his chest as he headed to the archive room. He was almost home.

Cal held his breath as the lock clicked, the handle turned, and the massive door moved.

The smell hit him first. A moldy dustiness that tickled his nose, a telltale sign of the old contents housed within.

He rummaged for a light switch, and the moment the fluorescent bulbs flickered to life, Cal shut the door.

Metal shelves filled a room no bigger than a small office. Most of the contents were hefty leather-bound tomes with *Franklin Sentinel* etched in gold along the spine.

The local newspaper was almost as old as Franklin, and he guessed the paper had handed over their archives for safekeeping.

He ran his fingers along the other works housed in the room, gleaning titles such as *Franklin During War*, and *Military Records of The Franklin Confederate Militia*.

He itched to peruse the pages of the Civil War documents, but time wouldn't allow it.

At the back of the room, a sign in red sat below a glass cabinet, which contained a system of white plastic pipes and two red canisters.

When alarm sounds, vacate room at once. Carbon dioxide will be released in thirty seconds.

Intent on getting on with his research, he moved toward a few metal shelves sitting almost empty at the back of the room. A cardboard box, dusty and bent on one side, had something scribbled across the top in black marker.

Elaine House Archives

Cal eagerly grabbed the box and removed it from the shelf. He went to the center of the room, positioning himself directly below one of the fluorescent lights, sat on the blue carpet, and opened the top of his prize.

"This has to be it."

Bella's heart pounded when a red light blinked on the right-hand corner of one of the two computer screens. The square with *LIB* across the top luckily turned black, but she became terrified the officer on monitor duty would spot the anomaly and want to check on Cal.

Bella had to do something fast.

The paper cup left on the folding table by the computers gave her an idea.

Bella knocked over the coffee, spilling it onto one of the keyboards.

"Oh, I am so sorry."

The burly man stood, turning his back to the monitors.

Bella hastily rechecked the screen, but the image with *LIB* was dark once again.

"Ms. Simone, what are you doing?"

Bella grimaced, summoned her courage, and did a little quick thinking before she turned and encountered a grim-looking Mason Dubois.

He marched into the study and saw the officer hastily cleaning up spilled coffee.

Mason came up to her, radiating concern as he scanned the study.

"Where is he? Where is Cal Broussard?"

Bella thumbed the paneled hallway behind her. "He went to the library with one of the officers."

Mason expanded his chest and then faced his officer. "You let the boy go to the library? I said to keep an eye on these two."

The tall officer, who Bella had found blunt and not very talkative, motioned to the monitor.

"He said he needed something from the archives. Kennedy went with him, and we've got the camera set up at the library for added eyes."

Her jaw trembled, making it hard to speak. She struggled to come up with an excuse, something to buy Cal time.

Mason walked up to Bella, eyeing her with a dubious glint in his green eyes.

"Tell me what you and Cal are up to."

Bella's insides turned to mush. "Cal wanted to get into the library archives. He said he found a clue."

The officer turned back to the monitors and shouted, "I've lost the feed from the library."

Mason charged toward the table. "Get it back."

Bella's knees knocked together.

"I can't." His officer typed commands into the keyboard. "It's cut off at the source."

Mason removed his walkie from his belt. "Kennedy, come in. Over."

Static filled the study, while rising tensions thickened the air.

"Kennedy, can you hear me? This is Sheriff Dubois. Over."

Bella's trembling grew worse. "Is Cal okay?"

Mason turned to his deputy. "Call Kennedy on his phone. Tell him to get the boy out of there."

The officer retrieved his phone from his pocket. "What are you going to do, Sheriff?"

Mason hastily scanned the camera images on their screens, searching for any sign of Cal. "I'm heading over there. Alert the others on campus. Tell them to go to the library."

Bella closed her eyes, wishing she could reach out to her last remaining friend.

Cal, come back to me. Please, before something happens to you.

A satisfied hum meandered through Cal as he perused the notes he'd scribbled down. The journal belonging to Ashton Dardenne, the last owner of Elaine House, had provided him with invaluable information. He might not have discovered the killer, but the property's history had offered a vital clue.

Cal gathered his legal pad and shoved it into his book bag. He'd spent more time than he'd intended in the archive room. Excuses formulated in his head, but Cal hoped the information he'd found would outshine his indiscretion.

He returned the journal and the faded articles to the cardboard box, and then hastily set it back on the metal bookshelf. Cal checked the lid, making sure it looked like no one had messed with the contents.

When he took a step back from the box, the red light above the glass case blinked.

Cal scanned the room, searching for any hint of smoke. Nothing.

His gaze then settled on a red sign below the glass box.

When alarm sounds, vacate room at once. Carbon dioxide will be released in thirty seconds.

He had not heard an alarm. Only the red light on the housing had gone off. Was it an error, a malfunction? Cal's uneasy stomach was encouragement not to wait around and find out. He had to get out of there.

Cal scooped his bag from the floor and dashed toward the door.

The moment he touched the cold metal of the doorknob, he relaxed, but when he tried to turn the handle, a wave of icy cold washed over him.

It didn't budge. He ran his hand over the door as a flashing red light filled the room, adding to his urgency. He searched for another keypad to open it, but he knew there was none. The door could only lock from the outside, so how had it—

"Your secret is mine now. No one will ever know."

The scratchy, growling voice came from the overhead speaker in the room's ceiling.

Who is that?

He blotted out the question, not wanting to consider his greatest fear. A vise of terror constricted his chest. The more he pulled at the door, kicking and fighting to get it to budge, the higher his sense of panic. Cal's rational thinking drowned beneath the riptide of emotions. His skin tingled, his muscles ached, and terror cut off his ability to plot his escape.

There was a click from behind. Cal whipped around and then froze when hissing erased the silence in the room.

He almost crumbled when he saw a stream of cloudy air escaping from the canisters housed in the gaseous fire compression system. Cal's time had run out.

He returned to the door, overwhelmed with fear. He banged, shouted, and yanked at the knob, desperate to get out. His fright propelled him to keep moving and looking for an escape.

A funny tingling rose in the back of his throat. He shook it off at first as he dropped to his knees, hoping to find a gap in the bottom of the door, allowing him some means to get air. The tingling turned into a cough, and then his breathing became labored.

Cal reached for his book bag. He would call Bella.

"Scared, little boy."

The ugly and almost demonic sounding words streaming through the speaker added to the numbness taking over his fingers.

He dug through his bag, yanking out his notes and laptop, rummaging for his phone.

He had left it in there. Why couldn't he find it?

The air thinned, and Cal found himself struggling to get in a deep breath. Sweat poured from his face and trickled down his cheeks. His heart sounded like thunder in his ears. Cold gripped him—the unearthly kind that sucked the energy from his muscles and left him paralyzed. Then Cal's rational mind kicked in. He had to maintain his reasoning no matter what his body felt, he had to battle to keep his mind sharp.

The room's lights dimmed, and his focus wavered. He stared at his book bag, willing it to remain in his sights. Darkness crowded his peripheral vision, and Cal's chest tightened, acid welled from his stomach, and a searing hot stab of terror nearly doubled him over. A headache rose between his eyes and quickly spread to the back of his neck. The nagging throbbing distracted him, drawing his attention away from his bag.

He turned for the door, desperate. He rammed his shoulder into it and clawed at the wood in a last attempt to be heard by the deputy outside. His limbs were sluggish, and his muscles burned with effort. He couldn't feel his fingers anymore, and when he saw smears of his blood on the door, he stopped.

His mouth went dry when he saw his broken and bleeding fingernails. He wanted to laugh and then couldn't remember why. How had he gotten in that room? He couldn't remember.

History. That was it. History had brought him to the room. He loved history, but Cal strained to remember why he loved it so.

Help. Get help.

The screaming in his head momentarily punched through his fog.

He spotted his book bag still in a heap next to him. Cal had to get to his phone.

Sweat soaked his shirt, sending a chill through him, but Cal's fear had vanished. He found that surprising and comforting. The almost euphoric feeling removed the clouds obscuring his judgment. He could think, and that was his greatest weapon.

Cal concentrated on getting his hand on his book bag. He couldn't understand why it was so hard to move. A buzzing erupted, blocking out the ringing in his ears. The light of his phone screen shone through the fabric.

They were looking for him.

Cal lurched toward his bag but ended up sprawled on the blue carpet, staring at his phone's light still coming through the canvas pocket. He wanted to get to it but couldn't make himself move.

Dizziness and nausea overtook him while he lay on the floor. The light in the room soon turned to hazy darkness, and that was when his fear returned. It wrapped around his heart, siphoning the hope from him. There was so much he still wanted to learn, to see, and then there was Bella. The first girl he'd wanted to kiss.

He heard a garbled voice and recognized his wobbly tone, but he sounded so far away.

When his vision returned, all he could see was a black figure hovering above him—Death? Who else could it be? He tried to reach out and swat the blurry shape away, but it was pointless. He had nothing left.

He tried to make a noise, but he had nothing left in him.

Cal prayed for justice and Bella.

Let one of us make it.

Darkness took over, immersing Cal in a soothing peace. He was never calm, and why would he be now when Death stood over him, waiting to collect him? But he went with the surge of utter tranquility. He would sleep for a while, and when he woke up, he felt assured that his nightmare would end.

ubrey sat on a cold stone bench outside the library, her arms around a sobbing Bella as she peered up at hovering Mason. The pink rays of dusk settled over The Quad, confounded her. How could the world seem peaceful with all the death and suffering surrounding her?

"It's my fault," Bella whimpered. "I sent him here. I didn't tell the officer when the library feed went out."

Aubrey pushed her sorrow aside and concentrated on Bella.

"No, don't you say that." She pushed the young woman's head away and wiped her tear-stained cheeks. "Cal would not want you to blame yourself."

"That's right. The killer is the one to blame," Mason grumbled as he stepped back from their bench. "Someone locked the archives door and activated the gaseous fire suppression system right under the nose of my deputy. The room flooded with a non-reactive gas, pushing out all the oxygen in the air, and suffocating Cal. Whoever did this knew none of us would figure out what was happening until it was too late."

"Do you have any suspects?" Aubrey demanded.

Mason pushed his hat back, appearing glum. "Samuel Collins was the one in charge of the library fire system. Sara Probst told me he had the only key to the gas casing in the archives room."

A tight feeling overtook Aubrey's stomach. "And where is he now?"

Mason pressed his lips together. "We don't know. He left the station with me over an hour ago."

"Which gave him plenty of time to come back here and kill Cal." Tears filled Bella's eyes as she peered into The Quad. "Every one of my friends was murdered by what they loved. Jenna had her horse, Cal his books, Hartley his four-wheeler, and London … well, Mr. Samuel knew of her reputation as the maneater."

Mason approached the bench. "We don't know for sure if it's him. Everything is circumstantial at this point."

"I can't believe it." Bella fidgeted and her hands twitched. "We trusted him. He knows our weaknesses. What chance do I have?"

Aubrey tucked Bella's head into her chest, attempting to soothe her. "We won't leave you alone again. I promise."

Mason stooped next to Aubrey and held up a small gold ring in a plastic evidence bag.

"Jeanne Caron's ring was found next to him. She was one of the three who went missing in the nineties, so there's no question it's the same person who killed the others. The jewelry ties all the murders together."

Aubrey took the bag and examined the gold ring. It was delicate and simple with small opals set into the band, but the name carved on the inside, *Jeanne,* sent a chill through her.

Mason took the bag and then handed Aubrey a legal pad, its pages thick with scrawled handwriting.

"Cal's notes. Must be what he came to the library to get. We found it in his book bag, not far from his body."

Bella pulled away from Aubrey and snatched the pad from her.

"He wanted to look into the old archives stored in the library from Elaine House." Bella scanned the top page. "He believed there was a connection there that linked the killings."

Mason motioned to the pad. "There were notes about the Newberry family, who owned the place, their lineage, and how their name changed through the years."

Bella flipped through the notes, gleaning every page.

Mason glanced ahead to The Quad and frowned.

Aubrey raised her head and saw the coroner's office gurney

approaching the library.

"Why don't you two go back to the dorm?" Mason suggested. "I'll wrap things up here."

But when Aubrey put her arm around the young woman, Bella didn't look up from Cal's notes.

She continued to voraciously read them even as Aubrey guided her back to the dorm.

"What is so fascinating?"

Bella handed her the pad. "You need to read this."

Aubrey stopped walking. She patiently read the first few lines of Cal's notes, trying to decipher his horrible penmanship.

"What am I looking at?"

Bella pointed at the bottom of the page. "The names. The Newberrys changed their name to Dardenne at some point in the 1880s, and then a Dardenne daughter married into the Chitimacha tribe. The same one who used to own this land. The family split into two factions—the Chitimacha line and the Dardenne line."

Aubrey shook her head. "I'm not following."

Bella took the pad from her. "In nineteen forty-five, the land was sold by the last of the Dardennes, Ashton, to Jacob Hill, who founded the Waverly School. The other surviving Chitimacha family members waged a court battle. They wanted to repurchase the property."

Aubrey read over Bella's shoulders, attempting to put the puzzle together. "But obviously, they lost their legal battle."

Bella held the pad against her chest. "Because they came from the wrong family line—the Chitimacha. Cal wrote that Ashton Dardenne admitted in his journal that the land and house should have gone to the other line, but the judge had been paid off by Jacob Hill. He wanted the land and was willing to pay anything to get it."

Aubrey watched the dark closing in around The Quad. "So, Cal thinks someone from the Chitimacha side is seeking revenge for losing their ancestral land. Any idea how we find them?"

"He didn't say, but he did leave this."

Bella flipped to the last note on the pad. She pointed at the words underlined three times.

Must check Newberry Graveyard.

Aubrey wiped her hand over her mouth, disbelief raging through her. "You've got to be kidding me."

"We have to go there," Bella insisted. "Cal died to get us this information."

Aubrey waved to the sky. "We can't go there in the dark. Tomorrow, with Sheriff Dubois and several armed officers, we will head out."

Bella tilted her head, seeming to weigh Aubrey's advice.

"Sure. No problem," she said in a flat tone.

A stitch of apprehension crept into Aubrey's chest. Getting through to Bella had turned out easier than expected, which was very unlike the determined young woman.

"Bella, promise me you won't do anything stupid. One more night won't change anything."

Bella peered up at her with bloodshot eyes. "You're right. We can wait a little longer."

Reassured, Aubrey put her arm around Bella and guided her toward the dorm.

The uniformed officer stationed outside opened the door for them.

Once inside the frigid lobby, Aubrey felt her fatigue reignite, fogging her mind.

"Let me get out of these damp clothes, and then you and I can sit and go through Cal's notes in detail. How does that sound?"

"Fine." Bella's monotone didn't change. "I will be waiting in the common area when you come down."

Her blank expression and lifeless eyes concerned Aubrey, but they had both been to hell and back in a single day.

Instead of questioning Bella's feelings, Aubrey heeded her exhaustion and trudged to the elevator. A hot shower and another coffee, and then she would be ready for another long night of worry.

Bella plowed into a low-lying branch while running through the darkened woods. She stopped and glanced over her shoulder before breaking into a jog. A few prickly thorns caught her shirtsleeves, but she pressed on, fearful of getting caught. The steak knife she'd kept in her dorm room offered some comfort—at least she wasn't defenseless.

Ms. LaRoux's reluctance to check out Newberry Cemetery convinced Bella she wouldn't get anyone to listen to her plan. If Mr. Samuel had somehow read Cal's notes, the first place he would go was the cemetery to hide evidence. If Bella could get a look at Mr. Samuel, even snap a picture, she could call for help and capture the sleazebag, ending the nightmare for everyone.

When Bella broke through the trees, the pines' scent faded while the eerie moonlight spread across the battlefield's tall grass. She pictured the dead men buried there, restless and crying out for vengeance.

Don't think about it. Move.

She hugged the edge of the field, following the path she had plotted in her head. She kept an eye out for a break in the terrain and any signs of headstones.

Instead of the land clearing, more woods crowded the way. The cold air rattled her resilience. Bella debated if she should go back. She raised her phone, shining the light on the ground, and into the clump of trees next to her.

She peered into the shadows. Her light flecked on something tall and white. With a shaky hand, she panned the phone back over the area, scrutinizing every break in the trees.

A square headstone cropped up. Slanted at an awkward angle, it sat nestled next to a black fence topped with decorative iron spears mounted on square bases. She slowly moved the flash from her phone to the side and spotted a pillar atop a raised mausoleum.

Bella's trembling eased. She took a few steps closer to the cemetery. The woods were uncannily quiet. No night birds, nocturnal creatures, or even a breath of wind stirred the hickory trees.

The closer Bella got to the site, the more well-maintained it appeared. No weeds or overgrown vines cluttered the headstones. The arched black gate didn't squeak when Bella pulled it open.

So who is keeping this place up?

She was about to step inside the burial ground when someone

grabbed her shoulder.

Bella dropped her knife, and her cry pierced the night.

"I told you not to come here."

Aubrey's frantic voice sent Bella scrambling for her knife. She wanted to hide her face, ashamed of getting caught.

"I had to." She kept her focus on Aubrey's jeans. "Cal's notes held a clue. If Mr. Samuel murdered my friends, he's coming here to hide the evidence before anyone finds it."

Aubrey lifted her chin. "Why didn't you tell me that?"

"Would you have listened to me?" she asked, sounding brittle.

Aubrey let her go. "You scared the crap out of me. I went charging out of that dorm, leaving the officer wondering if I was insane. And what if you had met up with Samuel or the killer?" Aubrey spotted the knife in Bella's hand. "Is that what you brought to defend yourself?"

Bella cradled her knife. "It's all I could find. I'm sorry I ran off, but we're here, so let's look around and find out what evidence Cal thought was here."

Aubrey retrieved her phone from her back pocket. "I'm texting Sheriff Dubois to let him know we're here."

Bella frowned as Aubrey typed. "He'll bring the entire force after us."

Aubrey finished her text. "God, I hope so."

"That could scare away Mr. Samuel, which defeats the purpose of my coming here." Bella walked through the gate. "Then everything Cal suffered would be ..."

"Let's see what's in here while we wait for the sheriff," Aubrey said behind her. "But if anyone shows up, you are to listen to me, agreed?"

Bella glanced back at her. "I came out here to stop the killer, not become the next victim."

Aubrey took the knife from her. "You could have fooled me."

Bella didn't want to argue. She'd accomplished her goal and made it to the cemetery. Now they had to uncover what Cal had found, and hopefully unmask the killer.

The faint light from her phone gave Bella a good look at the private cemetery.

Rectangular, with the black fence running the entire perimeter, the burial site had a variety of weathered upright tombstones, flat slab markers that covered the whole graveyard, and a few simple flush headstones. In the rear, a rising pillar stood atop a round mausoleum with weeping angels adorning three steps to a slab with several brass markers.

"This place is in good shape," Aubrey said, inspecting an upright monument. "Someone has been keeping it up."

Bella tried to make out a faded name. "Yeah, but who?"

Aubrey flashed her phone light over a few graves to the left of the gate. "These are all Newberry."

Bella moved deeper into the graveyard. "Same here." She inspected each grave, quickly passing on to the next once she spotted the Newberry name. Then the names changed.

"Got a Dardenne here," she called to Aubrey.

Aubrey's flashlight scoured several tombstones. "Over here as well."

Bella followed the Dardenne memorials until she came to one where the name carved there appeared slightly different from the others.

"This is odd. It says Caroline née Dardenne. Died 1908."

"This must be her husband." Aubrey shined her light on the grave next to Bella. "Nayati."

Bella turned to the grave. "That sounds Native American to me."

"It is. It means one who fights or wrestles."

Bella eyed her teacher as she went to another gravestone. "How do you know that?"

Aubrey kneeled and wiped a few leaves from a large slab. Then she took the knife and scraped away some of the dirt.

"Many Creoles married the native people in this area, including my grandfather. My grandmother was full-blooded Choctaw."

Bella admired the faint smile on Aubrey's face and the way it accentuated her delicately sculpted cheekbones.

"So I guess this is where the Dardenne family splits as Cal said in his notes."

Aubrey set the knife down as she searched more graves. "But what is the other family name?"

Bella became alarmed because they were running out of graveyard. Then she spotted the tall mausoleum in the back.

She hurried to the brass plates, hoping to find the name they needed. But before she got close enough to read the print on the mausoleum door, her phone reflected a name carved into the lintel above—Collins.

A lump formed in her throat. "Ms. LaRoux, I think you need to look at this."

Aubrey came alongside her. "What is it?"

Bella guided her hand holding her phone's light over the name carved deep into the stone.

Aubrey's loud gasp let Bella know she had spotted it.

"Do you think Mr. Samuel is part of the Collins family?"

Aubrey moved closer to the door, inspecting the plaques.

Bella waited for an answer, but Aubrey appeared intent on scouring the names.

Aubrey then paused and took a step back from the mausoleum door. "We have to go."

She took Bella's hand and pulled her toward the gate.

"What?" Bella demanded. "What did you find?"

Aubrey kept tugging at her hand, then let go the moment they reached the gate.

Bella then noticed the spot from a flashlight shining at the leaves in front of their feet. She followed the beam to the gate where Mr. Samuel, cradling the torch under his arm, stood grinning.

"What are you two doing out here?"

Aubrey's back stiffened, sending an electric charge of fear through Bella.

"Where have you been? Mason is looking for you. He has more questions."

Samuel opened the gate wider for them. "I've answered enough questions, Ms. LaRoux. The sheriff has all he needs from me."

Horrible nausea gripped Bella. She'd suspected Mr. Samuel was the killer and would arrive at the cemetery to hide evidence. But having him there, and the way he made Aubrey nervous, wasn't what she'd envisioned. How could sweet Mr. Samuel be the killer?

"Your father, Samuel Collins Sr., is buried here," Aubrey said with an edge of anger. "Why didn't you tell anyone you were descended from the Newberrys?"

Samuel maneuvered the flashlight into his hand. "Because no one cares. Old families with mixed blood are the norm in these parts, not the exception. You, above all people, should know that."

Bella crept closer to her teacher, the ramifications hitting her like a wall of falling bricks. Samuel was the one who had something to hide in the cemetery, and that he had shown up meant only one thing.

Bella shuddered. *He is the killer. But it can't be true. He is our friend.*

Then she remembered the knife Aubrey had left in the graveyard.

"What do we do?" Bella whispered.

Aubrey dragged her toward the gate. "Stick close," she muttered.

Bella wished the sheriff would hurry. Coming to the cemetery had been a big mistake because Samuel had probably been watching them all along. She'd walked right into his trap.

"The Collins family was denied the right to repurchase their ancestral home," Aubrey said in an accusatory tone. "You and your father both worked here when girls went missing. You admitted that you let Chitimacha tribe members on the land to perform rituals for their ancestors." She pointed to the mausoleum. "Did you mean those ancestors?"

Samuel held up a hand. "It's not what you think. Come with me. What I have to show you will explain everything."

"I don't think so." Aubrey grabbed Bella's sleeve. "Run."

Aubrey dragged her out the gate, and even as Mr. Samuel attempted to block their way, Aubrey drove her shoulder into him, pushing him back like a skilled linebacker.

They headed through the trees, following the edge of the battlefield. Brush slapped Bella's face, scratched her arms, but she didn't slow.

An icy fear seized Bella as they cut through the woods—someone she'd trusted was a killer.

Aubrey held up her phone, scrolling for Mason's number. "We have to tell Mason."

Bella wanted to snap the phone away, afraid the call would slow them down.

"Later, just run. We have to get through these woods."

A break in the trees sent a rush of hope through Bella. The school must be close, and if they could get onto the grounds, she became convinced they could outrun Mr. Samuel.

Bella picked up speed, pulling ahead of Aubrey.

Right before they reached where the moon broached the trees, Aubrey yanked at Bella's arm.

She fell to the ground, landing in a pile of pine needles. She quickly got up and searched for Aubrey, but she was nowhere in sight.

"Ms. LaRoux?"

A voice, quivering with fright, came from somewhere in the ground.

Bella scrambled to find her phone amid the pine needles, and when she hit the flashlight, she discovered a gaping hole inches away.

Round and lined with bricks, the opening was a few feet across with remnants of rotting wood boards still connected to the edges with rusty nails.

"Bella?"

She peered over the edge of the hole, putting her knees to the bricks, and shined her flashlight deep into the darkness.

The well went down about ten feet. The moonlight shimmered on the undulating bottom, and then Bella's phone caught on Aubrey's face.

She sat in a pool of water with floating twigs and leaves all around her. She appeared to tread water to keep her head above the mess. Aubrey's wide-eyed, stretched expression tightened Bella's throat.

"Ms. LaRoux, don't move. I'll get you out."

Aubrey waved at the gnats flying around her. She wrinkled her nose and raised her head toward the light. A greenish slime covered her skin and the water's surface.

"No, Bella, run. Head back to the school and get the deputies. Hurry."

Bella searched for something to throw down to her, desperate to get Aubrey out of there. "I can't leave you."

"Go before Mr. Samuel comes."

Bella's fear returned, and she turned her phone light to the darkness around her.

She stood, sweat dotting her upper lip as she strained to pick up the faintest footfalls. Bella scoured the woods for bobbing light, her jaw slackening as terror escalated in her chest.

"I'll be back." She peered into the well, wanting to see her teacher's face once more. "I promise—"

A hand closed around Bella's mouth, bile rose in her throat, and she fought against the strong arms closing around her and cutting off her scream.

The icy water, stinking of rot and mildew, collected around Aubrey's chest as she stared up at the opening, scouring the surface for any sign of Bella. The young woman's last words echoed in her head, slowing time as the gravity of the situation overtook her.

"Bella? Are you there?"

The silence was gut-wrenching.

Please, not Bella. She had been closest to Bella—losing her would be too much to bear.

Samuel—he'd been the killer. The one Lindsey said had been part of the school.

Incensed, Aubrey swam toward the wall. She palpated the uneven, slippery surface, looking for any groove where she could get a hold. Her fright compelled her to move quickly, but finding any footing took patience.

Finally, she found two niches thanks to the help of the moonlight streaming into the well.

Once she got her hands in place, Aubrey pulled her legs out of the water, but the moment she set her foot in the hole, her tennis shoe slipped.

She fell back. Her head banged against the stone, and she tumbled into the slimy pool.

Stunned, Aubrey endeavored to regain her senses. She sniffled and willed her tears away. She wasn't ready to give up yet.

Aubrey struggled to get a hold on whatever sludge covered the well's wall. She held on, trying not to think about what was in the filthy hole. Instead, she raised her head, clutching to the hope that someone would stumble across her.

Aubrey flexed her fingers and shifted her feet, fighting back against the numbness creeping along her limbs. The dizziness came in waves. A concussion would explain the ethereal visitor above the well, but it would also mean she couldn't trust her senses. Without her wits, she couldn't protect herself.

Aubrey prayed the officer who had seen her run out of the dorm had alerted Mason. They would be searching for her, and she held on to that hope, even though with each passing minute, she feared it might be too late to save Bella.

She leaned against the wall, exhaustion weighing her down. She longed to sit, rest her tired legs, but submerging more of her body in the water would mean her doom.

Stay focused. Keep fighting.

She repeated the mantra in her head until she picked up a strange warbling call.

Aubrey moved away from the wall, wading to the center of the well, craning her neck to pick up any sound.

"Aubrey!"

It was a man, calling from a short distance away.

Aubrey covered her mouth, so happy to hear something other than the drip of water. Then she questioned if her mind was playing tricks on her.

There's only one way to find out.

"I'm here!" She put everything she had into her cry. "I'm here. I'm here," she repeated, willing away the lump in her throat.

"Aubrey, keep calling out. I hear you."

The deep, sultry voice sent a warm rush of relief through every inch of her. She wasn't hallucinating.

"Help me. I'm trapped in a well. It's in a small patch of clearing between some thick pines. I can see the sky and the moon, so I know it's—"

A shadow crossed the opening.

"I got you, darlin'."

Tears warmed her cold cheeks as she made out Mason's broad shoulders and the outline of his Stetson.

"Mason," she croaked, unable to hold back her emotions. "I am so glad to see you."

"Are you hurt?"

She touched her temple. "I hit my head."

Panic flooded her system and constricted her throat as she remembered Bella's last moments.

"Mason, where's Bella? Have you seen her?"

"No." Mason set his hat aside. "I got your text and went to the cemetery, but you were already gone."

Guilt weakened her grip on the wall. "Samuel took Bella. He followed us to the cemetery and then said he wanted us to go with him, but we ran away. He chased us. I fell in here, and then he took Bella. You said he had the key to the ATV shed, and then there was the fire safety system in the library. You said he was the one who oversaw it. He has to be our killer."

"Did you ever think that someone could be setting him up?" Mason leaned over the top of the well. "The clues are too coincidental. Even the jewelry left at every scene seems staged to me."

Rage burned through her, chasing away the cold. "Don't you see? All the clues point to him. He has been an employee of the school through all the killings. His family was the one who lost this land in a court battle to Jacob Hill, the founder of Waverly School. The Collins family is buried in the graveyard. Samuel's father is there. He comes from the Chitimacha line of the Dardenne family, who owned the property. Isn't it obvious? He has the most to gain if the school closes. He gets his ancestral land back."

More light came from up top, and soon Aubrey could make out Mason's face and the two other officers who had arrived to help.

Mason removed a coil of thick rope from around the shoulder of one of his deputies. "Aubrey, let's talk about this after we get you out of there."

"But who else took Bella?" Aubrey shouted. "She was up there, and then she was gone. You must go and look for her. Find Samuel before he hurts her."

Mason unfurled the rope. "We will once you are safe."

He pointed at something beyond the well opening and directed his men to secure the rope.

Blinding flashlight beams bounced around the well walls, and when they landed on Aubrey, the brightness hurt her eyes and intensified the pounding in her head.

Despite the pain, the light comforted her until she got a good look at where she was.

Moss covered the walls, and the water was black, filled with leaves and twigs. She quickly raised her head, concentrating on the men above, terrified to discover what else might be lurking in the muck.

The end of the rope bobbed and swayed as it was lowered.

The moment she grabbed the thick cord, Aubrey's concern for Bella returned. No longer worried about getting out of the well, she wanted to find the young woman before it was too late.

"Tie the rope around your chest and under your arms," Mason called down. "Make sure it's secure. We're going to pull you up."

Aubrey checked the thick knot twice before she raised her head to the opening.

"I'm ready."

The hard yank sent a sharp twinge through her back. The fall must have banged up more than she thought.

Aubrey held on to the rope as they pulled her up, giving her a better look at the protruding roots coming through the round stones set into

—227—

the wall.

When she was only inches away from the top, the sweet, pine-scented air caressed her face, and she breathed deeply, thankful to smell something other than the polluted well water.

Bright lights hit her as soon as she breached the opening. She closed her eyes and turned her head away.

The men grabbed her arms, pulling her out, and the moment her feet touched the grass, Mason's arms went around her.

"Are you okay?"

His musky scent enveloped her. "I am now."

He held her back, inspecting her face, and then his lips smashed together. When he touched her forehead, a sudden sting made her pull away.

"You've got a nasty cut there."

She touched her forehead and then examined the blood on her fingers. "I hit my head when I fell, trying to climb out."

The mild aches she had not noticed in the cold water began to stab and sting. Her head, back, and left arm howled for attention.

Mason hurriedly untied the knot she'd made. "We need to get you to the hospital."

Aubrey shook off her growing discomfort. "No. We need to find Bella."

Officer Baxter came forward and touched her arm. "We'll find her. We will search for her. You go with the sheriff."

Aubrey wanted to argue, but reason told her she would slow them down and inevitably hurt Bella.

"Hurry. I'm afraid what Samuel will do to her now that he knows he's been found out."

"He can't hide for long." Officer Baxter nodded to Mason. "Get her out of here. We'll find the girl."

Mason took her hand and picked up his flashlight. "I'm taking Aubrey back to the house. I'll be on my walkie if you find anything."

Before she could thank the two officers who had come to rescue her, Aubrey stumbled.

"I think that knock on the head was worse than I thought."

Mason lifted her chin, examining her face. "Any double or blurred vision? Halos of light?"

She sucked in a few deep breaths. "No, but I can't feel my fingers."

Mason stepped closer to her, his eyes two green pinpoints of light. "I'm never leaving your side again."

She admired the shadows along his strong jawline, thrilled to be close to him. "You promise?"

He leaned in closer, his lips inches from hers. "When this is over, we're going to make some arrangements."

A lump swelled in her throat. "Will it ever be over?"

"Don't doubt me, darlin'." He pulled her along. "I won't let you down."

The trek to the manicured grounds of Waverly felt like forever to an exhausted and weak Aubrey but moving warmed her muscles and kept her from trembling. The numbness in her fingers and toes had evaporated, and when she spotted the lights from the school buildings, she longed for some hot coffee and a hot shower to get rid of the well's stench.

"You sure you saw Samuel taking Bella?"

She remembered the fright that had enveloped her. "There was no one else following us from the cemetery."

He stopped, and the moon's silvery rays lit up his face. "How do you know it wasn't someone else? You were in a well and didn't get a clear view of what happened."

"It had to be him." She recalled how Bella's voice cut off and her sudden disappearance from atop the well. "We should go back and look for her."

He motioned to the woods. "I've got ten men in there. They will find her and Samuel."

"Before or after he kills her?"

He wiped his face, appearing frustrated. "You need a doctor, not hours traipsing through the woods. When will you let me help you?"

"I let you help me," she argued. "You pulled me out of that damned well, didn't you?"

His heated glare made her regret challenging him. "Only after you ran off and almost got yourself killed."

Aubrey touched the tender spot on her forehead, wishing her nightmare would end. She was tired of being cold, frightened, and angry all the time.

"I'm sorry. I shouldn't have done that, but all I could think about was saving Bella. I don't want to lose another student, Mason. I've watched ..." Tears crowded her eyes, and she hated herself for becoming emotional. "I've watched innocent kids die and couldn't stop it."

Mason's chest expanded as he inhaled. Then he wrapped her in his arms.

"I get it," he whispered into her hair. "But you have to hold on a little while longer. We're close. I know it."

She curled into his chest, not realizing the embrace was what she needed. His warmth chased away her misery. It was a needed respite after her time in the well and too many sleepless nights.

Aubrey stood, feeling safe and protected. Mason's arms slipped from around her, and she was about to protest when a grunt tumbled from his lips. His flashlight toppled to the ground.

He fell in a heap, landing awkwardly in the grass. His hat rolled away and came to rest a few feet away.

Raw, icy terror spread from the center of her chest. "Mason? Mason, talk to me."

She kneeled at his side and touched his face, eager for any sign of consciousness.

"He can't help you now. No one can."

The throaty, ugly voice came from behind her.

She had never heard anything so hideous, but she could guess who it belonged to. The killer had followed them from the woods.

A blazing panic erupted in her chest. Aubrey stiffened, afraid to turn around.

She spied Mason's Glock, still holstered to his side.

Get the gun.

While she slowly attempted to stand, Aubrey stayed close to Mason's gun belt. She unclipped his sidearm and eased it out of the leather holster before rising.

Aubrey kept the gun close, her trembling finger on the trigger as she turned to meet whoever was behind her.

She held her breath, praying she had the strength to fire the gun. But then flashes of Hartley, London, Cal, Jenna, and Bella infused her with a determination to kill.

Aubrey prepared herself, but when she faced the woods, no one was there.

A punishing, burning sting erupted from the back of her head.

She wobbled, dizzy, and unsteady on her feet.

The grass came up quickly, but she could not stop her fall.

Aubrey did not feel the impact when she hit the ground. She fought to keep her eyes open, not wanting to give in to the overwhelming desire to sleep.

Black crowded her vision, narrowing the moon's light like a collapsing tunnel. Her heart broke. She had failed everyone, even Mason.

The tear that slipped down her cheek was the last thing she felt before the world faded away.

The sound of rushing water added to the god-awful throbbing in her temples. Aubrey's head rolled as she struggled to come out of her fog. Pins and needles radiated from her hands to her shoulders. She attempted to move her fingers, but they were numb. That was when she became aware of the burn on her wrists. Aubrey's eyes flew open.

Everything was fuzzy at first, but then she picked up the red brick color around her. Hurricane lanterns sat in a circle, their flickering flames casting ominous shadows along the remains of the crumbling walls and debris-strewn floor. The stench of rot and decay blended with the pungent aroma of kerosene while the rumbling of water grew louder.

The mill.

Aubrey recognized it even in the dim light. She tried to move, to see more of where she was in the structure but found herself unable to work her limbs. She raised her head and spotted the oily, dirty rope securing her hands above her, and tossed over a rough hued beam set in the roof. Aubrey lowered her gaze to her feet, where she found the same discolored rope holding her ankles together.

Her breath came and went in ragged gasps as she attempted to stem the sickening cascade of terror ripping through her every molecule. She wiggled, desperate to get free, but the ropes remained in place.

"Glad you're awake. I was getting impatient."

The cold, ragged voice came from a shadowy section.

Aubrey battled to get her head around, desperate to face her attacker.

A figure moved in the darkness. Tall and agile, it moved into the light.

A woman's long legs and torso took shape. The cut of her tweed suit and the slim fit of her skirt took Aubrey's breath away.

Sara Probst held up the voice changer on her hand. "I always find it scares your victims more when they don't recognize you."

Fury bubbled beneath Aubrey's skin. "You? You killed my students?"

Sara dropped the device to the floor. "I had no choice. I must keep Waverly's reputation untarnished, and your students had something I needed to silence—a secret. Something Lindsey Gillett learned about her sister's death and shared with her special group of friends."

Sara moved in front of the lanterns and stooped. When she rose, the light caught on the machete in her hand.

Aubrey focused on the glint of the blade. "Lindsey never told my students anything. They would have shared it with me and the police."

"Oh, they knew," Sara snapped. "I saw Lindsey whispering with those deviants in the halls. They would stare at me as I walked by. That's when I became convinced they knew about what I had done. I had to eliminate them. I couldn't risk my secret getting out. I became obsessed with killing them. I even dreamed of it at night."

Aubrey shifted her attention to her tormentor's face. "You're doing all this because you killed Marjorie and Lindsey?"

Sara's cruel snicker circled the dilapidated building. "You always were a little slow to figure things out. It's one of the reasons I hired you. I didn't think you'd become this much of a problem for me."

Aubrey twisted, still fighting her binds. "But why kill anyone? What could Marjorie possibly have done to you?"

"She didn't keep my secret," Sara screeched and then gentled her voice. "When her little sister arrived on campus, snooping around, I knew Marjorie had told her the truth. I silenced Lindsey, but then I would never be completely safe until I took care of her friends, too."

Aubrey scoured the walls, the ground, the open ceiling, desperate for a way to escape.

"My students were innocent."

"Innocent? They were liars and cheats, just like the others." Sara walked up to her, waving the machete like a baton. "My father was like you. He refused to see the evil in his students. I had to show him how wrong he was."

Sweat trickled down Aubrey's temples, despite her shivering. "Is that why you eliminated the others? Because of your father?"

Sara stopped in front of her, frowning. "Warren Probst was a great man, but he had one weakness—young girls. They were all pretty, blonde, popular, and willing to do whatever the headmaster wanted. The first one was Jeanne Caron. When I read her blackmail note, I knew I couldn't let her destroy my father's reputation." She ran her finger along the edge of the blade. "I hacked her into pieces and dumped the remains in Bayou Teche. And after my father took up with other eager girls, I killed them, too. Waverly had to be protected no matter the cost."

Aubrey wilted as the depth of Sara's depravity hit her.

"And Samuel? When did you decide to make him take the fall?"

Sara's dark eyes glinted in the lamplight. "The second I knew Lindsey had to die. He's worked at Waverly since the first girl disappeared, making him a likely suspect. All I had to do was plant clues that pointed to him. The sheriff's team will find a key to the shed by the mill after he is arrested. And when the remaining jewelry is discovered in Samuel's office at the stables, he will be as good as convicted."

Aubrey had to buy time. Mason's deputies must have discovered him by now. They had to be combing the grounds for her.

Keep her talking.

"Sheriff Dubois doesn't believe Samuel had anything to do with the murders. He doesn't buy your evidence."

Sara put the machete blade against Aubrey's cheek. "But you told him Samuel was the killer. That's why you and Bella ran from him at the cemetery. Your death will compel the sheriff to go after my head groundskeeper."

Aubrey closed her eyes, not wanting to see the metal against her skin. The idea of Mason ever believing such horrendous things upset her more than Sara's psychotic tale.

"You two were so disgusting. The way you rubbed up against each other," Sara hissed into her face. "I always knew you were a whore."

Aubrey's outrage swelled. She opened her eyes, glowered at Sara, and spat in her face.

Sara raised the blade of the long knife, tracing it over the front of Aubrey's stained shirt.

"I've gotten good at cutting people up. I can make someone live quite a while as I slice off parts." She bared her sharp, pointy teeth. "Let's see how long you last."

Movement came from outside the remains of a window. Someone hunched over, and sticking close to the exterior wall, crept toward the gap of collapsed bricks. An electric charge of anticipation spread out to Aubrey's limbs, picking up her heartbeat and awakening her hope.

She kept her attention on Sara and the machete pressed against her chest, but Aubrey concentrated on her peripheral vision, anxious to see who had come to save her.

A young woman inched her way through the break in the wall. Long legs and flowing brown hair were the first things Aubrey noticed. She walked in, careful of stepping on the debris, her footfalls covered by the rushing river behind the mill.

Then a pair of fiery green eyes flashed at Aubrey as the young girl picked up a brick. She put her finger to her tightly drawn mouth and made the sign for quiet. Aubrey had seen her sunken cheeks, sad gaze, and strong jawline before.

Shock riveted Aubrey and she froze, not wanting to give away her rescuer.

Sara raised the blade of her long knife, appearing ready to strike a blow. "I'm going to enjoy this."

Aubrey opened her mouth to scream as the blade drew near.

Lindsey rushed ahead. The headmistress turned to confront her, but it was too late.

When Lindsey landed a hard punch to Sara's temple, her head popped backward, causing her to drop the machete. Sara stumbled and dropped to her knees.

She touched the gash on her brow. Blood ran onto her hand and through her fingers, dripping onto the floor. Sara fought to get back on her feet, swaying as she stood.

Aubrey wanted to warn Lindsey, but the young woman had the machete perilously poised over her feet about to slice the rope.

Then Sara took a shaky step, coming toward them.

"Lindsey, hurry!"

The restraint loosened around Aubrey's ankles, but she still wasn't free.

Lindsey furiously sawed the machete blade across the ropes.

Sara was almost on them when she stopped and picked up one of the kerosene lamps. She came at Aubrey and Lindsey, brandishing it like a weapon.

"Behind you," Aubrey shouted.

Lindsey turned, still carrying the blade. The second she saw Sara, she swung the machete hard.

A *thwack* carried across the mill when the blade connected with her hand.

Sara's agonizing animal cry reverberated through the rafters.

The lamp fell against Sara's tweed skirt, the kerosene spilling out of the front and drenching her clothes. When the glass chimney shattered against the ground, it dumped the rest of the kerosene over the dried wood, old birds' nests, and trash on the mill floor.

Sara clamped her wounded hand, and her venomous gaze turned to Aubrey.

Lindsey cut through the last section of the rope, allowing Aubrey to kick away the coils around her ankles.

The floor ignited in a burst of flames fed by the wick from the lamp.

Lindsey raised the machete. She hacked at the rope suspending Aubrey's hands.

Aubrey crumpled, pins and needles coursing through her hands.

"You're mine!"

Sara lunged toward Lindsey, stepping over the spreading fire.

Lindsey arched away from her, and as she did, Sara's skirt ignited. A flare of red exploded, covering Sara's waist and hips.

Lindsey grabbed Aubrey and dragged her away.

"We have to get out of here."

Aubrey leaned on the young woman, her hands still bound with the rope dragging behind her.

A shrill shriek came from the room as Aubrey reached the gap in the wall.

The flames from Sara's skirt had engulfed her cream-colored blouse.

Black, noxious smoke billowed upward. The heat from the mounting fire pushed Aubrey back.

Sara spun around, slapped at her clothes as her horrific cries grew louder.

"Leave the bitch," Lindsey yelled, taking her arm.

They ran, dodging clumps of weeds, piles of trash, broken beams, and iron boiling pots to get away from the mill.

Aubrey's hands burned as the feeling came back. She longed to rest and catch her breath, but Lindsey urged her on.

"We have to get out of here before the whole place goes up!"

The stench of smoke wafted off her tattered clothes while Aubrey rubbed her sore wrists, keeping the lights from the school buildings in front of her. Occasionally, she glanced back at the growing smoke cloud rising in the sky. With every step, the terror Sara had ignited eased a little more. She wasn't over her nightmare, but she could finally start living.

She eyed the profile of the pretty young woman next to her.

"*Find out what happened to Marjorie and the others, then you will find me.* I saw the note you wrote."

Lindsey chuckled. "Yeah, I left that behind to get the others digging into the past. I never figured they'd give it to you."

"Where did you go?"

"Probst came after me. She meant to kill me like Marjorie, but I outran her. She was right on me in the end, but I dove in the Bayou Teche and stayed underwater. I guess she thought the current got me, but I'm a strong swimmer." Lindsey pointed toward the stables. "I hid there until I could sneak away. I was too afraid to talk to anyone, so I stole enough money for bus fare from a guy's wallet at the coffee shop and got on a bus heading out of town."

Aubrey stopped walking. "But why didn't you tell anyone where you went? You could have called the police, or your friends and warned them."

"I believed that as long as I was missing, they would be safe." Her slender shoulders drooped. "I was in Dallas when I saw the news about London and Hartley. I called the sheriff's department in Franklin, but they didn't believe I was Lindsey Gillette. That's when I got on the next bus and came back here as soon as I could. I arrived a few hours ago and went to the first place I could think of—Mr. Samuel's office at the stables. I knew he would help me."

"Why didn't Mr. Samuel notify anyone?"

Lindsey motioned to her right. "Ask him yourself."

Two approaching figures, one tall, one short came from the path leading to the stables. They remained hidden by a cloud crossing the moon. Aubrey stiffened, eager to see who was with Samuel. When the cloud passed, the moonlight shone down on Bella.

Aubrey held out her arms, her lower lip trembling as her student ran to greet her.

She embraced Bella and held her, wanting never to let go. She had saved at least one of her students. She hadn't let them all down.

"Where did you go?"

Bella pointed at Lindsey. "Mr. Samuel surprised me at the well. Then he took me to the stables to hide."

"I had to get her somewhere safe because I knew Probst was looking for her."

Aubrey rushed up to Samuel and hugged him, relieved but ashamed she'd doubted him.

"Why didn't you call someone the moment you found Lindsey?"

He held her back. "I was, and then I saw Bella running toward the woods from my office window. When I found you two at the cemetery, Lindsey wanted me to draw you away, someplace safe where Sara couldn't get either of you. That is what I wanted to show you—Lindsey hiding in the woods close by. Once I had you, Bella, and Lindsey together, I would call the sheriff and send him after Sara." He glanced at the orange light coming over the trees. "I'm guessing we don't have to worry about Ms. Probst anymore."

Aubrey nodded. "She's gone, but I still don't understand how you knew about her."

Samuel repositioned his cap. "There was always something off about Sara and her father. Warren Probst was an asshole to students and faculty. She was a lot like him, but when the girls started disappearing all those years ago, I suspected her old man." He nodded toward Lindsey. "It wasn't until I found her in my office that I knew I was right."

Aubrey faced Lindsey. "Why not go to the authorities or your parents if you knew Sara Probst killed your sister?"

"I didn't know for sure until she chased me to the river. When I was under the rushing water, I found a human skull. I was so terrified—all I could think of was getting away. Even after coming back, the thought of confronting Probst petrified me. But then I saw what she was doing to you at the mill, and I wasn't scared of her anymore. I was angry and wanted her to pay for what she did to my family and friends."

"I believe Sara planned to dump me in the river with the others." Aubrey rubbed her arms. "After she cut me up into little pieces."

Shouts and the bouncing beams of lights came from across the manicured field behind the school.

Lindsey looked ahead. "They must have spotted the fire."

Aubrey noticed the lines of worry across her forehead. She took the young woman's hand.

"It will be all right. We'll talk to Sheriff Dubois and tell him everything. No one will blame you for anything, Lindsey. I promise."

The girl squeezed Aubrey's hand.

"Marjorie told me about you right before she died." Lindsey turned to the lights closing in on them. "She wished she could make it up to you for all the mean things she said and did. She made me swear to never be like her—a bully. I made sure when I came here to make friends with everyone, especially the ones who were ridiculed. I had a promise to keep."

Her words cut across Aubrey's heart. The admission might not have erased Marjorie's cruelty, but knowing Lindsey had taken her sister's advice gave her some solace.

Aubrey glimpsed the fire rising into the sky and remembered Cal,

Hartley, Jenna, and London.

"Your sister would be proud of you."

Bella joined them. "Hey, you two took out The Prober." She put her arms around them. "Marjorie would be proud as shit."

CHAPTER 30

The bandages made Aubrey's wrists itch and her forehead hurt under the Band-Aid. Still, as she sat on the porch steps of Elaine House and surveyed the parking lot packed with students heading home, worried parents, and busy law enforcement officers, she felt glad to be alive.

The hum of conversation, the hugs, the tears warmed her. One day soon, Aubrey hoped to see Waverly return to the scholarly place it had been before all the violence and death.

Mason appeared at the steps, his Stetson in his hand, and red mud all over his boots.

"You find her?"

He glanced at the parking lot, watching the activity, and then climbed the steps. He sat down next to her and set his hat aside.

"Firemen found remains in the ashes. The divers in the river have found a few bones and one skull. It's going to take time to ID everyone, but yeah, we have Probst."

Aubrey picked at the dressing on her wrist. "I never in a million years thought she was the killer."

Mason leaned back. "I suspected something was up with her the moment we met."

Aubrey furrowed her brow. "You did?"

"Any woman who resists my charms the way she did has got to have a screw loose."

Aubrey snickered. "Seems to me, she had more than one screw loose."

She browsed the array of minivans parked next to fire trucks, and sleek sports cars pulled in behind patrol cars. Harried-faced parents stuffed trunks and suitcases into vehicles as they glared at the grand edifice of Elaine House. Aubrey could almost feel the animosity emanating from them. The school would have a long road back to building its esteemed reputation.

It saddened her to see Waverly cast into such a disparaging light. She wanted Sara to suffer for what she'd done, but not the school. The students and faculty deserved better.

"What will happen now that the press knows about the killings?"

"Waverly might take a few hard knocks, but it would survive with the right person at the helm."

She wrapped her hands around her knees. "Who would want to? Sara Probst will be a hard act to follow."

Mason nudged her with his shoulder. "You could do it."

She shook her head, and her stomach rolled at the suggestion. "I'm not an administrator. I'm a history teacher."

Mason leaned in, letting his warm breath tease her cheek. "What better person to run the school. You know the past and can learn from others' mistakes to give Waverly a new start."

A new start. Aubrey wanted that. A chance to begin again and put the past behind her.

"You can rebuild the school and stay in Franklin with me."

She arched away. "With you? We haven't even gone on a date yet. How can you be so sure it will work between us?"

He bobbed his eyebrows. "Then let's find out. Saturday night, my place. I'll cook steaks. You bring the wine."

She smirked at his optimism. "Fine. One date. But I warn you, if I stay, I'll be too busy to spend time with you. If I'm going to fix Waverly, it will need my full attention."

"Of course, Headmistress LaRoux."

She glanced around the porch of Elaine House. "I like the sound of that, but I don't know if I would want to live here. Too many bad memories in this house."

"We can make new ones together."

She gazed into his sparkling eyes. "When do you suggest we begin?"

He cupped her cheek. "How 'bout now?"

Mason touched his lips to hers, and Aubrey became lost in his kiss. He curled his arms around her and pulled her close.

For Aubrey, the noisy parking lot, the sound of harried parents, and students' probing gazes disappeared. All that mattered was Mason's embrace and her newfound dreams for the future.

EPILOGUE

Six Months Later.

The warm hints of spring chased away the dampness in the home as Aubrey strolled through the entrance of Elaine House with Mason's arm around her shoulder.

"You have to stop taking me out to lunch. I can never get through my afternoons without longing for a nap."

He kissed her forehead. "I told you I wasn't going to let you out of my sight. So get used to having lunches and dinners with me from now on."

She tapped the dimple on his chin. "I'm not complaining. I just think we should eat more salads, so I don't end up weighing three hundred pounds."

A grinding sound brought Aubrey to a standstill. It wasn't like the groan of the old hardwoods she'd grown used to in the home.

She glanced down and caught the sunlight glistening on fragments of blue and white pottery scattered along the hallway floor.

Aubrey toed a shard and mumbled, "What's this?"

Mason stooped and regarded the broken pottery.

"Where did these pieces come from?"

She raised her head to the toppled pillar where one of the blue and white Chinese vases had stood in front of her office entrance. The shards spread in a pattern across the hardwood floor.

A shudder ripped through her. "How did that happen?" Aubrey hurried toward the office.

"Wait," Mason pleaded as he followed her into the former parlor.

The same dusky gray walls greeted her, and the deep scowls and discerning gazes of the previous headmasters' portraits stared back as if disapproving of her new appointment. She stepped into the room and caught a glimpse of Sara Probst and her father, Warren. Aubrey had debated keeping their images in her office, but despite their crimes, they were part of Waverly's legacy.

Nothing seemed out of place. The barrister bookcases along one wall were intact, and the leather furniture in front of the immense walnut desk sat in the same spots since before she'd left for lunch with Mason.

The light from the brass chandelier glinted on something spread across her desk. That was when Aubrey spotted the broken gold frame.

One portrait lay face-down, shattered, and its backing ripped apart.

Mason came up beside her and removed his Glock from his holster. "Stay behind me." He crept toward the desk.

Aubrey's impatience flamed as she stepped around glass shards scattered across her red rug. When they reached her desk, she eagerly inspected the portrait's back.

Mason went around her, his gun out in front of him.

Her laptop and tablet remained right where she had left them. None of the files she had left out seemed disturbed—only the broken portrait.

Mason checked under the desk. He stood up, his attention on the room's entrance. "I'll sweep the rest of the house."

He was about to walk around the desk when he nodded to the painting. "Any idea who did this?"

Aubrey didn't like the worry lines cutting across his forehead. "Perhaps an angry student?"

"A student wouldn't leave behind one destroyed picture." Mason turned to the office. "Can you tell if anything is missing?"

Aubrey shook her head. "I have no idea. I've only been in this office for a month."

Mason motioned his gun toward the back of the painting, laying across the desk. "Why is this picture on your desk? Why put it here and break it up?"

Aubrey hovered over the back of the portrait. "I have no idea."

Mason went to an empty spot between the portraits of the other former headmasters. He traced the brighter outline where the picture had hung. "They took this picture down, took it to your desk, broke the frame, ripped off the back, and then left it. Why?"

Mason returned to the desk and ran his fingers over the portrait's backing. He lifted the torn paper in the back and checked the hollow behind the canvas. "Something must have been in here. They wanted to get to the back of the picture for some reason."

He set his gun aside and gently turned the picture over. The glass plinked as it fell across the desk.

The man in the painting had a slash across his face where the robber's knife had sliced into it. His noble brow, stern brown eyes, and long chin set off an unsettling ripple in Aubrey.

"Do you know who this is?"

She stood back from the desk and folded her arms. "Jacob Hill. He was the first headmaster in 1950. He bought the plantation from the Dardenne family to turn it into a school for girls."

Mason retrieved his gun. "How do you know that?"

Aubrey gave him a fleeting smile. "I read about him in Cal's notes that day you found him in the library. He read Ashton Dardenne's journal."

Sorrow cut through Aubrey's heart. The images of her students' mangled bodies still came to her in nightmares. She doubted they would ever go away. Aubrey concentrated on the problem at hand, putting the past to rest, for now.

Mason scoured the portrait on her desk. "So why would someone want to destroy his picture, and leave all the others?"

Aubrey recalled Cal's notes. "Jacob Hill rigged the legal proceedings so he could overrule the rights of the Collins family. They were the black sheep of the Dardenne line because they were descended from the

Chitimacha Indians. The Hill family still owns the land. Maybe someone wants revenge or to erase Jacob's memory."

Mason inspected the slash across Jacob Hill's face. "Taking out a picture doesn't strike me as the best way to get revenge." He slipped his hand inside the slash. "There might have been something hidden in this artwork. Something someone was desperate to get at."

Aubrey reviewed the face and the back of the portrait. "But what?"

Mason picked up his gun. "Whatever it was, it had to have been placed in this picture when it was framed. This portrait has been there for a long time, judging by the faded paint on that wall."

Aubrey exhaled in a rattled breath as the room closed in around her. "So, they waited until I became headmaster to make their move? Why?"

Mason's lips thinned into a grim line. "Or they just learned about whatever was here. Who knows? It couldn't have been big. Not enough room behind the canvas."

"So how do we find out what it is?"

Mason removed his phone from his back pocket. "We'll dust for fingerprints and see if we can find anything else. Perhaps our intruder left some clues."

Aubrey's fingers tingled as she stared at the portrait on her desk. "We already have a clue—Jacob Hill."

Mason hit the number on his phone. "I'm sure he can't help us. He's probably been dead for years."

Aubrey slowly traced the back of the painting, taking care not to tear or bend the paper. "Well, it seems someone knows a lot more about what's in this house than we do."

Mason glowered at her. "Reason enough to relocate you someplace safe until we investigate."

Aubrey stood next to him as he spoke with a commanding voice to his deputy on the phone. She should have felt reassured that Mason would take care of the mystery, but somewhere inside her, Aubrey knew there would be more to come.

"I'm at the house now," Mason barked. "Get everyone out here ASAP." He hung up and gazed at her. "They're on the way. We'll figure it out. I've got a crack group of deputies."

An overwhelmed Aubrey rested her hip against the desk. "I'm not sure it's going to be that easy. Whatever was hidden in this picture was never meant to be found."

Mason slipped his phone into his pocket. "I'm not leaving your side until we get to the bottom of this."

She smiled despite the slow churn of acid in her stomach. "Promise?"

Mason sucked in a deep breath and put his lips close to hers. "You're stuck with me."

Fear cut through her like an icy wind. "What if bad things start happening again like before?"

Mason put his arm around her. "That won't happen, darlin'. Lightning doesn't strike twice, even at Waverly."

ABOUT THE AUTHOR

Alexandrea Weis, RN-CS, PhD, is a multi-award-winning author, screenwriter, advanced practice registered nurse, and historian who was born and raised in the French Quarter of New Orleans. Having grown up in the motion picture industry as the daughter of a director, she learned to tell stories from a different perspective. Infusing the rich tapestry of her hometown into her novels, she believes that creating vivid characters makes a story moving and memorable.

Weis writes romance, mystery, suspense, thrillers, horror, paranormal, and young adult fiction and has sold approximately one million books. She lives with her husband and pets in New Orleans where she is a permitted/certified wildlife rehabber with the Louisiana Wildlife and Fisheries and rescues orphaned and injured animals.

She is a member of both the International Thriller Writers Association and the Horror Writers Association.

www.AlexandreaWeis.com